Fah X
Faherty, Terence.
Raise the devil

1st ed.

$ 23.95

W9-DDK-387

RAISE THE DEVIL

RAISE
THE
DEVIL

TERENCE FAHERTY

ST. MARTIN'S MINOTAUR / NEW YORK

Design by Heather Saunders

Library of Congress Cataloging-in-Publication Data

Faherty, Terence.
  Raise the devil / Terence Faherty.—1st ed.
    p. cm.
  ISBN 0-312-26640-5
  1. Elliot, Scott (Ficticious character)—Fiction.   2. Private investigators—
California—Los Angeles—Fiction.   3. Motion picture industry— Fiction.
4. Hollywood (Los Angeles, Calif.)—Fiction.   5. Las Vegas (Nev.)—Fiction.
I. Title.

PS3556.A342 R3 2000
813'.54—dc21

                                                                00-031816

First Edition: October 2000

10 9 8 7 6 5 4 3 2 1

For my friend Jerome Donahue,
in memoriam

RAISE THE DEVIL

1

I checked the tape holding the belt holster to the wall one last time. It was fine, or would be, if I could get myself to stop fooling with it. I picked up the tray of sandwiches I'd laid on the floor and rang the bell for the Grand Suite.

The door opened without prologue—no footsteps, no challenge, no fussing with the locks—and I was facing a man shorter than I was but broader by half. I saw black eyes, razor stubble as heavy as Fred Flintstone's, and a bony brow that glistened with sweat in the cool, conditioned air. Dillon, according to my briefing.

I wanted to size him up, but that wouldn't have gone so well with the part I was playing. So I stood there while he sized me up. He patted me down for good measure, checked the sandwiches on my tray, felt under the tray. Then he poked his head out into the hallway, shoving me backward a step to do it. I forced myself not to look to my right to see how well the doorframe's molding hid the gun. It hid it well enough. Dillon grunted and waved me into the suite.

It was nice. I already knew the layout by heart, but the little plan I'd studied—front hall leading to living room with desert view, bedrooms to the left, kitchen and dinette to the right—hadn't captured the atmosphere of the place. In an example of the detached way your mind can work when your sweat glands have taken over, I fell into a meditation on the decor. The muted grays of the carpeting and wallpaper, the inoffensive abstract art, the clean lines of the space-age furniture all reflected a civilization that was—like the year, 1962—in its high summer. I even had time to glimpse the irony of this: that all this style and refinement had gone into the creation of a town in the wilderness where the jaded rich could gamble their money away.

I glimpsed the irony, but didn't work out what it said about the world. I was in the little dining room by then, facing another irony. With a brand-new casino ready and waiting downstairs, the group of businessmen before me had chosen to do their gambling in the penthouse. As their common business was this casino or another like it, they probably knew their chances were better in a private game.

I ignored all but one of the half-dozen faces around the table. As far as my job was concerned, there was only one man in the room. His name was John Remlinger, and he was seated, as I'd expected, at the table's head. Remlinger was thin and boyish, if you could call a guy with dead eyes boyish. It was chiefly the black hair that created the impression. He wore it long and brushed back in an open imitation of President Kennedy.

"Finally," Remlinger said, cutting short my examination. Dillon nudged me toward a buffet table. I moved a very nice collection of bottles and a silver ice bucket and set the tray down. I was still there, bent forward at the waist, when Remlinger froze me with a question.

"Don't I know you?"

It was as much an accusation as an inquiry. The only answer I could make was to straighten my back and turn to face him. I kept my expression blank, which took some doing when he stood and circled the table. He didn't stop coming until we were toe-to-toe. I was suddenly remembering boot-camp inspections, and I put the memory to work for me, squaring my shoulders and looking straight ahead.

"A little old to be bellhopping, aren't we?" Remlinger asked.

I was. He was about the right age, twenty-five or so; nobody seemed to know for sure. He was about right in the aptitude department, too, though I was too polite to say so.

He had his face stuck right into mine. I could see one blue eye, perfectly clear and just as empty, an unmemorable nose, and the faint scars left by some middle-tier plastic surgeon. "Let's see a hand."

I held my right one up, palm raised. He turned it over and examined the knuckles.

"You've been a fighter, right?"

"Now and then," I said.

"I thought so." He turned to the table. "It's what I always say. The fight game's for suckers. A couple of decent paydays and you end up a flunky who has to look down on the front of his uniform shirt to remember his own name."

The other players laughed—one or two of them genuinely—and Dillon nudged me in the ribs. I was dismissed.

On our way back across the living room, I let my eyes stray to the hallway opposite the poker game, the one that led to the suite's two bedrooms.

Dillon noticed the glance and grunted: "Eyes front."

Another ex-G.I., I thought. Well, there were a lot of us kicking around.

We reentered the suite's front hall. It wasn't much more than an alcove, formed by a closet to the right of the entry and a powder room to the left. As I opened the front door, Dillon said, "Wait a minute."

I didn't wait. I took a step out into the hotel hallway. Then I half turned with my right hand on the molding next to the gun. Dillon had his right in his pocket. It came out with a money clip, and he dropped his eyes to it. When he looked up again, I was pointing the gun at his stomach.

"We'll go back in," I said.

He shrugged and turned around. I hit him as he took his first step. I put more into it than I normally did, because the thirty-two was a lighter gun than I usually carried and because, with a customer like Dillon, it was better to err on the generous side. He went down in a noiseless heap on the expensive carpet.

I stepped over him and paused at the threshold to the living room. The dining room's louvered doors were partially closed. Only one man at the table had a clear view of the space I had to cross. He was a little guy who resembled the politician Hubert Humphrey. He'd laughed the loudest at Remlinger's fight-game joke, and I was counting on his host to distract him now. Sure enough, when Remlinger began to reminisce about some killing he'd made in a poker game back East, Humphrey all but turned his back to the living room. I was across the open ground in three steps and into the hallway.

The second door I came to was locked, which made it the one I wanted. I used the passkey that had come with my uniform to open it.

Beyond the door was a king-size bed that had been made up for the day. The young woman stretched out on the bed hadn't been made up, but she wasn't the worse for that. Her short hair was golden blond and all the skin I could see was darkly tanned. That was quite a bit of skin, as she was wearing only panties and a bra. I would have known her without a briefing; she was a Hollywood starlet named Beverly Brooks.

Brooks didn't know me. When I slipped inside the room, she took in a breath that might have gotten us both killed. Before she could use it, I said, "Marcus Pioline sent me."

Brooks slid her long legs off the bed and stood up, less self-conscious than I was about how she was dressed.

"Do you want out of here?" I asked.

"What do you think?" she whispered, her voice saw-toothed.

"Where are your clothes?"

"I don't know. They took them."

There was no time for a search. I slipped out of my uniform blouse and handed it to her. The jacket covered her from her neck to her thighs. She reminded me of the dancers who'd advertised cigarettes in the early days of television, the ones who'd tapped away in boxy costumes painted to look like cigarette packs, with only their legs showing. Or maybe I remembered those dancers just then because I was desperate for a cigarette.

I led Brooks by the hand into the hallway. Time had taken a break while I'd been in the bedroom; Remlinger was still telling his story. We crossed the living room and squeezed into the first two feet of the alcove. The prone Dillon was using the rest. I stepped over him and held my hand out to Brooks, who hesitated.

"He's not dead," I whispered.

"Too bad," she said, and stepped across.

I shut the suite door behind us, peeled my holster off the wall, and stopped Brooks just before she hit the elevator's call button.

"The operator's not on the payroll," I said.

I led her to the far end of the hallway, to an unnumbered door that I opened with another passkey. Beyond that was the service elevator, open and ready. On the same ring as my passkeys was a smaller one, as brassy as Brooks's hair. I inserted it in the elevator's panel, turned it, and hit the button for the underground garage.

Standing in the back of the car was some castoff furniture: a dresser missing a leg and a couple of chairs, each minus an arm. On the trip down, Brooks looked herself over in the dresser's mirror, pulling at the dark skin under her eyes. "Damn," she said. "What's Marc going to say?"

"Worry about that when we're out of here," I said, killing the chitchat. Brooks drew the unbuttoned jacket tight abound her like a beltless robe.

A little bell signaled our arrival in the basement. I raised my gun as the doors opened, ready to scare Mr. and Mrs. Tourist of Omaha, Nebraska, to death. They weren't there; no one was. I glanced around the dark concrete bunker and stuck the thirty-two in my belt. It was the first mistake I'd made.

We'd gone about three cars down the first row when a voice behind us barked, "Hands up." I felt a sharp poke in the back as my gun was yanked from my belt. Then the man in charge said, "Turn around."

Brooks and I did our turning toward one another. Like me,

she was holding her hands up in the approved cowboy-movie fashion. The pose made her look like a little girl, helped by the fit of my coat and the size of her hazel eyes.

We ended up facing a little man holding a big gun. He looked as scared as Brooks had, but that was only a trick of the light. He laughed easily and said, "What do you know, bank night."

A house phone hung on the bare concrete wall of the garage. The little gunman limped over to it, lifted the receiver, and jiggled the switch hook. "Grand Suite," he said.

"Let's talk first," I said, but not as a serious opening for negotiations. Someone had stepped from the shadows behind a concrete upright. He was a big man in a straw fedora, and he was coming up on the gunman's blind side.

Brooks saw him, too, and drew in another of her fatal breaths. She held this one in all by herself. Better than that, she spread her arms a little wider, which caused the front of her coat to swing open like the doors of a barn.

The man holding the phone would have been lost in that landscape for ten minutes at least, if someone hadn't picked up on the other end of the line. "Right," the gunman said. "It's me. Down in the garage. Your little birdie's flown—"

He folded up then as thoroughly as Dillon had, but with a little more noise. The man in the panama hat, whose name was Paddy Maguire, was swinging a leather sap back and forth contemplatively. "What a way to earn a buck," he said. "Howdy Doody's got more dignity."

I collected my thirty-two and slid the little man's cannon under the nearest car. I straightened up in time to hear Paddy speaking on the phone.

"The weed of crime bears bitter fruit," he was saying. "Or didn't your folks have a radio?" I took the handset from him and hung it up. "Sorry, Scotty," he said. "I couldn't resist. Where'd we park the chariot?"

Our chariot was a rented Chevy Impala. It was a boxy, nondescript sedan, but it had a 327-cubic-inch V-8. I was using every bit of that displacement by the time we'd traded the parking lot's ramp for the blinding light of the street. It being early afternoon in Las Vegas, the street was all but deserted. A block later, it turned into dusty highway, and I gave the car its head. I didn't touch the brakes until we reached the turn for a private airstrip, ten miles west of town.

A plane sat on the tarmac, a red, white, and blue number whose twin props were turning so slowly you could almost see the blades. I pulled the Chevy up close, left the keys in the ignition, and collected Brooks and my bag from the backseat. Paddy was holding the plane's door open for us. He grabbed his hat with his free hand as the engines revved up.

"Not a moment too soon," he said. He gestured toward the highway with the unlit cigar he held clamped in his teeth. Two black sedans were flying toward us above the shimmering asphalt.

I was the last one aboard. The plane was moving before I'd gotten the door latched. A minute later, we were away.

2

The plane was a luxury conversion of a World War II transport—a Douglas C-47. It revealed its wartime roots with its takeoff, which combined a hell of a lot of vertical with a modest amount of horizontal. So much so that it seemed for a while that we had climbed aboard a P-47 by mistake. When I finally got my head unstuck from my seat back, the airfield was still in sight behind us, but the black sedans were scale models and the men around them—one of them Johnny Remlinger—were no more threatening than my boy's toy soldiers.

I checked the other passengers. Opposite me, Paddy was tossing the remains of his cigar, which he'd chewed mightily during the takeoff. He actually used a waste bin for once, a chrome one that popped out of the cabin wall like a miniature laundry chute. Brooks was strapped in on an upholstered bench near the cabin door. As I watched, her golden head drooped.

I undid my seat belt and worked my way back to her, easing myself down the aisle of the still-climbing plane. "You okay?" I asked, lifting her chin.

"Dead," she said.

She looked it. Her bright eyes were staring up at me from a depth. A reaction to our narrow escape, I told myself. "Lie down, why don't you?"

Brooks unbuckled her belt and lifted her bare legs onto the

little couch. In a wire rack by the door, I found a neatly folded blanket with "MP" embroidered on its silken edge. I used it to cover those legs, regretfully.

When I did, Brooks closed her eyes. "I haven't thanked you," she said, and fell asleep, leaving me to wonder whether she'd meant to thank me or just wanted to point out that she was still thinking it over.

I rejoined Paddy, taking the seat that faced his, club style. He'd opened a little cabinet next to the cigar chute and extracted a bottle of rye and two glasses. He poured us each a drink without bothering to ask if I was thirsty. I knew Paddy wasn't, that his drink was purely medicinal. He'd almost rather be back on the ground, explaining himself to Remlinger, than six thousand feet in the air, bouncing along like John Glenn.

"How'd it go in the suite?" he asked me when he'd gotten his first dose down.

He listened to my story up to the point where Remlinger claimed to have recognized me. Then he smiled. "This Remlinger's a movie fan, Scotty," he said. "Movie crazy, my sources tell me. Remlinger probably saw one of your pictures. Maybe both of them. He was probably remembering you from the late show."

If Remlinger had recognized me from a movie, he would have to have caught it on television. He was too young to have seen any of my work in a movie theater, my acting career having ended with a jolt on Pearl Harbor Day. Paddy's had ended when Al Jolson said, "You ain't heard nothing yet," but I never rubbed that in. It wasn't because I worked for him, either. I hated to see the years ganging up on Paddy, hated to know he was on the dangerous side of sixty.

The object of my concern searched the pockets of his linen suit jacket for a handkerchief, ignoring the fancy one in his breast pocket, the one that matched the yellow stripes in his blue tie. He used the plain handkerchief he eventually found to mop his big Pat O'Brien-issue face, the operation causing his thinning silver hair to stand up in front, something it had done all by itself once upon a time.

As I watched, Paddy shifted his gaze to a point above my right shoulder and gave out with the smile he reserved for paying customers. A short, swarthy man dressed for a round of country-club golf had come up behind me.

"You like that takeoff?" the man asked. "That was a Marcus Pioline special. What do you think of my *Argo*? Isn't she a thing of beauty?" He kept moving in a bowlegged shuffle until he reached the sleeping Brooks. He examined her briefly and then came back to us, sitting down across the aisle in the seat I'd used for the takeoff.

"So far so good, gentlemen, eh?"

"Thanks to this magic carpet of yours," Paddy said. He raised his refilled glass in Pioline's direction.

The little man shook his head. "I just provided the—how would you say it?—the getaway car. You two did all the work. From what I'm told, you've pulled off this sort of rescue so often you've lost count."

"Not yet we haven't," Paddy said. "I'd give you our running total, but it would destroy your faith in your fellow man."

Pioline laughed at that, a hearty laugh that went so well with his earthy persona I could picture him practicing it in front of a mirror. He looked like he'd been in front of one recently, passing a comb through his hair, which was as black as Remlinger's and maybe as thick. It was tough to say, given all the hair oil Pioline used. He had a gold tooth, which set his face off the way a beauty mark sets off a beautiful woman's. He was fond of joking that the tooth was his savings account, all he'd stashed away from a career in pictures.

"It's a miracle we have any faith left, we three," he said, "after all we've seen."

Pioline had seen plenty, if half the stories about him were true. He'd been a Hollywood fixture since the early fifties, when he'd arrived to promote one of the films he'd produced in England. The word on the street had been that he was a refugee who'd escaped to England when the Nazis overran Greece, and that afterward he'd worked his way into the British film industry, which had been soldiering on during the war despite losing its best and brightest to the services.

The film Pioline had come to America to pitch had starred his wife, Lillian Lacey, a statuesque redhead whose exaggerated height and more than exaggerated figure had relegated her to supporting roles and cheap comedies in staid England. Pioline had bet that Lacey would be less a curiosity than a standard of beauty in the big, freewheeling USA. It had been an especially safe bet, as he'd arrived at the dawn of the decade of Monroe and Russell and Mansfield. Lillie Lacey could more than hold her own in that chorus line, and she'd prospered. She'd stuck to comedies, but now they were sophisticated ones in which she had developed a new trademark: playing hard to get.

Pioline had explained it to me once at a party. "The men in the audience can't touch Lillie; they can only look. So you don't lose anything by making her a virgin. In fact, you win over the half of the audience that isn't interested in touching her, the women, I mean. How do you American chaps put it? We're working both sides of the street."

That phrase also summed up Pioline's master plan. After installing himself in Hollywood, he'd alternately produced Lacey comedies and historical epics designed to take advantage of the wide-screen craze. As far as I knew, he'd succeeded at both endeavors. He was currently combining his two specialties. His latest historical spectacular, *Warrior Queen*, would feature Lacey, now his ex-wife, in a rare dramatic role.

Warrior Queen was intended to ride the coattails of a blockbuster in the making, *Cleopatra*, which was filming in Italy under the direction of Joseph Mankiewicz. *Cleopatra* had an all-star cast and a bigger budget than the space program, a sizable chunk of which would be spent on publicity. Pioline was planning to exploit that campaign with *Warrior Queen*, the story of another beautiful woman who had mixed it up with the Romans and ended by poisoning herself. Pioline's queen was Boudica, a Briton who'd lived a century or so after the Egyptian temptress, not that the ticket-buying public would quibble over details like that.

Unfortunately for Pioline's peace of mind, his cast included Beverly Brooks—Bebe Brooks to the gossip columns and fan magazines. Somehow Brooks had disappeared from *Warrior*

Queen's shooting location in central California and run afoul of a small-time gangster named Remlinger, which is how Hollywood Security, Paddy's company, had gotten involved. We specialized in the discreet untangling of other people's knots, the other people being actors nine times out of ten. We weren't the only company in that field, though we might have been the oldest. Pioline had selected us at the recommendation of my wife, Ella, who happened to have written the script for *Warrior Queen*.

Pioline drew Ella into the conversation by opening his cigarette case and offering it to me. "Go ahead, Scotty, take one. Your wife isn't here to chide you about it. She even gives me a hard time, do you believe it?"

I didn't answer him. I was too busy succumbing to temptation. Pioline lit my cigarette and his with an elegant silver lighter that wasn't much bigger than a stick of gum.

"I'm glad Ella suggested calling you," Pioline said to me. "And not just because you pulled this off. You've always been cagey about what you do, Scotty. Secretive, almost. I've half believed that you didn't do anything, that you lived off your wife's considerable talents. You mustn't take offense at that, not when it comes from me. I've been accused of the same thing myself. In my case, there is some truth to it. What have I done but sell pictures of my once wife? Moving pictures, if that makes it more respectable.

"I'm glad to know you have your own job in this world," he said, patting my hand. "And that you are good at it. And I'm glad to make your acquaintance, Mr. Maguire," he added to Paddy. "I've heard of you and your company, of course, but I never connected you with Scotty, my friend who likes to hide in the corner at cocktail parties."

He crushed out his cigarette and got to his feet. "Now I must rejoin our pilot, Mr. Ford. I've spoiled him enough, letting him fly my baby so long. Besides, left to his own devices, he will simply land the *Argo* when the time comes. A success like this requires a special arrival. Something dramatic!"

When Pioline had shuffled away, Paddy passed me his blackjack. "Do it when I'm not looking," he said.

3

Pioline had gotten Paddy worrying with time to spare, as our flight had only begun. When we finally started to descend an hour later, I roused Brooks and had her strap herself in. I was afraid Pioline might try to duplicate some RAF victory roll he'd seen in England during the war, though I was careful not to mention this to my boss.

As it turned out, the worst we had to endure was a low pass over the little valley where the exteriors for *Warrior Queen* were being filmed. We came in from the west, through the wide mouth of the valley. Just as it started to narrow, we flew over a circle of trucks and trailers that marked the day's shooting site. Off to our right was a little town nestled against the brown hills.

"Sherwood," Paddy said. "All three streets of it."

Pioline ignored the town and continued down the valley, losing altitude if not speed. The tops of the nearer hills—the ones to our left—were level with the cabin windows. I caught a glimpse of some ruins on the highest hill, the remains of a fort or a mission. Then we were banking to the right, aggressively. Directly below us were a collection of buildings and a corral full of horses, unhappy with the noise we were making.

"Crowe Ranch," Paddy said, affecting nonchalance at the sight of all that dirt whizzing by. "Where you've been addressing your love notes to Ella."

Before I could pick her out in the group of people craning their necks to watch us, they were gone, replaced by a dizzying sweep of grassy ground. The engines changed their tone, and I felt twin thumps as the wheels were lowered, one after another. The airport was set very near the far hills, making it the last corner of a square whose other three were the town, the shooting site, and Crowe Ranch.

The actual landing was so uneventful I wondered whether Pioline's pilot had wrestled the controls away from him. We taxied back along the grass strip and ended up very near the single hangar.

Paddy insisted that he and I exit the plane first, telling Pioline that Remlinger could have called ahead to arrange a reception. That assumed that sleepy Sherwood had it own branch of Murder Incorporated, but I didn't raise the objection. I suspected Paddy of combining his usual thorough approach with a sincere desire to be on solid ground again.

My boss and I stepped out into a hot, dusty California afternoon. We found a reception committee of two waiting for us. One was a gentleman with antique sideburns who identified himself—when I asked politely—as Charley Gavin, the airport manager. His companion refused to identify herself however I asked. She was a brunette, Brooks's age and roughly her build, but even more tanned. She was wearing blue jeans and a sleeveless burnt orange top, but she was prepared for a more formal occasion: Over one arm she carried a peach dress. A pair of matching heels dangled beneath it. In her other hand was a square case that contained either fishing tackle or makeup.

"It's all right, Scotty, let her pass," Pioline called to me from the plane. "I radioed ahead for her. Come in, Nikki, come in."

She sauntered past me without a second look. Paddy tipped his hat to her and then went back to questioning Gavin about men in sharkskin suits. He needn't have bothered. I could see there was no one else on the airfield. No one within miles of it. Someone was headed our way, though. Dust was swirling above the road that came up from the east, from the narrow end of the valley.

By then Pioline had climbed down from the *Argo*, followed

by a tall rangy guy in coveralls who was blushing like a bevy of brides. Pioline introduced him as his "copilot," Clay Ford. The producer explained their presence and Ford's discomfiture with two words: "Bebe's dressing."

"We've got company," I said, pointing east. Two cars had topped a rise and were coming our way.

"Don't worry," Pioline said. "They're from the ranch."

"The ranch is north of here."

"Very observant of you, Scotty. Always be sure of your ground, eh? Yes, Crowe Ranch is due north, but the miserable road follows a little river, a creek really, that bends away to the east. They're our cars. I flew low over the ranch so they would know we're here. I told Charley to bring back Nikki and no one else when I radioed. I wanted Bebe to have a change of clothes."

Brooks made her entrance about ten minutes later, looking ready for cocktails at poolside, except for an accessory she carried: my bellhop's jacket. She crossed to me and handed it over.

"Thanks for the loan, Galahad," she said. Her voice, which had been raw in the suite, was still husky, but the huskiness now had a practiced quality, like Pioline's peasant laugh.

Everything about her was less natural. Her tomboy hair was ratted into a golden pile, her eyes were dark from mascara instead of fatigue, her very full lips had taken on the color of her frock. The exceptions were her breasts, as full as her lips and then some, which now looked extremely natural. The wear-anywhere bra I'd grown so fond of must not have worked with the low-cut dress.

Though it wasn't getting any cooler, I put on my jacket for something to do. Brooks brushed at its lapels.

"There may be a blond hair or two hanging around," she vamped. "Hope they don't get you in Dutch with your wife."

If Brooks had really been concerned about my matrimonial relations, she wouldn't have done what she did next, which was to stand on tiptoe and kiss me, just as the two cars from the ranch—identical Plymouth Furys—pulled up to the plane. Paddy, whose wife was safely down in Los Angeles watching Huntley and Brinkley, had to make do with a handshake.

As I'd feared, Ella was in the lead car. She'd been driving it, in fact, her lone passenger Lillian Lacey. Lacey got out first. She was almost ordinary-looking in a sack of a dress and flat shoes, her red hair hidden by a scarf. She conferred with her ex-husband and Paddy, Brooks and her dresser looking on. Ella walked around the group and followed me out to the *Argo*'s right wing tip.

We hadn't seen one another for two weeks. That was far from our longest separation, but it was enough to make me wish for a more private reunion, even with the wry look she was giving me.

"You and Bebe got on well," she said to start the ball rolling. Instead of kissing me hello, she wiped some of Brooks's lipstick off my mouth with the back of her hand. Its peach color didn't go well with what she was wearing, a madras shirtwaister.

"She's a sucker for a man in a uniform," I said, holding up one sleeve to show off its phony braid.

"Uh-huh."

Brooks didn't have to worry about a stray hair of hers getting me into trouble. After a couple of weeks at the ranch, Ella's was nearly as golden. She was generally golden, I thought as I examined the laugh lines around her very pale blue eyes, lines she hated and I secretly loved. She was giving me a sidelong look—perhaps secretly admiring my wrinkles. The look was a habit of hers. She'd broken her nose roughhousing with her brother years before I'd met her, and it wasn't exactly straight. She had a way of pointing her nose at you while she listened, which meant that the rest of her face was pointed slightly away. It gave her a skeptical air, but that may only have been self-consciousness on my part.

"How bad is it, Scotty?"

"I'll get over her in a year or two."

"I meant, how much trouble are we in with this Remlinger guy?"

"I don't know." I didn't say that I was glad our two children, Bill and Gabrielle, were in Indiana visiting my family or that I wished Ella were with them. It seemed silly to even think of

Remlinger as that dangerous, but I did. It had been easy enough to dismiss him the day before as just another Eastern hood come West to sow some wild oats. But I'd seen him since and looked into his eyes. I hadn't shaken the aftereffects.

The driver of the second car, a bespectacled guy I didn't recognize, sounded his horn, and we all turned his way.

"Danny Irwin," Ella said.

I knew the name Daniel Irwin, even if I didn't know the face. He was Brook's novelist husband. I'd even tried a book of his once, when I'd gotten far enough from the war to be interested in reading about it.

"We finally sobered him up," Ella added.

He was sober and unhappy, from what I could see of him. With a parting glance at us, Brooks walked to the car and got into the front seat. The woman Pioline had called Nikki managed to get into the backseat just before the car peeled away.

I asked Ella about the brunette.

"That's Nicole Cararra. She's Bebe's stand-in and companion. Bebe's paid companion, for all I know. How did you and Nikki hit it off?"

"We didn't."

"That's funny. She's been asking about you all day."

"What did you tell her?"

"Among other things, that you're the John Payne type. She actually asked me who John Payne was. Poor guy."

"I'll feel sorry for him later," I said.

Ella had her next line ready, but she never got to use it. Lillie Lacey was addressing us. "Conference time, children," she called, her Mayfair accent as out of keeping with her housewife disguise as it was out of place on the sunbaked airstrip.

Ella waved to her without turning. "Too bad," she said. "I was hoping for a little time alone with you."

"You were?"

"Yes. Bebe's not the only sucker for a man in uniform."

She brushed at my lapels in a conscious imitation of Brooks. Then she stood on tiptoe and kissed me.

"Bebe who?" I asked.

4

The drive to the ranch got me queasier than the flight. Pioline had told me that the road followed a meandering stream, but he'd neglected to mention the ruts, which made the Plymouth meander itself, even at low-gear speed.

Crowe Ranch at ground level lived up to what I'd seen of it from the air. If anything, it looked larger and plusher, a dude ranch more than a working ranch, but that wasn't doing it justice. It was a working ranch whose work was the movies and whose livestock included both horses and actors. More than one of the directors of my acquaintance would have considered that a bad deal for the horses.

The people part of the ranch, the part that wasn't pasture, was divided three ways. The main compound occupied the highest ground and consisted of three good-size buildings: Crowe House, where the owners lived when they were in residence, set square to the main gate; a combination cookhouse and dining room to the left of the main house and perpendicular to it; and a bunkhouse for the ranch hands and the less exalted guests, hidden behind the cookhouse.

To the right of this threesome as you entered the ranch and down a sloping path was what Ella called the "cottage grove," a grouping of little frame cabins, bigger than those of an old-style motel but less orderly in their arrangement. The haphazard layout was due to the locust trees around which the cottages had been built. The trees screened them from the buildings on the hill and—to a lesser extent—from one another.

To the left of the main house was another slope that started behind the bunkhouse and ran down to the corral and barns. "Downwind most nights, thank God," as Ella delicately put it.

On the slow drive from the airfield, Pioline had told us that our council of war would begin immediately. Nevertheless, when Ella and I finished our brief tour of the ranch, I borrowed the key to her cottage and headed for her shower. I was hoping she'd join me—in the cottage at least—but she didn't want to miss anything. I was nowhere near as anxious. I'd been in many such meetings with Paddy, and I knew he would do my talking for me, in between bouts of his own. Besides which, I was in a hurry to be a civilian again.

So I stood under the little shower in Ella's little bathroom until its little water heater gave up the fight. I went on standing there after that, the water feeling better the cooler it got. Then I dressed in the suit I'd worn to Las Vegas, a Dacron polyester, three-button job in a color called "black olive." I tucked the thirty-two under Ella's mattress, replacing it with a gun from my bag, a Colt 1911-A1. The gun was war surplus, like its owner. I wouldn't normally have worn it to a social gathering, but I found the weight of it reassuring. I could only hope I got over my willies by bedtime. I was too old to sleep with the lights on.

The conference was being held in the communal dining room. I would have considered that too public, if I hadn't known Pioline. I was certain he'd rented the entire ranch for the duration of the shoot. The dining room was a narrow wing of the cookhouse with walls that were no more than posts and wire screening. The matching screen door was spring-loaded—the better to keep out the horses—and I underestimated the spring's oomph. It turned out to have more than Ann Sheridan in her heyday, enough to slam the door behind me with a sound like the crack of a whip.

That sound effect made an entrance of what I'd hoped would be an infiltration. Six heads turned to watch me cross the concrete floor, four of which I'd expected to see. Marcus Pioline and Paddy were seated at opposite ends of a long table, each thinking, I was sure, that the other had graciously accepted the foot. Ella was at Paddy's elbow and Lacey at Pioline's, the actress sitting ramrod straight on her backless bench.

Lacey had lost her scarf and shaken some life into her hair, and she looked a little more like the famous *Life* cover that had introduced her to America in 1951. That photo, which had shown her in a low-cut evening gown knee-deep in a California surf, had been in black-and-white, which meant it hadn't even capitalized on Lacey's flaming tresses or her other Technicolor feature, her eyes, which were unusually green and unusually large. All her features were oversize: the sloping, ski-jump nose, at which she poked fun during television guest appearances with Bob Hope; the expressive mouth; the perfect teeth, which she called Marc's teeth since Pioline had paid to have them capped.

Lacey had told me once that whatever claim to beauty she had she owed to proportionality. "Grow one thing larger than anyone ever saw," she'd said, "and they put you in a circus. Grow everything big, and they put you in CinemaScope."

The two participants I hadn't expected sat facing one another at the middle of the table. One was a hardcase named Lange, a steel-jacketed round of a guy who had once worked for Hollywood Security. He'd left us to start a uniformed security operation, Lange Limited, which catered to independent producers like Pioline. Lange's parting with Paddy hadn't been a kiss-blowing competition, which meant that he'd probably opposed the decision to call us in. The brief nod he gave me didn't confirm my hunch or deny it.

Across from Lange sat a man in faded cotton and a straw cowboy hat. I suppressed a desire to remove the hat for him in deference to Ella and Lacey and shook his callused hand instead. He identified himself with a short name, Bud, and a long job title, ranch foreman and representative of the absent Crowes.

In place of handshakes, I received pointed looks from Paddy and Pioline. I didn't take them to heart. As I'd cleverly foreseen, the brain trust hadn't reached a consensus on the question of what to do about Johnny Remlinger. I could have taken a long nap and not missed that dawn. When I'd entered, Lange had been reciting a thumbnail sketch of Remlinger's career. He'd been addressing the ranch foreman, but I'd had the impression that the speech was Lange's way of reclaiming the turf where Paddy was currently squatting.

After I'd settled myself comfortably on a neighboring table, Lange took up the story.

"So Remlinger went from Gus Graffino's hatchet man to his heir apparent in the Cleveland mob. The word we got is that Graffino all but adopted Remlinger, which shows how bad his judgment is."

I'd missed the part where Remlinger joined the Graffino organization as a runner, worked his way up to gunman, and then single-handedly saved Graffino during a shoot-out with a rival business leader. Luckily, Paddy had already given me the basic continuity. I looked for Paddy to be squirming during Lange's lecture, but he was gazing on contentedly, like a proud teacher enjoying his reflected glory.

"There are a lot of stories about Remlinger," Lange was saying. "Too many for them all to be true. One that probably is true bears on our current situation. After the attempt on Graffino's life, Remlinger figured out that there had been some inside help, people in Graffino's own camp who had either actively participated or looked the other way. According to the story, which the Cleveland cops believe but could never prove, Remlinger set about cleaning house. He tracked the traitors down one by one and hung them. Only instead of using rope he used piano wire, the way Hitler did with those German officers who tried to blow him up. Remlinger didn't quit until he'd gotten the very last one, Graffino's own brother."

Lange paused to let that sink in. Then he said, "The Cleveland mob is deep into Vegas, so it was only a matter of time before Remlinger headed west. It was a short hop from there to Hollywood. A very short hop for Johnny Remlinger, since he's sort of big on the movies."

Paddy gave off blowing smoke rings and considered his cigar. "We've all of us made the same hop for the same reason."

"That's right," Pioline chorused in. "We're all movie-crazy outsiders who have elbowed our way in out here. Why should this Remlinger put the wind up us so?"

"Because when he stabs you in the back," Lange said, "it's with a real knife. He's not some Hollywood type you can outmaneuver or buy off. You'd do as well waving money at a live grenade."

"Nobody said anything about waving money," Pioline shot back. "We haven't a nickel to spare for that."

"Which is why we should call in the police, Marc dear," Lacey drawled. "They work for nothing."

"If Remlinger took Bebe across the state line against her will," Ella added, "we can get the FBI for the same price."

"We don't know if it happened that way." Pioline was holding his hands out a few inches above the table, as though he were expecting it to jump into the air. "All we know is she slipped away from here and went down to LA for some nightlife, that she met this Remlinger at a party and disappeared for a week—a very expensive week—and now she's back."

And we could all live happily ever after. I knew by then how the opposing sides had sorted themselves out. Ella and Lacey and Lange were for calling in the police. Pioline and Paddy were for keeping them out, the producer because he had a pile of money invested in a Bebe Brooks movie and my boss from force of habit.

My vote hadn't been counted, but only Lillie Lacey seemed to notice. "What do *you* think, Scotty, now that you're finally here? You're the only one besides Bebe who's actually met this gentleman from Cleveland."

I was curious about my opinion myself, but Paddy had gone back to blowing smoke rings. So I winged it. "Call in the police and the FBI and the National Guard while you're at it," I said. "They're not going to scare this gentleman off."

Ella shot me a glance that put Paddy and Pioline's earlier

attempts at browbeating in the shade. Then she switched it off, having read something in my own expression that I'd thought I'd bottled up.

I had time just then to rearrange my poker face. Lacey stirred in her seat, the movement writ large, like her every gesture. We all turned to follow her gaze and saw a delegation of two climbing the path from the cottages: Beverly Brooks and her husband.

It was easy to tell who had won their private debate. Brooks looked as cool and collected as she had when she'd stepped off the *Argo*. She was bathed in the kind of golden evening light cinematographers dream in, her peach dress and brown skin absorbing it and her golden hair batting it back toward the west.

Daniel Irwin was immune to the benefits of good lighting. He slouched along a half step behind Brooks, the outline of his clenched fists visible through the jacket pockets where he'd hidden them. I'd had my fill of studying Brooks for the day, so I concentrated on her husband as they finished their walk and negotiated the trick door.

Irwin was just under six feet tall, with no visible flab or paunch, which wasn't bad for a guy who had to be in his forties. I guessed it was nerves and not handball keeping his weight under control. Nerves and a bad stomach, to judge by his grim expression, which seemed to be the only one he'd packed. He wore black horn-rims, the same shape as the eyeglasses that had transformed poor George Reeves from Superman to Clark Kent. Above the glasses were a high, unmarked forehead and the remains of a curly head of dark hair.

Once inside the dining room, Brooks made straight for the conference table. "I want to apologize to everyone," she said, her sweeping gaze as she delivered the line taking in even the surprised Bud. "Especially to you, Marc. I made a big mistake and I'm sorry. I hope you'll take me back. I'd really like to finish the picture."

Pioline had half risen when Brooks entered the room. He jumped to his feet now. "My dear, my dear," he said. "Take you back? Didn't we just go get you? Of course you'll finish the picture. We were discussing what to do about Mr. Remlinger, not you. With you there is no discussion. You will continue in your part absolutely. But now you must rest. You are still tired."

"Not yet, Marc," Brooks said, with a hard edge to her voice I hadn't heard before. "Not until I talk to you about John— about Mr. Remlinger. I've decided I'm not going to press charges against him. I don't care what anyone says." Here the effort of not looking at Irwin made every neck in the room throb. "What happened was as much my fault as anybody's. I just want to make it right. The only way I can do that is by getting back to work."

Pioline had looked like a proud grandfather as she'd apologized. Now, as she carried the day for him, he positively beamed. "My dear, of course. It's settled then absolutely. No police, no publicity. You just let me handle it. You get some rest. Your eyes are closing by themselves."

"Okay, Marc." Brooks briefly looked my way as she turned to make her exit. I saw that Pioline was right. His starlet was suddenly as dopey with fatigue as she'd been on the plane.

The screen door slammed behind her, but Daniel Irwin held his ground. "This whole thing stinks," he said, his words a little slurred. "You should have called the police days ago, instead of risking Beverly's life with your silly rescue."

"I'm sorry you weren't . . . available to be consulted," Pioline said.

"Nuts to that," Irwin replied. "Now you're leaving Beverly's neck on the block for the sake of your stupid movie. Nuts to the whole bunch of you."

He turned and stomped out.

5

"Writers," Pioline muttered. Then he remembered his company. "Sorry, Ella. I should have said 'novelists' or just plain kept my mouth shut."

"But when is the last time that happened?" Lacey asked politely.

Pioline laughed the loudest of anyone, but ignored the implied advice. "So the matter is settled for us," he said. "We don't call the police. What do we do?"

"I can bring in extra men," Lange said. "Luckily, we're pretty isolated here. The shooting site is even better. We should be able to spot trouble from a fair way off."

"Good," Pioline said. "Very good. I will authorize it of course. 'Millions for defense, but not one penny for tribute.' That's our motto. But is there anything we can do of an offensive nature?"

All eyes turned to Paddy, even Lange's bloodshot ones. I found myself suspecting Pioline and even Brooks of working to Paddy's script.

"If you'd like," he said. "I can have a word with some contacts I have in Los Angeles. One of them is a man in the same line of work as Gus Graffino but with more seniority. If I can persuade him that this Brooks business is all bad press and no profit, he might call Graffino and arrange to have Remlinger's leash shortened."

"How will you convince this contact?" Lacey asked, genuinely curious.

"Let's say he owes me a favor," Paddy replied with enough false modesty to plug up the screen walls. "Of course, I'll have to move quickly. Remlinger could be halfway here already."

He'd overreached for once. Pioline was on his feet again. "I'll fly you down this evening. Right now, in fact. I have business in town myself. You and Scotty will be my passengers again."

Paddy recovered his composure quickly. "If it's all the same to you and Mr. Lange, I'd like to leave Mr. Elliott here. He can be my eyes and ears, and he's handled Remlinger once."

By which he meant, I was the man who had pulled the pin from the grenade. Despite that distinction, I had been on the point of demanding the assignment Paddy was slipping me. It would be safer and easier than the only alternative I could think of: attempting to drag the mother of my children away from the scene of the action.

"Is that acceptable to you, Lange?" Pioline asked. "Scotty? Good, Scotty stays. He'll need some things from home. Mr. Maguire, can you arrange that?"

I couldn't wait to see what Paddy—a man who'd made color blindness a fashion statement—would pack for me. If I was lucky, his wife and former business partner, Peggy, would come out of retirement long enough to handle the job. "I'll need a car, too," I said.

"I can hire another one locally or I can have yours driven up with your things," Pioline said. "Sending yours up might be easier."

He meant cheaper, but that was fine by me.

"Is that everything? Good. Meeting adjourned, I think."

Pioline was referring to the general meeting. He immediately scheduled another one, a one-on-one with his director, Max Froy, who was on his way in from the shooting site. Pioline promised Paddy that they would leave directly afterward. My boss took his stay of execution gracefully. Very gracefully, as he left with my wife on his arm. I hung around long enough to say a genuine hello to Lacey.

"I don't like this, Scotty," she said. "I don't like it one bit." She held my hand while she said it. It was the gesture of a person who doesn't want her audience to wander away before she'd finished, a gesture no one with emerald green eyes ever needed to use. "I feel as though it's 1940 again and I'm back in uniform. I'm glad you're staying."

The sentiment was less than universal. I'd just stepped out of the dining room and started after Ella and Paddy when Lange collared me from behind. He didn't literally collar me; he had that much professional courtesy. And he could spot a gun under any amount of gabardine. He just whacked me on the shoulder with all the subtlety of my draft board.

"You and I need to talk, Elliott," he said. He led me toward the business side of the ranch, the barns and the stables.

Lange wasn't a big man, but he carried himself like one. I knew from experience that it wasn't a pose; it was a mind-set. He needed to be tough to get away with wearing the uniform he'd designed for his company. It consisted of a navy blue shirt and tie and gray slacks with a blue stripe down each leg. "Lange Limited" was embroidered in yellow script over the breast pocket of the shirt, which also had yellow buttons. The initials "LL" appeared in the same color above the patent leather bill on his service cap, which sat squarely on his square head.

I never saw the outfit without reflecting on an odd fact of human nature: Some guys actually missed being in the service.

We ended up leaning on the wooden fence of a small corral where two men were saddling a horse. Beyond the corral was the wire fence that circled the ranch. A man on horseback was leading three riderless horses through the wire via a small gate.

"I didn't know you'd landed the security job for this picture," I said. "My wife didn't mention it."

"You mean your boss didn't," Lange said. "I could see you were surprised when you spotted me just now. It took me back to my days on Maguire's payroll. He never told any of us the whole story, did he? He always liked to hold something back. It was his way of staying in charge."

I figured this was foreplay, that we hadn't come out there to discuss Paddy. I was wrong.

"I'll stay out of your way," I said.

Lange waved at that worthless promise with a hand so broad and stubby it looked like all the fingers had been trimmed to the first knuckle. "Maguire isn't going to get a damn thing done in Los Angeles. Him and his contacts and his favors. He still thinks he can finesse the world with secret handshakes and money under the table. Hell, he still thinks it's 1945. Why hasn't he retired?"

I didn't know the answer to that myself. It wasn't that Paddy was broke exactly. Peggy had managed to hide a small amount of his income from him over the years. It wasn't even that he particularly liked what we did. It had more to do with having the Marcus Piolines of the world calling him in their moments of despair, him, Patrick J. Maguire, the man the studios had once given a collective Bronx cheer.

That treatment was something Paddy and I had in common. Lange wasn't a member of our secret society, so I didn't share my theory with him. He wasn't done complaining in any case.

"For all we know, this Gus Graffino is just as past it as Maguire. He may think he runs Remlinger, the way Maguire thinks he runs you. They're both kidding themselves. Remlinger's probably been leading his old man by the nose for years, the same way you lead Maguire."

I was only listening with one ear. The men in the corral had gotten the saddle, an English saddle, on the horse. Now they were hiding it under some kind of animal skin. "Paddy does the leading," I said.

"He did once," Lange said. "In the old days. I can remember when it was shoulders back and mouth shut with him. I've seen him kneecap a guy without blinking, without losing the ash off his cigar."

I still wasn't taking Lange seriously. "Everybody's character softens over time," I said. "Look at what happened to Harpo Marx."

Lange grabbed a handful of my lapel. "Don't joke with me, Elliott. I'm telling you, you ruined the guy."

Being a slow-to-anger type, I replied as though things hadn't gotten physical. "I didn't talk him into passing on your plan for a uniform service. I thought it was a good idea. But Paddy hated every minute he spent as a studio guard at Paramount in the thirties. So he wouldn't buy in."

"Who gives a damn about that? I'm talking about the man, not his balance sheet. You've softened him up with a lot of romantic crap about old Hollywood. You've always been up to your ears in that, but Maguire used to see the town the way it is. Now he's almost as gone as you ever were. It would be bad enough if it was still '45. But while Maguire's gotten more dewy-eyed, the world's gotten more dangerous. That combination is going to get him killed. Maguire thinks this Remlinger is just a junior member of his men-of-the-world club. He's not. He's a whole new animal."

"I know," I said.

That simple acknowledgment took the fight out of Lange for the moment. He released my lapel—too late to save its looks, polyester or no polyester—and stepped back. "I'd hate to see something bad happen to Paddy," he said.

I waited for him to extend his regrets to me, but he left me hanging and marched off. I bummed a cigarette from one of the men fooling with the saddle cover. While I smoked it, I thought about my own regrets, large and small. Then I went in search of Ella and the man I'd ruined.

I found them in front of Ella's cottage, sitting in Adirondack chairs, sipping tall drinks that looked like iced tea but probably weren't. I collected my pipe from my bag, figuring I could use it to cover the evidence of my second illicit cigarette. There wasn't a third chair, so I sat on the cottage's single stone step.

"Been visiting?" Ella asked.

"Lange wanted a word with me."

I snuck a long look at Paddy while he and Ella discussed our kids. He certainly didn't look like a man headed into trouble, but that might only have confirmed Lange's diagnosis. I'd noticed a mellowing in Paddy myself, but I'd associated it with the election of Jack Kennedy, another Irish Catholic, to the Presidency. All had been right with the world for Paddy when that had happened, and the glow hadn't worn off yet. It wouldn't wear off, if I was right. Not until the end of Kennedy's second term in 1968.

"What do you think the odds are of getting Remlinger called off?" I asked him after Ella had taken their empty glasses into the cottage.

"It's a place to start is all," he said. "We'll soon know whether Graffino's calling the shots or no. And whether Remlinger's fallen for Hollywood or for our Miss Brooks. If it's Hollywood, he'll find himself another starlet and become another producer's headache. If it's Bebe or nothing . . . well, we'll cross that bridge when we're prodded.

"Speaking of Beverly Brooks," he added, glancing at the cottage door and lowering his voice, "how did she strike you?"

"Monroe's safe for the time being."

"Let's try again. How did she seem to you?"

"Scared at first. And tired. Mostly tired. Being scared takes it out of some people."

"It does," Paddy said. He scratched at his five-o'clock shadow for a time, alternating between chins. "I'd borrow your razor and clean up a little, but it might be dangerous. My hand's shaking just thinking about that damned airplane."

Then, without a segue, he was back to Brooks. "She was named for Louise Brooks, did you know that? I mean, Bebe's real name was Kowalski or something until some publicity hack decided she reminded him of the old silent movie star. The hair color's wrong, of course. But there is a resemblance. Do you remember Louise Brooks?"

"I met her once, I think. In '39 or '40."

"She was washed up by then. I meant, do you remember her from silent pictures? There was no one better. Her specialty was playing ordinary working girls, shop girls we used to call them, who had some great good luck and then ended badly. Tragically, you'd say."

"Any of them take up with gangsters?"

"Sure, gangsters were big in the twenties. I was just trying to remember whether Louise Brooks ever played a girl who'd fooled around with drugs."

I sat up. "What are you getting at?"

"Nothing probably. That fatigue we saw in Bebe might just have been a reaction to the excitement as you said. But I've been thinking of some of the lost souls we've run across who've fallen in with pills of one kind or another. Some of them were dead on their feet, too, no pun intended."

"You think Remlinger might have been feeding Brooks pills as a way of keeping her in line?"

"More subtle than hiding her clothes," Paddy mused. "Or is that a strike against the idea?"

He never worked it out. Pioline pulled up just then in one of the production-company Plymouths. Lacey was with him, disguised again in scarf and sunglasses. She addressed me through the open passenger window.

"Don't forget, Scotty. Cocktails at my place when I get back from this little errand. Ella knows all about it."

Pioline leaned around Lacey to join the conversation. "I offered to drop Danny Irwin somewhere, but he took it the wrong way, so you're stuck with him. Good luck, Scotty."

Paddy cast a wistful glance at the cottage, but there was no sign of his drinking buddy. "My love to her nibs," he said. "Make sure she remembers to duck."

6

As I watched the Plymouth waddle through the screen of trees on its way back to the ranch proper, I became conscious of music, very familiar music coming from the cottage behind me. It was Duke Ellington's "Prelude to a Kiss."

I was a longtime member of Ellington's fan club, though there had been times in the early fifties when that club had all but closed down. Then, in 1956, the Duke had made a comeback that was the stuff of movie scripts. It had happened at the Newport Jazz Festival, where Ellington and his orchestra had been placed late on the bill, so late that people had been heading for the parking lot when—around midnight—a saxophone artist named Gonsalves had stepped down front to do a solo in the middle of "Diminuendo and Crescendo in Blue." Six choruses later, the sleepy audience was waking up. Ten choruses in, the ticket holders were on their feet, many of them dancing. The better conditioned were still at it on chorus twenty-seven, when Ellington deftly reined the stampede in.

The whole evening had been one for a happy ending collector's book, and I had been there, a birthday present from my successful wife, who had been one of the first dancers to take to the aisles. No happy ending collector I, but the miracle evening had suggested that one might still occur now and then, that there might be some point to slogging through years and years of middle reels.

Ella's cottage was one of the smaller ones, the better accommodations having been reserved for the actors, the few on hand and those to come. The floor plan was front room with fireplace and, behind it, a bedroom with bath. Ella and Duke weren't in the front room, though I didn't lift the deerskin rug on the hearth to make absolutely sure. I did have a brief vision of my wife reclining on the rug, back lit by a roaring blaze, and that fantasy turned out to be part prophesy.

When I entered the bedroom, I found Ella stretched out on the bed, showing off her tan in panties and bra, the bra less fancy than Brooks's, but no less formidable.

"Weeks go by without this happening to me," I said. "And then there's a day like today."

Ella laughed. It was a throaty laugh, like Pioline's, but more spontaneous. "Paddy couldn't resist telling me how you found Bebe. I thought you might be in the mood to reminisce."

What she meant was, she was in the mood to eclipse whatever memory of Brooks I might have tucked away. Toward that end, she unhooked her bra and threw it at me. I passed it to the bedpost on my way to examine the portable hi-fi.

"How'd you find Ellington in this outpost?"

"One of the set hands is a connoisseur. He loaned me a couple of records. I thought it would put you in the mood."

Assuming the sight of a beautiful woman wiggling out of her underwear did not. "Have you forgotten the invitation you've accepted for cocktails?" I asked, though I was out of shirt and shoes and left sock.

"No," Ella said. "That will be an intermission. I figured you'd need one. You're not getting any younger, you know."

"Quite well," I said.

Getting younger—or at least staying young—was Ella's department. She often seemed to me to be too young to have a twelve-year old son and a daughter of ten. I was just as often afraid of being mistaken for the kids' granddad. A physical-fitness craze had infected the country, and Ella was a carrier, swimming every chance she got, horseback riding with the kids, and beating her husband at tennis. I had no idea how the rest of the country was shaping up, but Ella was doing nicely.

When I sat down on the bed, she was massaging the red marks left behind by the underwire of her late bra. I took over the job, helpful guy that I was. In exchange, she massaged the welts left on my thighs by my boxers, although I hadn't actually noticed any.

That led to a kiss, a long one. Afterward I tried to recite her old signature line, "If you don't have a good kisser, be one," but she cut it short by sticking her tongue in my ear.

"There's no dialogue in the rest of this scene, Scotty," she whispered when she'd finished. "And no mush either. I want passion, not romance. And we've only time for one take."

Lillian Lacey was installed in Crowe House in place of the absent owners. In fact, the presence of the movie queen might have explained their absence. The house looked to be the oldest building on the ranch, with much hand-hewn wood in evidence. Lacey's maid, who was also old and hand-hewn and whose name was Hilly, showed us through a large front room overshadowed by a balcony whose railing still wore its bark. Ella paused beside a stone fireplace that made the one in our cabin look like a backyard barbecue. Above the railroad-tie mantel was a deer's head. According to Ella, Lacey had christened the thing Leslie, after Leslie Howard, the English actor killed by the Nazis.

"She thinks it has his eyes," Ella told me as Hilly urged us on. "Or was it his ears?"

That irreverent observation was a lot of the house tour I got. Lacey received us on a stone patio behind the building. Not a trace of her potato-sack costume remained. She was wearing a blue cocktail dress cut to fit, which I didn't notice fast enough. She called me on it almost before she'd said hello.

"How was your sex, kiddies? Satisfying, I trust. Don't look so surprised, Scotty. I'm something of a detective, too, you know. If a man doesn't look at my knockers two steps into the room, I know he's had sex in the last little while. The actual time since he's had it depends on his age: ten minutes or so for a youngster and anything up to a day for an old goat like Marc. I'd say you're a forty-minute man, Scotty. Ella, am I right?"

Ella wasn't saying. She was too busy laughing through her nose.

Lacey was steering me toward a drink cart decked out like the bar at the Beverly Wilshire. "Here are all the necessaries," she told me. "Mix us up some of your famous Gibsons."

While I worked, she and Ella talked about the party where the Elliotts and the Piolines had met ten years ago and more.

"Good days those," Lacey said, raising the glass I'd handed her in an impromptu toast, as Paddy had done on the plane. "The old town's not the same as it was, though I dare say you were thinking the same thing about Hollywood ten years ago, Scotty. Sometimes I wish I'd been around here in the thirties, to see what it was like. Then at other times I think I was lucky that my career really hadn't gotten moving before the war, not even in English pictures. It was easier for me to start again when I was demobed. I was still a fresh face."

She looked into my unfresh face and went back to a more general discussion of Hollywood and its changes. "I'll say this for Marc, whatever his faults, he's trying to uphold the old standards. He may have been a late arrival in Hollywood, but he'll still be here when they turn out the lights. No foreign locations for him. Mind you, I wouldn't have turned up my nose at half a year in Spain. Or in Italy, with Liz Taylor and those lovely men she has along, Rex Harrison and Dickie Burton. Don't think they're not having a lark.

"You should hear what they're spending on *Cleopatra*. Marc has a spy who slips him the figures, and it's obscene. Our little production will come in for what they've budgeted for ostrich plumes."

She held out her glass, which had somehow emptied itself while she'd talked, and I refilled it from a sweating pitcher.

"Thank you, darling. If I sound jealous, Ella, it's only because I am. Marc tells me not to fret, that every dollar they waste is another dollar of free publicity for us. Still, it would be nice to be the one frittering it away for a change."

I thought I saw Ella's pale eyes flit between Lacey's necklace and her bracelet, the stones of which matched the blue dress, but I might have been mistaken. Ella's "Wouldn't we all?" sounded sincere enough.

The back door of the cottage opened and a young woman came out. I knew her at once, because I'd been reading about her in Ella's letters. I think I would have known her anyway. She was Jewel Lacey, Lillie's daughter from a pre-Pioline marriage. A wartime marriage, if I was remembering right. That would put Jewel somewhere in the neighborhood of twenty, just old enough to be making her acting debut in *Warrior Queen*. She was playing one of Boudica's daughters, the other being Bebe Brooks. In Jewel's case, the casting was perfect. Her resemblance to her mother was striking, though her features and figure were more delicate and her eyes were an ordinary brown. She had her mother's red hair and pale complexion, and she would have had her height, if she'd carried herself with Lacey's assurance. As it was, she slipped in between her mother's chair and Ella's like a maid who'd come in to tidy up.

"There you are, Jewel," Lacey said. "I wondered where you'd gotten off to after I'd invited Mr. Elliott over especially so you could meet him."

Jewel said "Mother!" and blushed and sat down on the arm of Ella's chair.

"It's true!" Lacey countered. "She's been dying to meet you, Scotty, a real gumshoe and all. And she picked up a rumor—don't ask me where, she never goes out—that Alfred Hitchcock nicknamed the detective in *Vertigo* Scotty as a tribute to you, because you'd gotten Hitch out of some scrape. Is it true? Was the Jimmy Stewart character based on you?"

"I dunno," I said. "But I've heard a rumor that Kim Novak's eyebrows were based on mine."

"Don't encourage him by laughing," Lacey said to her daughter. "And don't be fooled. That isn't how real detectives talk. That's how actors talk when they're playing detectives in the movies. And out of the movies."

Jewel didn't appear to get that reference to my past life. I did. I would have said touché if I'd been the kind of guy who says touché. I poured myself a second Gibson instead and asked Jewel how she was liking the movie business.

"I'm not," she said, blushing again and looking apologetic, first at her mother and then at Ella. She hurriedly added, "There's so much sitting around waiting for things to happen."

"Now she's trying to fool *you*, Scotty," Lacey said. "The reason she doesn't like being in this movie is that the costume designer Marc hired has Jewel and Bebe wearing things that look like bikinis manufactured by the village blacksmith. Jewel doesn't like showing off her . . . legs. Do you, kitten?"

Jewel didn't react, because it wasn't possible for even a red-head to blush any harder than she'd been blushing. I noticed that Ella was patting her hand. She'd been making a habit of it, if I knew Ella.

"Jewel is right about the sit-around-and-wait syndrome, of course," Lacey went on, "but that's always been the way of it with pictures. It's been particularly bad on this picture because, in addition to the standard delays and confusion, we've had Bebe Brooks, a woman who has all the temperament of Judy Garland and not one whit of the talent. It's been weeks of 'What will upset Bebe today?' and 'Which of Ella's deathless lines will refuse to stay in Bebe's little head in this scene?' You won't believe this, Scotty, but one day the line was 'Hold, the Romans come!' Ten takes at least before the damn Romans got there.

"And now we're sitting around waiting for some boy gangster to descend on us like all the ten plagues. Waiting to see which one of us he'll pop off first. The whole ranch is waiting; the whole valley is in a state of nervous expectation."

Ella had been looking up at Jewel in concern. When she broke into Lacey's speech, it was in part, I thought, to reassure the young woman. "I'm not in a state of nervous expectation myself," she said. "How about you, Scotty?"

"Perfectly relaxed, thanks," I said.

"But as I observed earlier," Lacey said, "you two have just had sex."

"Mother!" Jewel said again, but Ella's plan had worked. The tension of the moment was heading west. I thought the occasion called for another Gibson, but Ella moved the pitcher away as I reached for it.

"That's all, brother," she said. "Your forty minutes are about up."

"Why Ella," Lacey said. "You glutton!"

I was ready to echo Lacey later that evening. It was after our second intermission, this one occasioned by the arrival of dinner, which Ella had arranged to have delivered surreptitiously by a friend she'd made in the cookhouse. Dinner by candlelight had been the romantic portion of the evening. We were now back to passion, accompanied by more commandeered Ellington. "Do Nothing Till You Hear from Me," appropriately enough.

Ella was sitting atop me, her hands holding my shoulders against the deerskin rug. She was gyrating her lower body gently and rocking her head from side to side in a counter rhythm, as though she was trying to work out a particularly large kink in her back. It was my favorite view of her, and not just because of the foreground interest supplied by her swaying breasts. She was momentarily unself-conscious, aware of me—I hoped—but also oblivious on some level, of me and the world at large. It was like watching her sleep, only more interactive, as I had some insight into the little smiles and grimaces that alternately moved across her wide mouth. I could have watched that show for hours, by which I mean I always wished I could enjoy it for hours. The actual record was nowhere close.

Over dinner, we'd discussed *Warrior Queen*, Ella recounting the hopes she'd once had for it and describing her disappointment when she'd realized that Pioline was transforming her serious script into something she'd called "a bronze brassiere fest." The biggest of Pioline's many concessions to the box office had been his casting of Beverly Brooks and the subsequent beefing up of her part at the expense of Lacey and Jewel and historical accuracy in general. In exchange for which, Brooks had done nothing but make trouble for Pioline, saving her worst outbreaks of temperament for those rare days when the busy producer flew in to visit the shoot.

That coincidence came back to me now. Though it was no moment to bring the subject up, I did.

"You say that—except for today—Brooks has always been at her worst when Pioline's been around?"

Ella stopped rocking her head but kept the rest of her in motion. "You've still got her on the brain?" she panted. "Damn, this is going to be harder than I thought."

"I was wondering if Brooks could be playing up to Pioline. Maybe the two of them have an affair going on. Marc and Lillie are divorced remember."

"As though being married ever stopped Marc," Ella said.

She straightened her back and moved my hands up from her hips to her breasts. Her own hands explored me, encouraging me to focus a little more sharply. At the same time, she started talking like a telegram.

"Give me one more minute . . . of your undivided attention . . . then we can chat . . . and if you say . . . 'Hold, the Romans come' . . . one more time . . . I'll make you start . . . from the beginning!"

7

Way too early the next day, I was seated under a scrap of awning, watching Brooks and Jewel Lacey rehearse a bit of business with the picture's stunt coordinator. I'd spent a restless night, despite Ella's effort to wear me out. I'd gotten up at one point to check on Lange's sentries, but their boss had intercepted me and sent me back to bed. At first light I'd borrowed the cookhouse phone and called Paddy. He'd told me my clean socks were on the way and acted coy about the real point of my call, telling me only that his attempt to go over Remlinger's head with the mob was moving ahead.

So, for lack of anything more constructive to do, I spent the morning keeping an eye on Brooks. Seated next to me in a matching canvas chair was Daniel Irwin, there to keep an eye on me.

I couldn't blame him for wanting to chaperone. In addition to practicing a few basic thrusts and parries with short, broad swords, Brooks and Jewel were getting used to moving around in the costumes Lillie Lacey had spoken of so disparagingly. She'd called them bikinis, but that wasn't accurate. They were certainly two-piece, the pieces a breastplate that shone like metal but probably wasn't and a short skirt of what looked like animal hide and probably was. But the breastplate was long enough to meet the skirt, so there were no bare midriffs to upset anyone's grandmother. There were bare backs, as the breastplates lacked back pieces. That would have been a serious disadvantage in a fight, but aesthetically it was all to the good. The chest pieces were held in place by crossed thongs, a motif repeated by the sandals the women wore, which were laced up to their knees.

Brooks already looked plenty comfortable in the outfit, but then I knew that self-consciousness wasn't one of her failings. It was Jewel's whole act, and I couldn't help feeling sorry for her as she stood stiffly under a golf umbrella held aloft by a flunky assigned to see that she didn't burn in the sun.

"Of course," Irwin suddenly said, picking it up in the middle as though we'd been talking all morning, "Boudica's daughters were royal princesses and probably priestesses too, like their mother. They wouldn't have been caught dead dressed like that. Or, to make better use of the cliché, they would have been dead shortly after being caught dressed like that."

I tapped out the pipe I'd been nursing. "Ever see the statue of Boudica and her daughters in London?" I asked. "What they're wearing in that chariot makes these outfits look like Edna May Oliver's Mother Hubbard."

I waited for Irwin to counter that the statue in question was the fantasy of a Victorian sculptor who'd spent too much time in the Rubens gallery, but the novelist was busy looking at me like he hadn't really noticed me before. He pushed his canvas butterfly-hunter's hat back on his head and sat up.

"I forgot for a minute that you're Mr. Ella Englehart," he said, using Ella's pen name. "You've probably lived through a dozen drafts of the script."

"At least," I said, trying to ignore the crack he'd made at my expense. To give me something to take my mind off kicking his chair from under him, I trotted out a thumbnail version of Ella's scenario.

"Boudica was the queen of the Iceni, a tribe that had held on to a little of its independence after the Romans conquered Britain. The king of the Iceni, Boudica's husband, was named Prasutagas. When he died, in 61 A.D., he left his kingdom jointly to Nero, the Roman emperor, and to his daughters, hoping by that gesture to put his family under Nero's protection.

"The plan backfired. When the news reached Rome, Nero threw a fit over not getting the whole pie. He ordered his men in Britain to grab everything Prasutagas owned.

"The actual dirty work was done by a procurator named Decianus. Decianus went overboard, not only emptying the Iceni coffers but publicly humiliating Boudica and her daughters. The queen was flogged by the procurator's soldiers, and the two princesses were raped by his slaves.

"The Iceni went nuts over that. They revolted. With Boudica leading the way, they sacked a Roman town called Colchester, took a breather to slaughter every man, woman, and child they'd captured, and then wiped out most of a Roman legion marching against them. All the time, Boudica was picking up new allies faster than Maury Wills collects stolen bases. The combined tribes took London and beheaded so many people the skulls have been turning up ever since.

"That was Boudica's high water mark—or high blood mark if you want to be literal. After that, she marched her army out to meet the Roman governor, Suetonius. He'd been off conquering Wales when the fracas started. When news of the revolt reached him, he beat it back and lined up every legionnaire he could find. He was still outnumbered ten to one, but he decided to stand and fight. He arranged his army on a piece of high ground with his flanks protected by forest.

"Boudica threw her troops right at the Roman's massed swords. The legionnaires hit them with javelins, then answered with cavalry when Boudica fired off her chariots. Finally, the Romans counterattacked. They pressed Boudica's army back against the Britons' own supply wagons and did some slaughtering of their own.

"Boudica escaped, but only so she could poison herself in peace. She was buried in secret by what was left of the Iceni. Her grave has never been found but may be somewhere near Bakersfield. Fadeout."

I wasn't sure Irwin had been listening. He'd been throwing eye daggers at a stuntman who was showing Brooks how to hold her sword.

But then he said, "That's your wife's script all right. Pretty accurate as Hollywood whey goes. Except that she has Suetonius, the Roman governor, in love with Boudica, a woman he probably never saw. Not to mention the fact that Suetonius was past sixty when all this occurred, making him one unlikely love interest. Our esteemed producer got around that by casting Richard Egan in the part, a man twenty years too young."

Pioline had wanted John Wayne or Robert Mitchum, but he couldn't meet either's price. I would have been just as happy discussing that bit of gossip, but Irwin had moved on to his next complaint.

"And she has Boudica finishing off Procurator Decianus in London when the guy actually escaped to Gaul."

I shrugged. "You have to kill off Basil Rathbone," I said, naming the veteran heavy Pioline had tapped for the part. "People expect it."

Irwin shrugged right back at me. "As I said, not too inaccurate as far as the bare facts are concerned. But Miss Englehart managed to miss the real spirit of the story. I mean, the story's real spirituality. For your wife, it's the tale of an extraordinary woman, grievously wronged, who seizes command of a revolt and comes within a hair of defeating the greatest empire of the age."

"So?"

"So, Boudica was more than a wronged woman or even a wronged queen. She was high priestess of her tribe's cult, a cult that worshipped a goddess."

"Andrasta," I said. "She's mentioned in the script."

"Glossed over in it, you mean. The script makes her sound like a wood nymph. She was a Celtic war goddess. She demanded human sacrifice and plenty of it, which is why the Iceni didn't take prisoners. Their sacred groves soaked up rivers of Roman blood because Boudica was the representative on earth of a vengeful, orgiastic goddess."

"Orgiastic?" I didn't know what it meant, but I liked the sound of it.

Irwin ignored me. "That's probably why she and her daughters were abused in the first place: because they represented a religion the Romans wanted to stamp out. It's surely why the Iceni rose and why they fought like nothing the Romans had ever seen. They were defending the religion of their fathers. When they failed, Boudica *had* to kill herself. Andrasta had proven to be no match for the Roman gods."

It was my turn to give Irwin a closer look. "How'd you get to be such an expert on Roman Britain? You teach literature, don't you?"

"You get that out of my dossier?"

"No, off the jacket cover of one of your novels. The one about the bomber campaign over Europe, *Blue Hell*. I always thought you guys in the Air Force had it made until I read that. It made me a lot happier to have been in the field artillery."

"It wasn't the branch of the service you were in that mattered," Irwin said. "It was whether you were occupying the wrong spot at the wrong time. If you managed never to do that, you've got no cause to complain."

"That's what I thought, once," I said. "I really believed the rest of my life would be one long Sunday afternoon, that nothing would ever bother me again."

Irwin laughed humorlessly. "Didn't we all? It turned out to be one long Monday morning for some of us."

He seemed to be in the mood to work himself over. I decided to take advantage of that to add a page or two to the dossier he'd spoken of. "How did you meet your wife?"

"She met me," Irwin said. "It was part of her plan to become Marilyn Monroe's doppelganger."

"Excuse me?"

"Her double. Anything Monroe does, Beverly has to do. Monroe married Arthur Miller, so naturally Beverly had to find herself her own man of letters. It was my bad luck to be passing by the library that day. Talk about being in the wrong place at the wrong time."

I looked out to where Brooks was being coached on her swordplay. Her long tanned legs were spread wide for balance, and her golden hair shone brighter in the noonday sun than her ersatz armor. "Some bad luck," I said.

I didn't bring up the sad fact that Monroe had divorced Miller, since Irwin was already slipping downward in his chair.

"I guess you have to be in my shoes to appreciate it," he said. "Or rather, my bed. You'd find it a little crowded most nights, I'm afraid."

I thought about apologizing, but the novelist wasn't finished.

"Or you can read all about it in a book I'm thinking of writing, *Blond Hell*. It'll make you glad you're a washed-up actor turned hotel peeper."

I went back to thinking about kicking him, and he went back to sulking. I'd refilled my pipe and lit it before he spoke again.

"I said earlier that the Iceni were fighting for the religion of their fathers. It might actually have been the religion of their mothers. You asked me how I came to know about Roman Britain. I didn't know anything about it until I read the script for *Warrior Queen*. That got me interested enough to do some research.

"One thing I came across was the possibility that the Iceni monarchy was matrilineal, that the crown passed from mother to daughter instead of from father to son. That was often the case in earlier times, when the patrimony of a child was problematical at best. It was even more common in societies that worshipped war goddesses like Andrasta. A king like our Prasutagas might have been a consort, whose power came only from his place in the queen's bed. In fact, in some of the earliest matrilineal societies, the king wasn't even a permanent fixture. He would serve for exactly one year, following which he'd be sacrificed to the local goddess."

Irwin pulled his hat down over his eyes. "Sounds a little like the prototype for Hollywood, don't you think?"

8

Two exciting events wrestled for dominance that afternoon. One was the arrival of my car. The other was dinner.

My car was a 1961 Thunderbird convertible, white with a red interior. Being a family man, I'd held off buying a Thunderbird until they'd given it four seats. Then I'd waited a few more years until the car got back a little of its looks. The '61 was a redesign, a reaction to the '58 through '60 models, which people had nicknamed "the squarebird" for good reason. The '61 was happily lacking in right angles. In fact, the front end was so pointed that Ford's brochures called it a "prow," its designers' intention apparently being that the quad headlights and the hood should run interference for the vestigial bumper, which was tucked safely beneath them. The obligatory fins were also vestigial, at least in height. In length, they were striking, their chrome caps running from the recessed headlights all the way back to the very unrecessed and very large taillights. The door handles were built into the tops of these fins, a styling cue taken up in the car's interior, whose dashboard blended into the door panels without a pause. The front seats were buckets divided by a console. The steering wheel swung to the right when the car wasn't moving, to allow the driver to exit without the indignity of sliding. That indispensable item had really sold me on the car, that or the 390-cubic-inch V-8.

The T-Bird was delivered to the ranch by one of the reinforcements Lange had called up, a kid who was still smiling from the drive when he handed me the keys. "Three hours flat," he said.

His boss was less pleased when he arrived a moment later. "My men aren't chauffeurs, Elliott," he said.

There wasn't much fight behind the words, as Lange was almost as fond of a nice car as I was. He worked at not licking his lips while I unpacked the suitcases that were jammed into that portion of the trunk not devoted to the automatic convertible top.

"Let me know if you boys land dates for the prom," I told Lange and his apprentice when I'd finished. "I may let you drive it."

Paddy had done a better job of packing for me than I'd dared hope. I found the reason inside the second case: a detailed list in Ella's handwriting. She wasn't around to thank, having gone off to hide somewhere and work on the latest rewrites Pioline had requested.

I didn't see my wife until I reported to the screened dining room for dinner. It was an especially early dinner, as the whole company had an unusual evening call.

Lacey, who seemed to be presiding over the meal, explained it to me after I'd squeezed in between Ella and Jewel. "We're having a bit of Guy Fawkes tonight. That's a bonfire to you colonists. But first we're going to shoot my descent from the temple of Andrasta at sunset. If there is a sunset."

"There's always a sunset." Lacey's debating partner was Max Froy, the German-born director, who was on his way out of the dining room. He stopped long enough to say hello to me and to reminisce about the evening we'd met. The event had taken place on the soundstage of an ill-fated movie Froy had been directing for Warner Bros. He and some stagehands had stormed the trailer belonging to the picture's star and found me standing over a body with a gun in my hand. The kind of introduction, in other words, that makes a lasting impression.

"Care to entertain us with that story?" Lacey asked when Froy had gone.

The offer was tempting. Daniel Irwin, stuck between his wife and Nicole Cararra on the opposite side of the table, actually looked interested. Cararra did, too, backing up Ella's claim that she'd been curious about me. Brooks, who like Jewel had changed back into civvies, was wearing her sunglasses while she ate, so I couldn't measure her curiosity.

"Sorry," I said. "I'd be breaking two or three oaths."

"That's all right, darling," Lacey said. "We'll get the story out of Ella later. We women have become very close here in our isolation. It was a regular hen party most nights until Mr. Irwin arrived and then you, Scotty. Next week we'll have Mr. Egan and dear old Basil Rathbone joining us. I'll miss the sorority-house feel, won't you girls?"

That it had been a sorority house with cowboys and, more recently, armed guards wandering around hadn't spoiled it for Lacey. But then, she'd never been within a mile of a real sorority. Neither had Brooks, but she gave her costar an answering smile. Brooks was sticking to her agreement to get on with the job. If she felt as uneasy as a certain member of her bodyguard did, she wasn't letting on.

During dinner, I tried to chat up Jewel, but it was heavy going. Ella fared better, leaning across my fried chicken and potato salad to draw the reluctant actress out. She managed to get Jewel to talk about the school where she'd been studying art when opportunity, in the form of *Warrior Queen*, had knocked. Jewel spoke so wistfully about the place, I got homesick for it myself.

After the meal, I walked Ella back to our cottage. On the way, she kicked stones and I passed along Irwin's criticism of her take on the Boudica story.

Ella shrugged it off, but her stone kicking got positively antisocial. "That Joan of Arc angle is nothing new. The Roman historians leaned on Andrasta and all that Celtic mumbo jumbo too, Dio Cassius, the old potboiler, and Tacitus, though he was more restrained. It helped them explain how a mere woman almost kicked their imperial butts back to Gaul. Not to mention that it was a great justification for what the Romans did to the Iceni and the other tribes. There's never been a rationalization for conquest as surefire as 'my god's better than yours.' I didn't want to plead the Romans' case for them, so I toned that stuff down. I certainly didn't need a supernatural explanation for Boudica's success. She was a tough, intelligent woman. Period."

Another stone took flight, this one coming dangerously close to my car. "I expected some men to have problems with Boudica's story," Ella said, "but not Daniel Irwin."

"His current marital difficulties may have prejudiced his thinking," I replied.

We'd arrived at the shady spot where the Thunderbird was parked. Ella patted its hood. "I think Danny's still sore that we didn't send him along with you guys to rescue Bebe. But honestly, Scotty, we couldn't have. He was blind drunk from the day she snuck off to LA looking for trouble."

Which she'd found in the person of Johnny Remlinger. I scanned the ranch for him for the fiftieth time that day. "How was Irwin before Brooks took off?"

"He was only here for a couple of days. He wasn't drunk when he got here, but he started in pretty soon after that. It was nothing like the drinking he did after Bebe ran out though. Why?"

"I'm wondering why Brooks really went to Los Angeles. Did she really meet Remlinger by accident or was it set up in advance?"

"She's sticking to the story that she bumped into him at a party."

"Then why was Irwin drinking before she ran out?"

"Don't read too much into that, Scotty. It may only have been because Bebe is tired of Danny and he knows it. The poor jerk."

An hour before sunset, Ella and I drove out to the shooting site. Most of the production vehicles and vans I'd seen from the air were still there, circled like a wagon train. Around them, Pioline's technicians had erected several sets, giving the place the look of a miniature back lot. Ella pointed out Andrasta's temple and sacred grove, the doomed Roman town of Colchester, and a small battlefield where one of Boudica's successful ambushes would be filmed by the second unit.

They'd chosen their ground well. It combined just enough wooded land to suggest ancient Britain with long vistas of grassy plain that were less authentic but would look like a million bucks on a wide screen.

May Froy joined us briefly while his assistant director coached the extras and bit players who had been bused in from Sherwood. The assistant was using a bullhorn, but he barely needed one—it wasn't exactly a cast of thousands.

Froy read my thoughts. "They will look like many times their number on the screen. Wait and see how we do it."

I knew the trick, such as it was. It consisted of herding the extras around so they formed the background of every shot, their ranks shuffled so different faces were in front for each angle.

"Pioline has promised me an army of extras for the climactic battle scenes," Froy said. "Two armies, in fact."

A Hollywood veteran, Froy could live for months on a promise like that, even though he knew in his heart there'd be fine print. I watched the doubt chase the hope around his lined face. Then he was off to capture his sunset.

He got a beauty. It built up slower than Ravel's *Bolero*, going from a gentle rose to a bloody red riot and then to an afterglow that leaned toward orange and hung on for take after take. Froy didn't really need more than one take, since the action he was filming consisted entirely of Boudica and her daughters descending the wide temple steps three abreast. Brooks at her most forgetful couldn't screw that up, and this was Brooks at her best: attentive, cooperative, restrained. Jewel fielded more of Froy's comments. One comment, actually, but that one repeated over and over: "Lift your head, Miss Lacey, and remember you are an Iceni princess!"

She was dressed like a princess this evening, in a long wine-colored robe, a twist of golden wire in her hair. Brooks wore the same outfit, but made it look like a Paris original. Neither princess was a patch on the queen mother. Lacey was wearing a flowing robe of multicolored cloth, like a tartan plaid but less regular. Across her broad shoulders was a purple mantle, secured by a golden brooch. Above that, her neck was encircled by twisted gold, the necklace so broad it looked like a very expensive brace. There was more twisted gold in her wig, which was as red as her own hair but much longer, cascading down to the small of her back. Not a trace remained of the Lillian Lacey who had once traded pies in the face with Lucille Ball. She moved with the stately dignity that only the truly tall can achieve, a dignity she'd played against through all her long career.

When Froy finally lost his light, the crew set up for the second shot of the evening, and I fidgeted around, getting in people's way. The presence of the extras, even the modest number the cost-conscious Pioline had provided, made me uncomfortable. I would have been snatching wigs off their heads, searching for Remlinger and his beetle-browed sidekick Dillon, if Ella hadn't taken me by the arm.

While she paced with me, she explained that the next shot would be a pep talk delivered by Boudica to her people, with a roaring bonfire as a backdrop. It was a shot that called for skillful lighting. The candlepower from the fire would try to turn the actress in front of it into a tall, English silhouette. The challenge was adding enough fill light to keep that from happening without adding so much that the eerie, midnight quality of the scene was lost. Froy's cameraman had worked it all out the night before, and he got everything organized now with amazingly little fuss.

Lacey took her place in front of the fire for a final lighting check. It looked too bright to my eye, but to the camera it would all be shadows and highlights moving in a dance dictated by the flames. When the cameraman was ready, Lacey gave the first of what I was sure—knowing Froy—would be many readings of the same speech.

"Iceni," Lacey almost whispered the word. There wasn't a hint of her posh accent in her suddenly raspy voice. She'd been given a prop spear for the scene, and she started off using it as a staff. "I present myself to you as an ordinary woman striving to avenge my lost freedom, my lash-tortured body, and the violated honor of my daughters. Roman lust and greed has grown until now our very bodies are polluted. But the goddess Andrasta will grant us our revenge." She was holding the spear at shoulder height now, and her voice had risen higher than that. "I call on Andrasta to swell our numbers with the spirits of our dead heroes, with her own inhuman and indestructible minions, with every restless demon of the night hours.

"Our enemies won't stand up to the battle cries of our thousands, let alone endure our blows! Think of our numbers and the reason why we are fighting. Then conquer or die in battle!" Here she raised her spear above her head, the tip glinting in the lights. "I, a woman, am resolved to do so. You men, if you like, can live as Roman slaves."

There followed a scripted roar from the extras. It was followed in turn by applause from the cast and crew that the Teutonic director cut short.

"They can print that one and go home," I said to Ella. "If I were a Roman, I'd be booking a stateroom on the next galley out."

Before she could give her own review, Daniel Irwin loomed out of the darkness behind us. "Good speech," he said to Ella. "Damn good."

When he'd wandered off again, Ella whispered to me: "I lifted most of it from Tacitus. Hell, Shakespeare did it all the time."

9

My early call to Paddy on Thursday had gotten him out of bed. He paid me back for that by placing a call to me at an even earlier hour on Friday. The Elliott cottage didn't have a phone. None of the cottages did. I was escorted to the one in the cookhouse by the kid guard who had driven the Thunderbird up from LA.

As we crossed the predawn ranch, moving like two visitors to a cathedral, the youngster, one Hank Knific, introduced himself. He was big and broad-shouldered but a kid for all that, with hair worn the way my son wore his: shorn close everywhere but right in front, where it stuck straight up. I guessed that Knific had just gotten out of the service or graduated from some junior college football squad. Guessed but didn't bother to ask.

As we approached the cookhouse, we were hit by the competing aromas of coffee and frying bacon. That was enough pick-me-up to turn Knific belligerent.

"I wouldn't mind this Remlinger dropping by," he said. "I could use some action."

I remembered that lament from my army days. It had often won the lamenter a thrown helmet or worse. I settled for saying, "Be careful what you wish for."

The cookhouse phone hung in a comparatively quiet corner. "Morning," I said to the handset. "How's your insomnia?"

"Fine now," Paddy boomed back, knocking sleeping birds off telephone wires across three countries. "I was just calling to cure yours. I got a message last night from that gentleman who owed me a favor."

"Owed?"

"That's right. As of now, we're square. The word's gone out to Mr. Remlinger that Beverly Brooks is off limits. He's also to let bygones be bygones regarding our visit to Las Vegas. In exchange for which, Brooks won't press charges."

"The charges she wasn't going to press anyway?"

"The very same."

I would have asked Paddy what he thought the chances were that Remlinger would take the deal seriously, but his delivery had already told me that he didn't share Lange's pessimism.

"Mind if I hang around up here until we're sure?" I asked instead.

"As long as Marcus Pioline is willing to pay, I insist on it. Get yourself a little sun. And give my best to the missus."

I could have gone back to the cottage right then to deliver Paddy's message, or at least to shave, but I entered the dining room instead. The ranch hands were having their breakfast, and they made a place for me.

As I sat down, they were discussing a horse-grooming problem that threatened the hands' Friday night in Sherwood. Bud, the foreman, was of the opinion that one of his precious charges hadn't been cared for properly the night before. He'd found the horse still marked with dried sweat when he'd made his predawn rounds. The more combative of the hands defended their honor, saying that the corral was crowded with extra horses for the shoot, that they were mixing it up as a result and undoing their careful grooming.

I found this down-to-earth squabbling remarkably restful after the day I'd spent with creative types. And I needed restful just then, almost as much as I needed bacon and eggs. Paddy's call was having the opposite of his intended effect. I'd been comforting myself with thoughts of Remlinger on the run or holed up somewhere waiting for Robert Stack to kick his door down. Now the gangster knew that nothing very bad was going to happen to him. And he knew where we were. I thought back nostalgically to the earlier part of the week, when we'd been the invisible men plotting against him. He was doing the plotting now, and I was waiting for the second shoe to drop, convinced it was going to drop on my head.

It landed about an hour later, just as I was getting out of the shower. When I'd gone in, Ella had been in the doorway to the bedroom, talking happily about the picture's prospects, now that Paddy had come through for us. When I pulled back the curtain ten minutes later, I found Lange leaning in the same doorway, holding my towel.

He pointed to my shoulder, more specifically to the white scar of the bullet wound that had ruined my golf game. "I remember that one," he said.

"Me too." I held out my hand for the towel and he passed it over. "My wife ask you to lifeguard?"

"She's up at breakfast with Lacey and the others. They'll all be heading out to the shooting site soon. I don't see any reason to hold them here. They're as easy to look after out there, except that letting them go divides my men. But if I cancel the shoot, I'll have to tell them."

"Tell them what?"

"Remlinger is in Sherwood. One of the extras who's billeted there spotted him and hotfooted it over here."

"How does an extra come to know about Remlinger? I thought we had the lid on this."

"That was Pioline's pipe dream, not mine." He handed me a folded newspaper. "Here's how the extra knew about Remlinger. And how he was able to recognize him."

The paper was that day's edition of the *Hollywood Spy*, a daily that made the *Hollywood Reporter* read like the *London Times*. Under the headline STARLET ESCAPES LOCKED LOVE NEST was the whole story of Brooks's elopement to Las Vegas, ending with an account of her rescue that was sketchy but accurate. Accompanying the article were photos of Brooks, Remlinger, and Daniel Irwin, Remlinger's a posed studio number as polished as either of the other two.

"Leave it to that psycho to have his own press agent," I said aloud but to myself.

Lange said, "Some store in Sherwood has been bringing that rag in on the milk train every morning to sell to our people."

"Any copies here at the ranch?"

"Not that I've heard, but it's only a matter of time. Pioline knows all about it. I just got off the phone with him. I thought he might have leaked the story himself, whatever he said about not wanting a scandal."

I handed Lange the newspaper and wiped the steam from the mirror over the sink. I knew he'd be impressed if I could shave at that moment without cutting my throat. I would be, too. "What did Pioline say?"

"He denied it, mad and loud. He thinks your boss might have been the source. Paddy is mentioned by name in the article. So is Hollywood Security."

Paddy wasn't above that kind of free publicity, but I didn't think he'd jeopardize his relationship with Remlinger's elders for a little ink. They were men who took looking foolish very badly. "What did you say to that?"

"I told Pioline to keep guessing. He's flying up here this afternoon. He wants Remlinger talked to before then. I'm on my way to do that right now."

I noted belatedly that Lange was wearing a gun belt. The holster contained a thirty-eight whose bluing matched his uniform shirt. "Mind some company?"

Lange treated me to a rare smile, a twisted one too small for his meaty face. "If you let me drive that car of yours, I might be talked into it."

There were two ways to get from the ranch to Sherwood. One was to drive west to the shooting site and then make a left. The other was to take the winding, rutted river road from the ranch to the airport and head west from there. We chose the shooting-site route because the road was better and Lange would be able to get the T-Bird up over thirty. Also, it would let us escort the talent as far as Froy's outpost.

Ella rode with us in the Thunderbird. From the driver's seat, Lange briefed her on Remlinger's arrival. Ella and Lange went back a ways. He knew he could count on her not to lose her head, and he was right. Her only comment when he'd finished was a distracted "Hooray for Hollywood."

She had a little more to say when we dropped her near Lillie Lacey's trailer. She said it to me. "Here's another fine mess I've gotten you into. Don't punish me for it by getting hurt."

"I wouldn't want to let you off too easy," I said. "How about I get roughed up a little?"

I was resting my arm on the door of the car. Ella toyed with one of the buttons on the sleeve of my jacket. "Wise guy," she said.

That was all the parting scene Lange had patience for. We were in Sherwood fifteen minutes later. A sign at the point where the road turned from dust to dusty pavement told us so. It also told us that the town's original name had been San Ignacio and that the population was two hundred and nine.

Lange read that aloud and grunted. "Must be counting the tombstones."

We passed a garage whose original livery stable sign could still be read under several coats of paint and a general store that had to be the one that currently stocked the *Hollywood Spy*. They could have shot an episode of *Gunsmoke* in front of the place. After they'd covered over the photo someone had taped in the front window, that is. It was a magazine cover of Ernest Hemingway that had run shortly after his suicide.

Lange knew where he was going. He made a right at the general store and drove us up the hill that backed the town, the road winding through redwoods, not trophy-size specimens, but big. Beyond them was a building that looked almost as old, the San Ignacio Inn, a rambling, part-timber, part-adobe structure with a tile roof, the tiles every shade from apple red to dirt brown.

"How this one-horse burg ever rated a spread like that is anybody's guess," Lange said. "Must have been a stop on some stagecoach line between Los Angeles and Frisco."

Another mystery was how the inn had stayed in business after the stagecoaches went away. Lange knew its current source of income. "Pioline's put up the technicians and supporting cast here. And any extras who aren't driving in every day or locals. Most of them so far are locals."

We parked in a circular carriageway near a groaning olive tree, one of a pair that flanked the inn's front steps. The reception desk was in a cool dark room with a beamed ceiling and a stone floor, both of which needed sweeping. The girl behind the blackened counter, which might once have been a bar, looked up with alarm at Lange's uniform. Or maybe just at Lange.

"Could you help us?" I asked. "We're looking for a man named Remlinger. We understand he's staying here."

"There's no guest by that name," she said, her dark eyes never leaving the safe haven of mine.

"Mind if we see the register?" Lange asked. The girl never looked his way.

"He may be using another name," I explained. "He's about twenty-five, my height but thinner. He has blue eyes and black hair, kind of bushy in front." A brunette Dan Duryea, I would have added if I'd thought she could remember the actor at the right age. I hunted around for a more contemporary example and came up with Martin Landau.

I needn't have troubled; she was suddenly nodding. "Yes. I know him. That's Mr. Elliott."

Lange made a noise that was either a suppressed laugh or his breakfast hitting bottom.

"Is he staying here alone?" I asked.

"No, there's a Mr. Maguire with him."

"Describe him," Lange said. And then, "Please."

"He's like a refrigerator on legs. And his eyebrows meet in the middle."

Not an FBI Standard Description, but I recognized the gentleman. "What's their room number?"

"They're in a suite. Suite Eleven. But they're not there now. I just saw them on the verandah, having breakfast."

She gave us directions that sent us into the low-ceilinged interior of the inn. As we walked, Lange said, "Dillon, too, huh? Well, at least we know you didn't kill him with that whack on the head."

I quoted Beverly Brooks on the same subject. "Too bad."

"Why use your name and Paddy's?"

To tell us they knew all about us. Or to let us know that their side had the ball now and we were on defense. I didn't actually word a reply. We were exiting onto the verandah just then, a broad stone patio with half a dozen wrought-iron tables and matching chairs. The area was partially shaded, but it seemed very bright after the gloom of the inn.

Only one table was occupied, that one at the sunny center of the little plaza. Remlinger and Dillon were sitting there, lingering over their coffee from the look of things. The remains of at least two newspapers were scattered about the breakfast dishes, one of them a *Hollywood Spy*.

Dillon's little eyes were on us the second we stepped from the inn. He was in a rumpled dark suit and tie and a whitish shirt. It might have been the same outfit he'd been wrinkling when I'd left him napping in Vegas. Remlinger was wearing an open-necked shirt—very white—and a blue blazer that had a shawl collar and a phony crest on its breast pocket done in golden thread. He affected not to notice our approach until we were stepping up to the table. Then he raised his bushy head, cocked it to one side, and smiled.

"The real Mr. Elliott," he said. "Sounds like a movie title, doesn't it? Who's your friend? In that getup he must be an admiral in the navy. Or is it the space patrol?"

Nobody laughed at that, not even Dillon. He was too busy staring holes in me.

"I don't think he likes your hat," Remlinger said to me. "Those broad-brimmed models went out with the fifties. Dillon's very particular about hats. It bothers him that his haven't fit so good since you stopped by Las Vegas."

He tapped the front page of the *Spy*. "I was just reading about it. You don't come out very well in the article, Elliott, considering you did all the work. I'm puzzled. I was looking for something along the lines of 'the part of the bellhop was ably rendered by former Paramount walk-on Scott Elliott, who can be briefly glimpsed in such classics as *Second Chorus* and *Arise My Love*.' I knew I'd seen you before."

And researched me since. "Did you plant that article?" I asked before I'd really thought the idea over.

"Me? If I'd leaked that story they'd have gotten it right."

I would have asked what he meant by that, if Lange hadn't finally chimed in: "What are you doing here?"

"Who wants to know?" Dillon demanded. They were a perfect match, one trench mortar chatting to another.

"Cool it," Remlinger told his man. "It was a civil question. It deserves a civil answer. We're doing a little tour of movie locations. Have you ever seen *The Adventures of Robin Hood*? Sure you have. Well, some of the exteriors were filmed around here in 1937. That's why they changed the name of the town to Sherwood. They were that proud of it. It's all in the brochure."

He reached for the inside pocket of his jacket, causing Lange's hand to rise to his holster. "You should also cool it," Remlinger said. He produced the brochure. "It says that Errol Flynn and Olivia de Havilland stayed right in this inn. Of course, it wasn't such a fleabag back then. I was lucky enough to get Flynn's old room. How do you like that? There was some guy in it when we got here, but I talked him into swapping with me." He referred to the pamphlet again. "The *Robin Hood* crew also filmed up around Chico north of San Francisco. We may go up there next week. This week, we're here."

"You were told to stay away from here," Lange said.

"You're right, I was. Congratulate your boss for me, Elliott. He must have some pull. I had to promise to be a good boy and not go near Bebe. I won't either, unless she needs me."

"For what?" Lange asked.

I expected something scatological in reply. Instead, Remlinger said, "To look out for her. Don't ask me from what; she knows. And she knows I'm here by now; I arranged that. So everybody's happy. You gentlemen enjoy the rest of this beautiful day."

10

The rest of the beautiful day passed fairly quickly. Pioline flew in after lunch, announcing his arrival—as he had on his last visit—by bringing the *Argo* in low over the valley. Lange and I had split up after leaving Sherwood. I'd dropped him at the ranch to watch the livestock while I'd driven out to the shooting site to sweat in the sun in my unfashionable hat. When the *Argo* roared in, I slipped back to the ranch to eavesdrop as Lange briefed Pioline and Paddy.

Only there was no Paddy. Lange returned from the airstrip with one passenger: Pioline. The producer explained as he mixed himself a tall Scotch-and-soda in the front room of Crowe House, Lange and I looking on from opposite ends of a sofa whose leather had the look and feel of the original cow.

"Maguire wanted to work on things from the LA end. That's what he said. If you ask me, he couldn't face the tongue-lashing he was going to get from me. 'Everything's hunky-dory,' he says to me last night. Hunky-dory! I do not call it hunky-dory when I wake up to find the whole mess in the paper and Johnny Remlinger set to snatch Bebe the second our guard is down. Maguire had it coming from me and he ducked."

I thought it more likely that Paddy—who had been given ear calluses by every studio hoss in Hollywood at one time or another—had actually ducked another ride in the *Argo*. I would have spoken up for him, but Lange took on the job.

"Maguire delivered. Remlinger was warned off; he told us that himself. He said he isn't going near Brooks, that he's only here to look out for her."

"Look out for her?" Pioline repeated. "Protect her? From what? Drama critics? What does she need to be protected from, except eating too much?"

"Nothing," Lange said.

"Nothing is right. And that's what this gangster's promise not to go near her is worth."

I set my shoes on the Crowes' wagon-wheel coffee table. "If he meant to snatch her, he would have done it. Or laid low until he was ready to do it."

"What's his play then?" Lange demanded.

"He let Brooks know he's nearby. I think he's hoping she'll come to him."

"As though she would stick her head back into that noose," Pioline said. "Is he that crazy?"

"His ego is that big," I said.

"Is it?" Pioline stood, and his savings account, the gold tooth, glinted. "Well, my ego is big, too. Bigger than his, I bet." He tossed back his drink with a flourish. "I think it's time this Remlinger and I met."

It would have been an interesting event, had it taken place. We escorted Pioline to the San Ignacio Inn, arriving just as the hotel was rousing itself from its siesta. Remlinger and Dillon weren't there. They were off sightseeing, the manager of the inn personally assured Pioline, the best client he'd had since Jack Warner.

As the employer of the most interesting sights in the valley, the producer didn't take this news well. We spent the rest of the day at the shooting location, keeping watch on Brooks. Or at least on her trailer. The starlet had gone temperamental after lunch and refused to leave her dressing room.

"Like I told you," Ella said. "It's a pattern." She and I had walked up to a grassy knoll behind the temple set for a little privacy. "Pioline flies in, and Bebe cuts up rough. You can count on it, like 'arms' following 'charms' in a song lyric."

"You don't think it could have had anything to do with Remlinger following Brooks?"

"She knew about that early this morning. Remlinger paid one of the lighting guys to bring her a note. She was a little scared, but she was able to joke about it. You know, you saw how well she was doing before lunch. Then, within an hour of Marc's plane flying over, she was blowing her lines again and kicking assistant directors. Just like the Vegas business had never happened."

None of the actors was exactly focused. Even the horses, picking up on the general mood of nervous excitement, were misbehaving. As we watched, a stuntman doubling as one of Boudica's guards was thrown twice. The second time, Lacey's own horse was spooked. It was all the actress could do to rein him in. That was enough for Pioline. He told Froy to pack it up for the day.

There followed a minor rhubarb caused by actors who didn't want to go back to Sherwood for fear that Remlinger would murder them in their beds. I avoided that discussion by volunteering to drive Brooks and her husband to the ranch. I should have taken on the extras single-handed.

Irwin had received the news of Remlinger's return quietly enough. That had been both a relief and a disappointment to me. I certainly didn't want him gunning for the gangster, but I didn't like his defeated look and the whiff of whiskey I got when he climbed into the backseat of the Thunderbird next to his wife, pointedly ignoring Ella's offer of the passenger-side bucket.

Brooks liked the seating arrangement and her husband's aroma about equally. She was in her sunglasses again, with a shocking pink scarf tied around her hair.

"Smells like you broke a bottle back here, Galahad," she said before we'd driven a quarter mile. "Watch the bumps, or it'll smell like somebody puked his guts up. Try to lose that smell. I have; you can't."

"You can lose me anytime you want," Irwin said.

"You keep saying that," Brooks replied, "and here we are. Drive to Reno, why don't you, Galahad. You two can be our witnesses."

"Thanks, kids," Ella said sweetly. "But there are some ceremonies I'd as soon Scotty didn't know about."

The line was far from Ella's best work, but it set Brooks laughing like a studio audience. She went on laughing, until Irwin told her to shut up.

"It's 'shut the fuck up,'" she corrected. "You're supposed to be the big novelist, but you don't even know the proper use of fuck. What century are you writing for? How are you ever going to be taken seriously? How is your work going to survive? You're getting buried by even bigger losers than you are. Writers with nothing to say are leaving you behind because they squeeze a fuck into every other sentence. How hard a trick is that to learn?"

"Shut up," Irwin hissed.

"Shut the *fuck* up," Brooks said. "Jeez, am I talking to myself?"

I'd let the car accelerate in a subconscious effort to get to the ranch before a fight broke out. Ella reached across the console and rapped me on the arm.

"There's a dip in the road up ahead," she said. "Let's take it with the wheels on the ground."

That got Brooks laughing again. This time Irwin let her wind herself, the happy moment coinciding with our arrival in front of their cottage.

"Is it locked?" I asked Irwin.

"No."

"Wait here then."

"Go get 'em, Galahad," Brooks called after me.

Although the cottage was almost as unprepossessing as Ella's from the front—one door, one window, and a little gable roof trying to pass itself off as a porch—inside it was much bigger. I didn't work up any hurt feelings over that. I also didn't look very hard for Remlinger. I determined which bedroom was Brooks's by the simple method of locating the biggest. Then I searched it for the drugs that Paddy may or may not have been hinting about. I didn't find so much as the cotton plug from a pill bottle. I also didn't find any indication that Brooks was sharing her room with her husband. Or anyone else, for that matter. There was a framed photo on the dresser, but it was a publicity still of Marilyn Monroe inscribed by the actress: "To Beverly Brooks, a girl to look out for."

"Get in line," I said.

11

Dinner reminded me of the last one I'd had in England in 1944 prior to crossing the channel to join the fighting. Which is to say, I didn't get much of it down. The air was very still. Somewhere, someone was burning wood, and the smell of it was hanging just above our heads, like spent tobacco in a bar.

Only Pioline had any conversation, but then, he was flying to Los Angeles at dusk, leaving the rest of us behind. While we ate, the producer described the project waiting in the wings: an adaptation of Robert Graves's *I, Claudius*. That led to a discussion of a previous attempt to film the book, by Korda in England before the war. It had been interrupted by Merle Oberon's car crash and finally scuttled by artistic differences between Charles Laughton, the star, and Joseph von Sternberg, the director. At least that's the way Pioline reported the gossip. He was more convincing when he described the money he was hoping to save by reusing the costumes and sets from *Warrior Queen*. Lacey contributed some reminiscences about Oberon, but her heart wasn't in it. Her green eyes kept stealing to the empty places set for Beverly Brooks and Daniel Irwin.

About the time the desultory proceedings had dragged themselves to the coffee and cigarette stage, I happened to glance through the screen wall of the dining room and catch the eye of Hank Knific, security guard to the stars. That is, the kid caught my eye from a spot next to the cookhouse where he couldn't be seen by Pioline and the others. I excused myself, telling Ella I'd forgotten my pipe, and went out to talk to him.

Knific started off by asking for Lange. "He left orders to hush it up if Miss Brooks went . . ."

"Nuts?" I suggested.

"I guess. He didn't want Mr. Pioline and the others bothered. Now we can't find him."

"Where's Brooks?"

Knific took me to the source of the burning-wood smell I'd been enjoying with every bite of my dinner. It was a big tree stump, out beyond the horse corral but inside the boundary fence of the ranch. Sometime earlier, the stump had been doused with something flammable and set afire, one step in the long process of getting rid of it. The stump was only smoldering now, but it was putting out enough smoke to enable it to double as a bonfire in ancient Britain.

Beverly Brooks was standing before the blackened prop. She was surrounded—at a respectful distance—by four of Lange's men, who were looking worried. A little beyond them was an outer ring of ranch hands, who were cleaned up for a Friday night in Sherwood but in no hurry to get there. The cowboys were dawdling because of what Brooks was wearing: a one-piece, canary yellow bathing suit and an orange beach towel, which was loosely slung around her shoulders. The security squad was worried because of what she held in her hands: an ax.

The ax must have been left behind by the stump crew; I could see picks and shovels scattered about. Like the stump, the ax had been transformed, in its case into Boudica's spear. Brooks was treating her audience to the scene Lillian Lacey had done for the cameras the night before. It was Brooks's own version of the scene, with very few words lifted from Tacitus. When she spotted me, she said, "One more time from the top," and started in all over again.

"Iceni! You mud crawling shitheads! I present myself to you

as something you'll dream about all your fucking lives and never have: a really nice piece of tail. At least I was before the fucking Romans got to me and scarred my beautiful ass for life."

She tried to display the damage, but the towel/mantle defeated her.

"How do I get my perfect body back? And how do my daughters get their virginity back, the shitheads, after they were gangbanged by the fucking Romans? We can't, can we? Not in a hundred years.

"So here's the deal. I want you to cut the balls off every Roman you find. Every fucking son of a bitch's balls right off. If you haven't got any balls yourself, if you can't do it, bring 'em to me. I, a woman, will do it for you!"

She demonstrated with the ax, almost hitting her left leg. I brushed past the frozen guards. Brooks raised the ax again as I stepped up, but its weight slowed her movements to waltz time. I had a firm grip on the handle long before she reached the top of her backswing.

She dropped her hands to her sides. "All yours, Galahad. It was getting heavy anyway. Get me something lighter for the next take."

"That was a wrap," I said.

She looked up like she wanted to argue the point. Her eyes were so angry and alive now she barely resembled the woman I'd met in Las Vegas. Had she been sleepwalking then, or was she dreaming right now?

"Okay," she said. "Have it your way." The towel finally slipped from one of her shoulders. When I put it back, she seemed surprised to see it. "Oh yeah, I was looking for the pool. Did you know this swinging place doesn't even have one?"

"It's coming in tomorrow by helicopter," I said.

"Very amusing. Your arm, Galahad."

I led her back toward her cottage, taking the long way to avoid the dining room. I understood why Lange wanted Brooks and Pioline kept apart: to preserve the illusion that Lange Limited was on top of things. Hollywood Security had been in the same spot often enough, so I fell in with the plan.

"Don't tell your wife," Brooks said as we ambled, "but that was the way that speech of hers should have been written. Her version stunk. It sounded like an address to the Rotary Club. Any woman who gets beaten and has her daughters raped is going to foam at the fucking mouth, not recite poetry. Tell Ella she can use that 'cut their balls off' line anytime. She doesn't even have to give me screen credit."

"She may insist," I said.

"Not that the censors would let someone say 'cut their balls off.' Heaven forbid. Maybe someday, though. What do you think, Galahad? Will they ever let 'cut their balls off' into a movie?"

"No."

"I think you're wrong. I think the day is coming. I can see it. I can see the future sometimes."

"When you're on what?" I asked.

"Come again?"

"What are you high on?"

"Hormones, Danny says." She squeezed my upper arm against her breast. "He can drink, why can't I?"

"Is that what you're doing, drinking?"

"I'll tell you something else. I think the day will come when the movies will actually show balls being cut off. Show it in glorious Technicolor. Man, I can't wait to see that."

"What did Remlinger do to you in Las Vegas? Did he beat you? Or rape you?"

"He's still got his balls, doesn't he?"

"So what did he do?"

She squeezed my arm again. "Nothing that took, Galahad," she said. "Nothing that took. Tell me, what's the opposite of swinging?"

"I don't know. I don't speak Sinatra."

"Do you speak American, Galahad? Sometimes I think I'm the only one around here who does. Dead, that's the word I'm looking for. This place is dead. It's Lawrence Welk on the range. The drag of all possible drags."

That critique was the last thing I got out of her. We'd reached her cottage steps. I called for Irwin but got Brooks's other roommate, Nicole Cararra. She looked Brooks over without batting one of her very black lashes.

"Danny isn't here," she said.

"Where is he?"

"I should know? It wasn't my day to watch him."

"That's right," I said. "It's your night to watch her." I passed Brooks over. Cararra put an arm around the starlet. "Keep her inside until she sobers up. And make sure she does sober up."

Brooks got a laugh out of that. She was still laughing when Cararra shut the door behind them.

My wife was waiting in front of our cottage, the pipe I'd excused myself to find in her hand. As usual, she knew my explanation before I'd said it. "How was Bebe?"

"Higher than Eisenhower's hairline." I sat down in the free Adirondack chair, the one Paddy had hogged the night before.

"Booze?"

"I dunno."

Ella shook her head steadily through my somewhat edited version of Brooks's dramatic reading. Then she asked, "What makes people who have the world on a plate throw it over like that?"

"How would I know? My plate was delivered to Dana Andrews's table by mistake."

"Was it?" Ella asked, tousling my hair. "Or were you yet another actor who got scared that he might actually make it?" It was an old theory of hers, and it couldn't hold her interest.

"For once I agree with Lange," she said. "It's better that Marc didn't have to face Bebe tonight. He's got enough to worry about."

"He was fine at diner," I said. I was trying to fill the pipe with tobacco, but I was so tired I was making a mess of it.

"He was acting," Ella said. "I saw him just before he headed for the airstrip. He looked like hell. I wasn't crazy about him driving himself over there, never mind flying. We offered to take him, but he said no. He didn't want anyone wandering away from the campfires. He made a joke about it, but he was acting all the same."

"We do seem to be a little under siege," I said, tamping down the tobacco with what concentration I could muster.

"And all because of some pip-squeak gangster from Cleveland. What's this century coming to?"

"You sound like Paddy on the subject of Troy Donahue."

"Or you on prefabricated martinis," she countered.

I'd have set aside my standards and drunk a bottled cocktail right then. Maybe without a glass. "Did you hear the plane take off?"

"No." She'd removed her shoes, and she was poking my knee with a her big toe. "But then I don't recall hearing it the other night."

"You were busy saying 'Scotty' over and over in an urgent tone."

"Ah yes. I remember now. I was imagining I was Kim Novak in *Vertigo*."

"There's an odd coincidence," I said.

I smoked the pipe while we chewed over the day and dusk turned into genuine night. Then I smoked another one, leaning back against Ella's legs. Occasionally we heard voices from the ranch proper and once the sound of a car coming and going. None of it suggested an assault, though, so we stayed where we were.

We stayed there for another half hour or so, discussing our kids, Gabby's incipient rebellious streak and Billy's total lack thereof. Before we'd exhausted that subject, the wooden upholstery of Ella's chair finally got to her. She stretched and said, "What do you say we make it an early night?"

"I'll catch up," I said. "I ought to check on you know who."

I got up and headed for the cottage where I'd deposited Brooks. Before I'd gone far enough to work the stiffness out of my knees, I heard the sound of aircraft engines in the distance. I stopped and looked at the luminous dial of my watch, wondering if it could be Pioline's *Argo*, an hour and more behind schedule. The engines were going full out, the sound echoing from the hills that circled the valley. I turned in the direction of the airstrip just as the horizon beyond it was lit by a brilliant flash.

I stood there stupidly until the sound of an explosion roared over the ranch like a doomsday wave.

12

When I reached the airfield, I found it deserted. In the near distance, wreckage from the plane was still burning on a black hillside. I drove straight for it, hitting sixty on the grass runway. The strip ended in a gully that nearly rolled the Thunderbird on its back. I wrestled the car to a stop next to a pickup that was parked with its front end in the dry brush of the hill.

I left the car and climbed on foot, guided by the fire and by the sound of someone shouting Pioline's name. I slipped again and again on the rocky ground and cut myself on the scrub vegetation, which broke into razor-sharp pieces when I tried to push it away. The fire should have been racing through this brush, but it wasn't. I was stumbling over pieces of the plane long before I reached the flames, which had been contained by a rocky hollow. The shouting was coming from a man who was running back and forth before the fire, like a dog blocked by a fence. I called to him, but he didn't seem to hear me, not even when I grabbed his arm.

He swung around, and I grabbed his other arm, sure he was about to lash out. His bulging eyes were that wild. Mine might have been too, just then. The shouting man was someone I'd never expected to find alive: Pioline's pilot, Clay Ford.

"How did you get out of that?" I shouted.

He didn't answer me, didn't even see me. He was running

with sweat. I could feel his arm muscles twitching like a sleeper's beneath his coveralls. I shook him until the ball cap fell from his head. "Did anyone else get out?"

He nodded toward the darkness behind me. Before I could decide whether it was safe to leave him, a stray breeze handed me proof that at least one person hadn't escaped the flames. It blew smoke from the fire right into us. Smoke from burning gas and rubber and flesh. Ford shook me off and doubled over to retch.

I turned away from the fire and saw flashlights bobbing up the hill toward us. Farther off were headlights, two caravans' worth, a small one on the winding ranch road to the east and one from Sherwood that must have contained every car the town owned.

Ford was still kneeling in the brush. "Stay there," I said.

I set off in the direction the pilot had indicated, my eyes stinging, wishing I'd thought to bring a flashlight myself. I didn't need one. Before I'd moved out of the fire's range, I saw bare legs and then a familiar peach dress. It was Beverly Brooks, laid out like she'd already been visited by the undertaker. Her eyes were closed, and her golden hair was tousled again, the way it had been when I'd found her in the Grand Suite. It partially hid what might have been a bruise or a smear of grease on one temple.

"Her neck's broke."

I jumped at the sound of that matter-of-fact remark. It had been made by Charley Gavin, the airport manager I'd met the day Pioline had flown us in.

"Sorry," he said. "Didn't mean to scare you."

"Is that your truck down there?"

"Right, it is. Got here within a minute or two of the crash. You must have broken the sound barrier if you came from the ranch."

"Did *you* fold her hands?"

"Yes. That's all though. She was laying there peaceful when I found her. Been thrown clear when the fuselage cracked apart. Miracle that. She's not burned at all."

Just dead. "Clay Ford's back there in shock," I said. "I don't know how he managed to get out alive."

"He was never in, if you're meaning the plane. He drove here with me in the truck."

"Pioline left him behind?"

"Yes sir, he did."

"And Pioline?"

"Still at the controls, from what we could tell. The fire was already bad when we got here."

"What happened?"

"He flew right into the side of the blamed hill, both engines running strong. Damnedest thing I ever saw. Hell, you can damn near jump over this little hill. I've cleared it in planes with sixty-five horsepower. He had twenty-four hundred."

I heard my name being called by a voice I knew. An angry voice. Before I left Brooks, I loaned her my jacket one more time, laying it over her shoulders and face to protect them from the greasy ashes being carried by the shifting breeze.

When I found my pager, Lange, he was trying to interrogate Ford. He forgot the pilot fast enough when he saw me.

"What's the idea of trying to run down my men back at the ranch gate? Why the hell didn't you wait for us to get organized?"

I might have said that I hadn't known he'd come back from wherever he'd gotten off to, but there was no time for small talk. "You'd better throw up a perimeter before that crowd gets here. Pioline and Brooks are dead. We may be looking at a murder investigation. When word gets out that a star died up here, this hillside will be picked clean before we get a chance to look it over."

"Brooks too? Jesus. I've only got three men with me. I left the rest to watch the ranch. Jesus Christ."

The solution came from Bud, the ranch foreman, who'd panted up the hill after Lange. "Some of those Sherwood cars are my men. I'll cut them out of the crowd and organize a picket."

I stayed with Ford while they saw to it. The fire was dying

out, becoming several smaller fires and revealing the twisted shape of the cockpit and one of the massive radial engines. The little runway below us was bright with headlights now. A crowd had formed at the spot where I'd left the Thunderbird. Lange's men and the ranch hands, I hoped. I heard Lillie Lacey's voice yelling "Marcus!" and I knew that Ella must be down there, too. She'd elected to go to Lacey when I'd raced back to the cottage for my car. Listening to the actress's anguished voice, I decided I'd drawn the long straw.

Ford was stirring finally, blinking at the darkness like a startled dreamer. He was seated on a piece of stone. I took the rock next to his.

"Why weren't you on that plane?" I asked.

"Because she was."

"Brooks?"

"Mr. Pioline brought her back from the ranch on his second run."

"He made two trips between the ranch and the airport tonight?"

"That's why we were late getting away. He said he had to go back for something. Came back with her. Said he'd changed his mind about LA. He was going to Palm Springs instead. Didn't need me for Palm Springs."

Lange was coming up the hill again. There was a guy with him who could climb and smoke a cigarette at the same time. This wonder was carrying a medical bag.

"Why didn't Pioline need you?" I asked, whispering now.

"Palm Springs is where he liked to take . . . lady friends," Ford said, whispering too. "Never wanted me along on those flights. I should have been. I should have been with him."

The arrival of Lange and the doctor shut Ford up for the night. That is, the shot the doctor gave the pilot did. While the medico was working, Lange guided me a few steps away.

"We've got things under control, I think," he said. "The local law is helping us."

We were helping the law, but I didn't feel up to shifting Lange's worldview, so I just asked, "How's Lacey doing?"

"Thank God for your wife," Lange said. And then, "Who the hell?"

Charley Gavin had popped out of the stony earth again, this time at Lange's elbow. "I know why it happened," he was jabbering. "I know why it happened."

"Show us," I said.

He led us in the direction of Brooks's body, where Lange paused briefly, and then down the hill to a large piece of wreckage. It was the tail section of the *Argo*, looking huge now without the rest of the plane for perspective. Gavin was pointing to a little wing he called the horizontal stabilizer, almost jumping up and down in his excitement.

"It's here on the right elevator," the old man said, indicating one of the hinged panels on the stabilizer outboard of the rudder.

Lange raised his flashlight, training it on a length of red metal in the shape of an I-beam. It had been slipped into the slot between one end of the movable elevator and the matching piece of the fixed stabilizer, the top of the "I" above the wing and bottom below it. The beam—held in place by a cord hooked into an eyelet on the stabilizer—served as a rigid brace that prevented the elevator from moving even an inch.

"What is that thing?" Lange asked.

"Gust lock," Gavin said. "When a plane's parked on the ground, the wind can blow the control surfaces around, maybe damage them. Just moving them stretches the control cables if you let it go on too long. So we use gust locks to hold the elevators fast when the plane's tied down. You've got to take them off, though, before you try to go flying."

"Say you don't," I said.

"Then you've got no elevator control. You can't raise the nose, which means you can't climb. That's what happened to Mr. Pioline. He didn't know enough to pull his throttles back or didn't realize what was happening in time. So he flew right into the hill. Damnedest thing I ever saw."

"Are you telling me?" Lange began. Then he pushed me out

of the way and charged up the hill. I turned in time to see a flashbulb going off in the darkness at the spot where Brooks lay.

By the time I got up there, Lange had knocked the photographer down. The prone figure was rubbing his jaw and blaring out the name of his newspaper—the *Heston Herald*—like a college cheer. Lange was in the process of removing film from a camera, springing the back with the aid of his flashlight. Then he went for the camera's owner again. I stepped between the scrambling figure and Lange.

"He's only doing his job," I said.

"So am I." Lange flung the camera into the darkness. Then he bent to pull my jacket back over the starlet's face. "Doing it too damn late."

13

I awoke the next morning to a wonderful sight: Ella leaning over me, her crooked nose an inch from mine, her sun-bleached hair brushing my stubbly cheek. For an instant I forgot where I was and the darker parts of who I was, lost in the immediacy of those watercolor eyes and her fragrance, a combination of crushed roses and Ivory soap.

Then she said, "You told me to call you at eight," and it all came back to me. The long cold night on the hillside. The protracted interview with the local law, during which I'd tried unsuccessfully to interest anyone in Johnny Remlinger. The belated call Lange and I had paid on the Errol Flynn suite of the San Ignacio Inn, which had netted us nothing, Remlinger having checked out, apparently in some haste. The last thing I'd done before crawling into bed had been to call Paddy, who had already heard the news bulletin and was his usual calm self. He'd told me he'd try to trace Remlinger on his end—guessing the gangster was bound for Brazil or maybe Labrador—and we'd talk in the morning. Dawn had been breaking when Paddy said that, and now, just a couple of hours later, it was full day.

"How is it you look so good?" I asked my wife. "You didn't get any more sleep than I did."

"Less," she said, compounding the mystery. "I couldn't sleep.

I kept worrying about Lillie and Jewel. I went up to check on them just now."

"How are they?"

"Not so good. Jewel is acting like nothing happened, which isn't right. Marc was only her stepfather, but that still means something. Lillie's bad. I don't think she could have stayed down at all if that doctor hadn't given her a shot."

"Him and his needles," I said. Because of the doctor, Clay Ford had been unavailable for questioning throughout the preliminary investigation. That had left us with Charley Gavin as our only expert witness. Gavin had insisted that the crash had been a careless accident and nothing more, repeating his explanation of gust locks until I'd wanted to clamp one over his mouth. It had given the sheriff, a pensioner named Tyler, an easy out and he'd taken it.

"While I was up at Crowe House," Ella was saying, "I caught up on my reading. The crash happened too late to be more than a news flash in the state editions of the LA papers, but we're front-page news in the county rag, the *Heston Herald*."

Her use of the word "rag" and her tone—righteous disdain— told me Ella wasn't happy with the press we'd gotten. She'd been a studio publicist when we first met, and the job hadn't left her enamored with the fourth estate.

"They're probably sore because Lange broke their camera last night," I said. And tried to break their cameraman, a part-timer who'd been hanging around Sherwood when the plane crashed, hoping to get a picture of Lacey or Brooks visiting the general store.

"They're more than sore. They're out to get us. They said we constitute 'a menace to public morals.' "

"I asked you to pull the blinds the other night."

I immediately regretted the lip, as Ella pushed herself off me and began pacing the little room. "I'm talking about the cast and crew of *Warrior Queen*. Did you know this shoot was a 'haven of promiscuous sex and wild drinking, a microcosm of debauched Hollywood injected into the lifeblood of a pure county'?"

By then I was sitting up and seven-tenths awake. "I thought they loved the movies around here. They renamed the town because of one."

Ella paused in her pacing to give me a doleful look I knew quite well. "That was twenty years ago, Scotty. The whole world loved Hollywood back then. Significant segments have had a change of heart. Notably the *Herald* editorial writer, who sees us all as 'sun-tanned pill poppers.'"

I was wide awake now. "The paper used those words?"

"Yes. Worse than that, it tied them right to Beverly Brooks. It said her autopsy will show 'the presence of high levels of tranquilizers.' Will it, Scotty?"

"I wish I knew." Right then I would have settled for knowing how the *Heston Herald* knew.

Ella was moving on. "The paper insinuated that Marc was supplying the pills to Bebe. I can't imagine that. But then, I didn't believe your hunch about Bebe and Marc having an affair, and that was on the money. He was old enough to be her father. No wonder she did the spoiled-child number whenever he flew in. Or was that the drugs?"

I didn't answer, not wanting to concede that Pioline might have been involved with the hypothetical pills. Ella had been fond of the producer. For that matter, so had I.

Ella wasn't interested in my speculations in any case. She had a job for me. "Go see if Danny Irwin is okay. They put him in the cottage reserved for Richard Egan. It's the big one at the edge of the grove. And he'll need someone to go with him when he identifies his wife's body."

"She's been identified," I said. Pioline was a different matter. That identification would take a dentist with a strong stomach.

"When he goes to see her then. He'll need a friend, Scotty."

Or a stranger with acting experience, I thought. I showered and shaved before I stepped into the role, knowing a long day stretched ahead of me. I didn't think an extra thirty minutes would make any difference to Irwin. Lange's men had found him dead drunk in Sherwood's only saloon on a tip from some ranch hands who had enjoyed the sight of the novelist pickling his brains. The Lange Limited squad had tried to tell Irwin about his wife, but he'd been too far gone to acknowledge receipt of the message. So they'd hauled him back to the ranch and poured him into bed.

That's where I expected to find him when I visited the Egan cabin, but the unmade bed was empty. I headed up into the main camp, which was understandably quiet, given the late night everyone but the horses had had. The only ones stirring were Lange's guards, who must have been dead on their feet. Lange had reinforced the front gate against an expected onslaught of reporters, though few had shown up as yet. And he'd doubled his patrols of the compound's perimeter fence. While I was scanning for those sentries, I spotted Irwin.

He was seated in a canvas chair at the spot where we'd sat together watching his wife practice her swordplay. There was no one for Irwin to watch today, but he seemed to be finding much to consider in the dry, trampled grass of the yard. Sheets of newspaper lay at his feet, and others were blowing toward the fence like tumbleweeds. He held one paper clenched in his hands. I guessed what its name would be long before I could see its masthead.

Irwin hadn't brought out a chair for me, so I stood, getting in between the novelist and his reading light.

"What do you want?" he asked with no real interest.

For a moment, I was too taken aback to answer. I'd expected to find him in bad shape, physically and otherwise. He didn't seem particularly under the weather, but that I could accept. Hard drinkers were sometimes immune to hangovers, a gift that sped the unlucky ones straight to a sanitarium. It was Irwin's emotional steadiness that surprised me. He looked as though he'd unconsciously absorbed the news of his wife's death through last night's alcoholic haze and awakened in an advanced and quiet stage of grief.

"I'm sorry," I finally said.

I'd meant it as a condolence, but Irwin took it for a confession. "For bringing her back here from Vegas to die? You couldn't have known what was going to happen. You didn't know half of what was going on right under your nose."

"Did you?" I asked, nodding toward the *Heston Herald*. He had the paper open to the editorial Ella had quoted to me, the one that had found all the evils of Hollywood in the person of Beverly Brooks.

"It's hard to say what I knew," Irwin began. He'd traded in his Clark Kent specs for sunglasses, and he'd lost his safari hat. His thinning hair was currently trying to join the escaped news sheets in their race to the fence. "That's part of the curse of being a novelist. All the possibilities of a situation are always in your head. It's hard to concentrate sometimes on the single possibility that happens to be taking place."

"Must make driving fun," I said, having had enough literary theory. "How about the possibilities contained in that editorial?"

"Marcus Pioline was not screwing my wife. He wasn't her type. Beverly liked to pretend to be a nymphomaniac. She was far more . . . discriminating."

"Why was she in Pioline's plane last night?"

"Because it was her time to be."

That riddle took me back to Thursday morning, when Irwin and I had sat side by side in the sun, swapping wartime philosophies. "Her turn to be in the wrong place at the wrong time?"

"Yes. Did you see her last night? Afterward?"

I said I had.

"Lange was supposed to be taking me to her. But I've lost track of him."

"I'll take you."

"Is she in Sherwood?"

"No, in Heston, over in the next valley. It's the county seat."

"Good," Irwin said, looking oddly relieved. He read my expression and explained. "I hated to think that we'd been that close last night and I hadn't known it, that I'd been too drunk to even cross a street to see her body."

"How did you happen to be in Sherwood?"

"I was tired of drinking Pioline's booze."

"Was that the only reason?"

Irwin's sunglasses didn't need cleaning, but he gave them a once-over with a crumpled handkerchief, revealing eyes that were yellowed and red-rimmed. "Have another reason in mind?"

"I think you went looking for Johnny Remlinger."

"Don't try to make a hero out of me, Elliott. It's more job than you can handle. I did go by the San Ignacio Inn, but I wasn't after a confrontation. I was looking for a fruition."

"Come again?"

"I was looking for an ending, a result, a conclusion. A denouement, in my trade. I didn't find one."

"One found you," I said.

"If you're referring to Beverly's death, I'm afraid that won't conclude anything, not even for her." He held up the paper. "She'll live on in this medium for a time at least."

I spotted Lange marching our way, all spit and polish despite the night we'd had, and stepped up my questioning. "How about the drug angle? Was the paper right about that?"

"I don't know," Irwin said, lying and telling me to take it or leave it.

"How did the paper know so much?"

"As to that," Irwin said, "I've been developing a theory. I believe the newspaper's had us watched the whole time we've been here. Look at the top of that hill behind you. See anything?"

I looked and saw the ruins I'd spotted earlier from Pioline's plane. "That old fort?"

"A mission, rather," Irwin said. "The original San Ignacio. Several times since I've been sitting here this morning, I've seen a flash of light on that hill. Some wartime habits you can't shake. We were always looking for a light in the sky, sunlight glinting off a Messerschmitt or a Focke-Wulf. Of course, we were scanning the wild blue, not the high ground. You said you were in the artillery?"

"Right."

"What would you have thought in '44 if you'd seen flashes of light on a hill above your position?"

"That we were being watched through field glasses," I said.

"My guess is this is a telephoto lens on a camera. We may make the front page of tomorrow's *Herald*. 'Grieving husband consoled by unknown man.' Take my advice, Elliott. Stay unknown."

"Consider it done," I said.

14

Lange insisted on driving one of the rented Furys into Heston, convinced its hardtop would protect us against reporters and photographers. And maybe snipers in treetops. I didn't argue with him. Lange had taken the crash almost as strangely as Irwin, becoming obsessive about the tiniest precautions and details, as though if he got all his T's crossed and his I's dotted, his employer would spring back to life.

Heston by daylight was a little more impressive than it had seemed in the wee small hours, when the sidewalks had been safely tucked away. It was typical of the larger postwar California towns, which is to say it had clean wide streets laid out on a grid, nondescript buildings—squat earthquake-proof cubes, most done up in a sandy stone—and a business district that consisted of opposing strips of identical storefronts, the shops and offices they contained as interchangeable as the tubes in a television set. If less personable.

Heston Hospital was exactly the kind of facility you'd want nearby if your appendix felt tight, not that you'd be able to call the place to mind once your stitches were out. It was modern and antiseptic and death-scene quiet.

The staff was very happy to see Daniel Irwin. Though they didn't state their reason, it was easy to guess. His nonappearance had been holding up the real business of the day, namely

Brooks's autopsy. I had no desire to be there when they pulled the starlet from the cooler. So I slipped away from the procession as it headed for the basement morgue and asked at a nurse's station for Clay Ford.

The directions I got took me down a first-floor hallway, past a waiting area where a sheriff's deputy sat reading a newspaper. He didn't glance up as I passed. Ford did when I entered his room. The pilot was seated on the side of his bed, tying his boot.

He started to smile and then grew embarrassed, his reddened skin visible well into his crewcut. "It's Elliott, right?" he said. "Listen, Elliott, about the way I acted last night . . ."

"Forget it," I said. "You'd just lost your ship. Besides, everyone was shaken up."

"Everyone didn't end up in a loony bin for observation."

We looked around his room, the only loony bin I'd ever seen with open windows.

"I've been with Mr. Pioline for five years," Ford said, still trying to justify himself. "Flown his family all over. Flown right seat with him in the left more times than I bothered to log."

"Did you teach him to fly?"

"No, but I helped him get his multiengine rating. We went down to Texas together to pick up the *Argo*. It was a war surplus C-47, which you probably spotted. The double doors give it away. Ours was one of the planes they used on D-Day, according to Mr. Pioline's research. He was real proud of that, even though there were hundreds of them flying back and forth that day. After the war, it sat around in mothballs waiting to be turned into a flying yacht, which is what Mr. Pioline called it. Or the royal barge. The Howard Company stripped it down and built it up again according to our specs—Mr. Pioline's specs. It was a beautiful plane."

A nurse's aide entered the room carrying a tray that contained covered dishes and a little jug, whose escaping aroma had preceded her. "This is your last chance to eat something," she said to Ford. "You really should."

The pilot shook his head, but I waved her in. "Leave it," I said. "I'll see to it."

"I can't keep it down," Ford explained when the aide had left. "I'm still woozy from the shot."

"Let me cover for you." I poured out the coffee and rifled the dishes for something I could eat standing up. I found soggy toast that may have been the best I'd ever had.

"Anyway," Ford resumed, "that's why I was coming apart a little last night. A man I knew so well and liked so much. A plane I'd come to think of as my own. To see them fly into that hill for no reason." He shook his head. "If it had been anyone but Marcus Pioline, I would have thought he'd decided to commit suicide."

"Suicide and murder," I said. "Pioline wasn't alone in that plane."

"Right," Ford said. "I wasn't thinking."

He was giving me a shy, up-from-under, ingenue look, as though he really believed the suicide angle might be true but didn't want to say it. As I'd suspected, he hadn't been told of Charley Gavin's discovery.

"Talked to the sheriff this morning?" I asked.

"No. I'm on my way there now. A deputy just came for me. He's outside somewhere. Say, would you consider going with me, Elliott? I'm not half as windy about talking to the federal crash investigators as I am about facing this sheriff. I know what the feds want. I'm not sure about Tyler."

"He wants to ask you about gust locks."

Ford was suddenly on his feet, looking me square in the eye. "What about them?"

"Did you use one on the *Argo*?"

"Of course we did. Everyone who flies a C-47 does. Ours were custom-made cast-aluminum jobs painted red for visibility, with a little streamer of red silk attached to each one."

"How many were there?"

"One each for the right and left ailerons, one each for the right and left elevators, and one for the rudder."

"What were the silk streamers for?"

"Just an extra safety feature. The movement of the silk might attract somebody's eye if you taxied away with a gust lock in place."

"Where did you keep the locks when you weren't using them?"

"We stowed them in a compartment at the rear of the cabin. Next to the lavatory. What's this all about? Are they trying to blame that crash on a gust lock?"

"Yes," I said.

"That's crazy. I removed the locks myself. It's part of the walk-around you do before every flight. You remove the tie-downs, remove the gust locks, check the control surfaces, check the undercarriage, check the engines. Every time the same things. I use a checklist."

"Pioline didn't do his own checking?"

"Are you kidding? That's why I had to be so careful. Mr. Pioline never even bothered to kick the tires himself. Just jumped in and went. You'd have a second chance to catch a forgotten gust lock when you did your run-up before takeoff, when you checked to see that your controls were free and correct. You'd know from one of your controls being frozen that a gust lock was still on somewhere. But Mr. Pioline never even heard of a run-up. When I'd ride him about that, he'd say that every plane that had ever crashed had been checked by somebody and it hadn't mattered in the end. You'll never hear the shot that gets you, he liked to say."

Ford lost himself in some memory of his go-for-broke employer. "So you're sure you took both elevator gust locks off?"

"Damn straight I did," he answered, loud enough for half the floor to hear him, Tyler's deputy included.

I dropped my own voice to a whisper, hoping to set an example. "We found the tail section of the plane. The right elevator gust lock was still in place."

That news silenced Ford completely, but the damage had been done. Tyler's deputy appeared in the doorway, sulking like a kid whose party invitation had miscarried.

"We should be going," he said to Ford with one eye on me.

Sheriff Tyler's office was in one of Heston's newer stone cubes. The sheriff was as different from his smooth featureless building as it was possible to imagine. Tyler might once have been a medium-sized man, but he'd settled, becoming one of those older types who seem to be all legs and waistline and eyes. Watery, observant eyes, in Tyler's case. His face, with its lines on lines and gray bangs, reminded me of the old cowboy star Harry Carey. Or maybe it was Tyler's voice that brought the dead actor to mind. It was gruff, deep, and as flat as the top of a mesa.

Tyler's office was a little pocket of prewar decorating in the fluorescent-lit and vinyl-upholstered building. It looked like it had been moved in one piece from some older municipal structure, long since torn down. Or maybe they'd torn down the old building first, sparing Tyler, his leather-topped desk, and his hunting-lodge walls, and thrown up the new building around them.

"Morning, Mr. Elliott," he said when we'd seated ourselves, Ford and I on one side of the scrimmage line, Tyler and a stenographer on the other. The steno was old enough to call me sonny, and I wondered whether she and Tyler chased each other around the cuspidors when the taxpayers had all turned in. While I was wondering, the sheriff added conversationally, "Seen any gangsters this morning?"

"It's early yet," I said.

"Feels late to me," Tyler said. "Course I never did get to bed last night. How about you, son?" he asked Ford. "You feeling up to a talk?"

"Yes, sir," Ford said, sitting forward in his seat like an anxious applicant.

"Has Mr. Elliott been discussing his theories about the crash with you?"

"No, sir."

"Good. We're not interested in theories this morning. All we want are facts. One fact we have already is that Charley Gavin found this doohickey called a gust lock attached to the tail of the plane. Let's talk about that."

Ford ran through his speech about gust locks—what they were, where they were stowed, why he was sure he had taken them all off—while Tyler sharpened the stenographer's spare pencils with a penknife and I silently willed the pilot to settle down. He was talking too quickly, emphasizing his diligence too strongly. In Tyler's rheumy eyes I saw sympathy, the last emotion I wanted Ford's story to be inspiring.

"Relax, son," the sheriff finally said. "Nobody's accusing you of anything. I'm not investigating the accident as such. The Civil Aeronautics Board will do that. I just want to make sure before I step away from this that what happened really was an accident."

"It can't have been," Ford said. The very words I wanted, but not in the calm authoritative tone I needed.

"Are you saying there never has been an accident caused by a gust lock?" Tyler asked.

"No. Every pilot's heard about plenty. The first B-17 ever built crashed on a test flight because it took off with an elevator gust lock in place. I'm saying it couldn't have been what happened last night."

"Let's get our lines untangled a little. What time was it when you took this gust lock off?"

"When I did my walk-around, about eight o'clock."

"The sun was just setting, so there was still plenty of light," Tyler said. "Is that why you did it so early, for the light?"

"No, sir. I didn't do it early. Mr. Pioline told me to be ready to leave at eight-thirty."

"I recollect now," the sheriff said. "Charley told me last night there'd been a delay. Let's hear about that."

"Okay," Ford said, the change of subject giving him a chance to gather himself. "Mr. Pioline got there at eight-thirty. Drove himself out, which surprised me. He asked Mr. Gavin to run the car back when we'd gone.

"I thought we'd leave then, but Mr. Pioline wouldn't get on

the plane. He paced around for a while by himself out on the edge of the runway."

"How long a while?"

"A couple cigarettes' worth. Maybe three. Half an hour almost. I didn't think much about it at the time. Mr. Pioline had a lot on his mind. This movie they're making has some problems."

"So I've heard," Tyler said, not looking my way. "Did you have Mr. Pioline in sight the whole time you were waiting?"

"Most of the time. I went back into the office for my map case. I was there when Mr. Pioline came inside to make a call. I don't know to who. He asked Mr. Gavin and me to leave. He came out five minutes later and said he was going back to the ranch."

"What was his state of mind then?"

"He was agitated. I thought there must have been more trouble with the movie."

"But we know now there wasn't any," Tyler said, giving me another quick take. "So he drove away. What did you do?"

"I called to get the latest weather. Then Mr. Gavin and I played cards."

"You didn't put the gust locks back on?"

"No, sir. I didn't even bother to tie the *Argo* down again. There was hardly any wind."

"Go on."

"I was starting to think I would have to secure her, that we wouldn't leave that night. Mr. Gavin even offered to let me sleep in the office. Then, a little after ten o'clock, Mr. Pioline came back. We understood then why he'd been waiting."

It was the part of the story Ford had blurted out to me on the hillside. He repeated it now, showing by his halting delivery that he felt embarrassment for two people who were past feeling any themselves. "He had Miss Brooks with him."

"How did she behave toward Mr. Pioline?"

Ford shot a glance at me, his mute counsel. "Affectionately," he said. "Mr. Pioline told me he'd changed his mind. He wasn't going to Los Angeles. He was going to fly to Palm Springs. And I wasn't to go along."

"Why not?"

Ford gave me another hopeless look and then told Tyler of Pioline's regular trips to the desert resort with his "lady friends."

"I see. You're doing fine, son. We're about to the end. So Mr. Pioline and Miss Brooks got aboard the plane. Did Mr. Pioline do one of those walk-arounds first?"

"No."

"Did anyone?"

"No."

"It was dark by then, wasn't it?"

"Yes."

"So Mr. Pioline just fired her up and went."

"Yes."

"He taxied out onto the runway and flew right into the side of the hill. You and Charley jumped in his truck and drove to the fire. What were you thinking?"

"What?" Ford whispered.

"Charley said you were in bad shape before you ever got there. When Mr. Elliott found you, you were worse."

Ford cut the lengthy explanation he'd given me in his hospital room to four words. "I'd lost a friend."

"So it was natural for you to be upset," Tyler, the county's grandfather, crooned. "It would be just as natural for you to be thinking, 'How did this happen? Was it something I did? Or didn't do?' Were you thinking that, son?"

"I took that gust lock off," Ford said, and buried his face in his hands.

15

We all sat for a time, Sheriff Tyler waiting for another word from Clay Ford. When none had come after a couple of minutes, the stenographer cleared her throat, and Tyler said, "That's it then."

He addressed the person who had slipped him his cue. "You can add this, Sally. The statement given by Mr. Ford agrees in every particular with the one given after the crash by Charley Gavin—as Mr. Elliott can attest—with one significant exception. Charley did not witness Mr. Ford doing his preflight check of the plane at eight o'clock because he was busy with other work around the airfield. Ergo—"

"Ergo," Sally said, laughing girlishly.

"Ergo, he could not say whether Mr. Ford removed the gust lock."

Ford looked up at that, dry-eyed and mad. Tyler stayed him by raising a horny palm and continued dictating. "The repetitive nature of the walk-around is such that Mr. Ford could have omitted a step while having a clear mental image of performing it based on the many prior times he'd done it. There is also the possibility—though Charley Gavin denies it—that Charley replaced the lock himself, perhaps absentmindedly, when he saw that the flight would be delayed. Old Charley—Mr. Gavin make it—is getting a little forgetful.

"A third possibility is that Mr. Pioline, while out of sight of Mr. Ford and Mr. Gavin, replaced the lock, maybe to pass the time while he smoked his cigarettes, maybe to take his mind off the trouble his actors were giving him.

"In any case, the crash was an accident whose cause—the gust lock—is known but will probably never be explained."

"You're forgetting a fourth possibility," I said. I kept talking even though Sally, without any visible signal from Tyler, had stopped writing. "That the gust lock was replaced by someone who wanted the crash to happen."

"A young hoodlum who loved Miss Brooks so much he wanted to see her dead?" Tyler asked.

"A young hood who discovered that Brooks had betrayed him with Marcus Pioline, the man who paid to have her rescued from Las Vegas. And who then carried her back here in a certain C-47."

"I see how it fits," Tyler said. "At one stroke, this hood eliminates an unfaithful lover, a rival, *and* an airplane that had crossed him. Say, do you think he was really out to get the plane and the other two were just innocent bystanders?"

The steno cleared her throat again and shook her head disapprovingly.

I felt the same way. "What happened to the streamer on the gust lock?" I asked.

"The whatsis?"

"The gust lock had a strip of red silk attached to it, to help draw someone's eye if the plane taxied off with the lock in place."

Tyler looked at Ford.

"Yes, sir," the pilot said. "It does."

"It did," I corrected. "When Gavin found the lock last night, there was no strip on it. I'll testify to that. Someone pulled it off so there wouldn't be the slightest chance of anyone spotting the lock."

Tyler pushed gray hair out of his eyes. His forehead wasn't furrowed by horizontal lines like Paddy's. It's cuts radiated upward from the point where his shaggy eyebrows met.

"The strip broke off is all," he said. "The plane was going hell for leather before the end. This strip of silk can't have been meant to take that. So it broke off. It's out there now, wrapped around some scrub bush, fluttering in the wind."

"Why are you so anxious for this to be an accident?" I asked.

"That will be all, I think, Sally," Tyler said. "You can go, too, Mr. Ford. Sally will call up Charley Gavin, and he'll come and get you. You two will be talking to the federal crash investigators later this morning, I understand. Just be as straight with them as you were with me and you won't have any problems."

As the two left, I heard voices in the outer office, one of them Lange's. Then the door clicked shut, and it was just Tyler and me and the dead deer heads.

"You seem like a right guy, Elliott," Tyler finally said.

"It comes and goes with me," I replied.

"You a vet?"

"Yes."

"Pretty safe guess, a man your age. I'm a veteran, too. Different war. That disposes me to be patient with you. But my patience is like your good behavior. Apt to come and go."

"You haven't answered my question."

"Seen this morning's *Herald*?"

I nodded.

"You movie folks took quite a pasting in it. You're the four horsemen of the apocalypse in a Cadillac limousine, according to Doc Beard, the gentleman who wrote the editorial. Not that he's a gentleman or a doctor. He's the editor of the *Herald*. And a staunch supporter of the political party that's currently out of power in this county, which makes him no friend of mine. I've gotten the Beard treatment in the *Herald* so often my scars have grandchildren. I'm almost grateful to you folks for coming along to give him another target."

But not grateful enough to stick his neck out. "You don't want the word murder spoken out loud because the *Herald* might hear it."

"Exactly," Tyler said. "That would give Doc Beard a new stick to beat me with come this fall's elections. A Teddy Roosevelt autograph model. What you're asking me to take on is the kind of case that drags itself around forever and gets nowhere, one that's all hunches and no evidence. Beard would love that. He could call me nine kinds of incompetent and sound right every time. Even worse, he'd have me tied in with you movie types so tight, people would be blaming me for the price of popcorn. All that so you can ease you conscience."

"What's my conscience got to do with it?"

Tyler paused to do something I hadn't seen anyone do in years: roll a cigarette. He was adept at it, too, although he cheated a little, using the leather desktop as a workbench.

"Care to try one?" he asked, nudging his tobacco pouch my way. "No? Dying art, I guess. Two bad about your friend, Ford. Take my word for it, he's feeling guilty about that accident. Checklist or no checklist, his conscience is bothering him."

"We were discussing my conscience," I said.

"Well, aren't you two in the same boat? Even if Ford had nothing to do with that gust lock, he's going to feel bad for a time because he didn't do his job. He was hired to fly the plane, and the plane is gone. His employer is dead. You were hired to protect Miss Brooks. Now she's dead. Doesn't matter that it wasn't your fault, that it was something no one could foresee. You feel responsible. You wouldn't be much good if you didn't.

"Now you want to square accounts by bringing in this Rembrant—"

"Remlinger."

"Remlinger to justice. And you don't care whose life you make miserable doing it. There, I've said my piece. I wanted you to know I understand and don't hold any of it against you. You can show the next folks in, if you wouldn't mind."

I stood up. "What's to stop me from going over to the *Herald* and demanding an investigation?"

Tyler had been admiring his cigarette all this time. Now he lit it with something like a sigh. "Not a thing, if Beard's the kind of man you care to do business with. Just wanted you to know the lay of the land before you made up your mind. Of course, it's only a matter of time before Beard gets wind of this Remlinger, with or without your help. Surprised he hasn't already. From what you tell me, Remlinger's been tied to Brooks in the Los Angeles papers. Isn't that what got Mr. Pioline up here to be killed?"

"Yes," I said, though that crisis seemed a month in the past.

"Then they'll mention it, and Beard will know about it, maybe even start yelling murder all by his lonesome."

"Why the stall, then?"

"So I can have my answer finished, my report. Facts can sometimes carry the day for you, even against a newspaper. That is, they might if I have a day or so to find the facts."

He was a guy Paddy could have played checkers with for hours, but Paddy was elsewhere. I collected my hat and went out, stepping right into Lange and Irwin. The grieving novelist was as composed as ever, as far as I could tell with his cheaters in place. Lange was another matter.

"What gives?" he demanded, aiming his bullet head toward the office I'd just vacated.

"My conscience was bothering me," I said, and left it at that.

Once outside, I asked for the offices of the *Heston Herald*. They were a short pleasant walk through a park away, in a two-story brick building whose first-floor front had big display windows, the kind that were perfect for showing off the latest fashions from exotic Sacramento. The *Herald*'s windows were displaying front pages of the paper, some recent and some not so. One yellowed number announced V-J Day in monster type. Brooks and Pioline hadn't rated that size of headline, but their front page was getting more attention from the passersby. Score one for us.

I slipped through the little knot of readers without touching so much as a shoulder pad. I stepped directly into the newsroom, to the accompaniment of a tin bell mounted on the inside of the front door. No one looked up at the sound, which had been swallowed whole by the hammering of typewriters, the ringing of phones, and the clatter of a Teletype. It wouldn't get much busier at the *Herald* until World War III broke out.

A kid was making the rounds of the desks carrying a cardboard box lid full of cardboard cups of coffee. When he swung my way, I lifted one.

"Hey," he said, hitting a note an octave above the ringing phones. "This is for the staff. You out-of-town guys get your own."

"You may want an out-of-town contact someday," I said. "Or do you plan on being buried here?"

He thought it over while his tray sagged in the middle. "What paper you with?"

"None," I said. "But it's still good advice. Where's Doc Beard's office?"

The kid laughed at that. "Robert McNamarra couldn't get in to see Doc right now."

I sipped my coffee for timing purposes. "He could if he'd spent the night inside Crowe Ranch."

The cub reporter put the tray down without spilling a drop and took off up an open staircase that climbed one wall of the newsroom. He made so much noise on the wooden steps I could almost hear him. I followed at a more leisurely pace, enjoying my stolen coffee, which beat the cup I'd promoted at the hospital hands down.

By the time I got to the second floor, the kid was emerging from an office looking impressed. I handed him my empty and thanked him, for the coffee and because he was holding the door for me.

A second later, I wanted to take it back. The room he was ushering me into wasn't an office at all. It was a supply room, one wall of the narrow space lined with shelves. I had a glimpse of stacked paper, boxes of staples, paste pots, and rows and rows of those little glass bottles of mucilage with rubber nipples on the top that dispense the stuff when you least expect it.

I hesitated in the doorway, thinking I was being put on ice. Then I spotted the cot in the gloom at the far end of the room and on the cot the man I'd come to see: Doc Beard.

When the kid shut the door behind me, Beard lifted himself on an elbow and raised the paper shade on the closet's only window. "First sleep I've had today," he muttered.

He was younger than I'd expected. Based on Beard's folksy nickname and the fact that he was the ancient Sheriff Tyler's political adversary, I'd been expecting someone around Paddy's age, another member of what Lange had called Paddy's men-of-the-world club, a loose brotherhood of the successful and the survivors. Instead, I found another member of my club, the where's-half-my-life-gone? society.

Beard didn't spot our kinship. "Who are you?" he asked.

He didn't ask it in a friendly way, but that might have been the sand in his eyes. It took me a while to get past the Hawaiian shirt or pajama top he was wearing—an odd vestment for the guardian of the county's morals—so I could study the man himself. When I did, I saw veins bulging at hollow temples, yellow teeth, skin somehow untouched by sunshine in a state that had invented the stuff, and thin lips almost as colorless as the skin, lips that were kissed about as often as Nixon heard "Hail to the Chief."

"My name is Elliott."

"The security man from Hollywood," Beard said. "Or should I say professional kidnapper?" Tyler had been right. Beard had heard all about the Vegas angle sometime since today's *Herald* had hit the streets. "Sorry I didn't get your name in this morning's edition. I'll give you the front page tomorrow if you've brought me something good."

I'd brought a stick of dynamite big enough to blow Tyler a year into retirement, but I hadn't decided whether I'd hand it over to Beard, a man who would have been just as happy if Lillian Lacey and the rest of her troupe were sharing Brooks's slab in the hospital basement.

"I've come to ask a question," I said. "Where did you get your inside information on the *Warrior Queen* shoot?"

"From what we in the newspaper business call a confidential source. If you've come here to act tough, remember there aren't many people tough enough to win a wrestling match with a newspaper."

He sounded confident, but he inched his way closer to the open window just in case.

"Relax," I said. "I'm just curious about the timing. The crash wasn't six hours old when your paper hit the street. Was your confidential source wearing roller skates?"

"News isn't news forever. You have to move fast if you want to profit by your knowledge. If you've got something I can use, there's a twenty in it for you."

I made a mental note to have my suit pressed. "Are you sure you haven't been having the ranch watched?"

"If I have, it would be perfectly legitimate. Your charges are celebrities. Everything they do is news. If they happen to fry themselves, it's big news."

"You implied in your editorial that Marcus Pioline was using drugs to keep Beverly Brooks in line. That's not news, it's slander."

"You can't slander the dead, Elliott. Especially not dead Hollywood producers." He said Hollywood the way some people say Nazi, as if the word were burning his tongue. "Marcus Pioline managed to get himself a headline or two before this, with the help of other willing young women. If he wanted to keep that hobby a secret, he should have died alone."

"Who told you Pioline was supplying pills?"

"Get yourself a court order if you want to know that. Then I can laugh at you *and* the court order." He pulled the shade back down. "Now, if you don't mind, I've got a prior appointment."

I didn't mind. I'd decided I'd go after Remlinger single-handed before I'd have Beard on my side. I covered my walk to the door with a last question.

"What do you have against Hollywood?"

"Nothing. I'm just another scavenger like you, living off the giant's fat carcass. Or better: picking over the leavings of a dying empire. I think that's why these Roman epics are so popular now with what's left of the studios, because the big bosses—illiterate though they be—sense some parallel between the Decline and Fall and their own situation.

"Think about it," he said, warming to his subject so quickly that I decided he was quoting from the copy he'd written for tomorrow's editorial page. "Here's this once powerful entity dwindling away, the Julius and Augustus Ceasars gone, what's left of the show being run by pretenders to greatness like Marcus Pioline, while foreign barbarians bang at the gates. That makes me maybe a historian, another Gibbon. What does it make you, Elliott?"

Horatius at the goddamn bridge, I thought, and left.

16

As I stepped from the *Herald*'s building, I was mistaken for a journalist for the second time that morning. On this occasion the man with the bad eye was an out-of-town reporter, who took me for one of Doc Beard's gang.

"Hey, buddy!" he called to me from the window of a dusty Fairlane. "How about giving a couple of fellow hacks a break and telling us how to get to Crowe Ranch? I think your citizenry is playing games with us. We've driven halfway back to Frisco twice and not found the place."

I stepped over to the car and looked in. There were two people in the front seat, the onlooker a woman.

"I can show you, if you'll give me a lift," I said. Lange wouldn't mind. In fact, he'd probably prefer the arrangement.

"Hop in," the driver said.

I waited until we'd cleared the town before observing that the ranch residents weren't letting reporters through the front gate.

That was all in a day's work for the driver, who said, "We'll see what we see. Mabel here might turn the trick, if she'll excuse the expression. She's met Lillian Lacey."

Mabel's white linen hat was doing better in the heat than she was. It bobbed up and down when I asked, "Is that right?"

She started to turn in her seat, decided against it, and commandeered the driver's rearview mirror, twisting it around until she could see me and I had a view of one well-mascaraed eye. "Hollywood's my beat," she said. "I've interviewed Lillie several times. She's a darling woman."

"So I understand."

"I'd arranged to interview her next month in connection with this picture, and I will come back when shooting resumes. In the meantime, though, I want to be there for her."

"Shooting may not resume," I said absently. I was thinking of the *I, Claudius* stories Pioline had told us. That production had unraveled because of an actress's car wreck. It wasn't likely that *Warrior Queen* could survive a plane wreck that had taken out an actress and the producer.

"Oh, they'll finish the picture," Mabel said breezily. "Lillie will move heaven and earth to get that done. She has to. She's broke."

I didn't have to pretend to be uninformed now. "I heard she got a pile from Pioline in the divorce."

"Not as big a pile as she deserved. Not with his reputation. Then she tried to double what she got by investing it in some movies—all flops. I thought at the time that she might be trying to beat her ex-husband at his own game as a little extra revenge. She did it all on the QT, without her name ever appearing, so it isn't generally known. But take my word for it, she's got less in her pockets right now than the three of us."

That put Lacey in a bad spot, based on what I knew of a third of our pockets. I thought it over while Mabel described the problems facing the *Cleopatra* shoot in Rome. The list carried us right to the gates of the ranch.

The crowd of reporters and photographers had grown considerably since I'd left, reinforced by several television film crews. My driver pulled into a makeshift parking lot someone had set up on a patch of the Crowes' better grass.

"Might as well present our credentials," he said.

I hung back as he and Mabel closed on the guard at the gate. I arrived in time to hear Lange's man recite his piece about Lacey's indisposition and the possibility of a statement from her later that morning. My guess was, Ella had already written it.

Mabel was asking the guard to pass along news of her arrival when he spotted me. He touched the brim of his cap. "Mr. Elliott, your wife asked me to tell you you'll find her at Crowe House."

He opened the gate wide enough for me to ease through sideways. As I sidled, I caught Mabel's asphalt eye. "I'll tell Lillie you're here," I said.

She didn't believe me. The last thing I heard from her as I led the guard away from his post was a sotto voce speculation on the marital status of my parents at the time of my birth.

When we'd gotten out of earshot of the press corps, I asked the guard, "Who was on the gate yesterday evening before the crash?"

"I was, part of the time. Chet Harris relieved me around nine-thirty. He's the guy who almost ended up mounted on the front bumper of your Thunderbird."

"Pass on my apologies."

The man who wasn't Harris didn't promise anything.

"I'm trying to trace Pioline's movements after dinner last night. I'm told he left for the airport and then came back."

"Right. He went out of here about eight o'clock. Came back around nine-twenty. Just before I went off duty."

That had to be the car I'd heard coming and going while Ella and I chatted on the steps of her cottage. The car hadn't approached the cottage grove, which meant that Pioline must have come looking for Brooks on foot. That would have been the discreet way to do it. I tried to confirm the hunch without leading my witness.

"What did he do when he came back?"

"Drove straight to Crowe House." He indicated the dirt track that climbed the slight rise to the main house.

"Did you see where he went after he parked?"

"Nope. Too dark."

The darkness made Harris an unlikely witness to Pioline's movements, too. I'd have to find others.

"Thanks, chum," I said,

Crowe House was a fortress within a fortress, with its own

guard at its front door. This one wasn't wearing the navy blue uniform, leading me to deduce that Lange had subcontracted the work, to rest his own men or just to back them up.

I was saved the job of explaining myself to the new arrival by Ella, who came out the door as I trudged up the gravel path.

"What's for dinner?" I asked.

"It's not even lunchtime yet," Ella said, her "Where have you been?" forestalled for a time at least. Like the rest of us, she'd forgotten to pack her mourning attire. She was wearing a sleeveless dress that had vertical stripes above the waist and horizontal ones below, the stripes formed by a repeating pattern of pink roses on a green trellis, arranged against a white background. I experienced a strong desire to lay my head down among those roses and sleep.

"How's Lillie?"

"Come see for yourself. She's been asking for you."

Lacey and Jewel were together on the living room sofa, huddled on it, despite the building heat of the day. Jewel took one look at me and left, happy, I thought, to have someone to pass her mother to. Lacey was in bad shape, her face blotchy and swollen, her eyes dull, her head lolling on her neck. Her large hands were the only lively things about her, and they were too lively, kneading a soiled knot of handkerchief incessantly. She wore a long terry robe and wore it casually. The Leslie Howard deer head above the mantel was giving her a worried look with which I was much in sympathy.

"Tell me, Scotty," she said when I sat beside her, "have they found out why this happened?"

"No," I said. To comfort her, I fell in temporarily with Sheriff Tyler. "They think it was just an accident."

Lacey reached out to pat my hand, her own hand uncomfortably warm. I glanced at Ella, who nodded and said, "We've sent to Los Angeles for some decent help."

"She means she sent for my doctor," Lacey said. "She thought I was asleep when she phoned. She's afraid that bumpkin from Sherwood might have given me a rabies shot last night by mistake. Or was it rabies itself, darling?"

Her voice had a faraway quality that I liked less than her fever. "Why not let me take you to Los Angeles?" I asked. I felt Ella tense up beside me just before Lacey exploded.

"No! I won't leave! I won't leave Marcus!" It must have been an argument that the actress had already won that morning, because she calmed down as soon as Ella indicated, with cooing sounds and gestures, that no comment of mine should be taken very seriously.

"Sorry, Ella," Lacey finally said. "Sorry, Scotty. All morning I've been feeling like dear old Una O'Connor. Remember her from the Frankenstein movies and the *Invisible Man*? Nobody did a comic hysteric better than Una. Even so, halfway through every picture she was in, you wanted to slap her. I always did. Ella's been feeling that way about me all morning."

"I have not."

"Could you make us some tea, do you think, Ella darling? Ella sent Hilly to bed; she'd been up all night, poor thing."

When Ella had gone, Lacey drew herself up and tried to convince me things weren't as bad as they looked. "The press expects a bit of mourning, Scotty. And you have to please the press. Marc would give me a right hiding if he knew I'd passed up a chance for free publicity. Publicity to die for," she added, and a single tear rolled down her cheek. Being a Lacey tear, it was demitasse-size.

"Not that Marc didn't deserve at least a show of sorrow, for all his faults. I've often asked myself where I would have ended up without him. I wouldn't have made it to America, unless I'd come over to break into burlesque. I know that much.

"He lifted me a peg or two, Scotty. A vulgar little man the toffs laughed at behind their manicured hands, but he knew every trick in their book. Couldn't be bothered speaking like anything but a fisherman himself, but he corrected me every time I dropped an H. Do you know what my nickname was in English pictures before I met Marc? 'Lacey Knickers,' because in every picture they'd find some excuse for me to appear in a teddy or some other gauzy underthing. Five years after Marc started managing my career, they were calling me 'Lillie White,' everybody's favorite virgin. You don't mastermind a move like that if all your brains are in your pants. Poor Marcus."

I was more interested in a move that had everything to do with Pioline's pants. Ella would give me a right hiding—whatever that was—if she knew I was questioning Lacey, but Ella was still in the kitchen.

"I've heard that Marcus came back from the airport last night."

"Yes." Lacey was suddenly self-conscious about the gaps in her robe. She pulled it tight around her. "He popped in sometime after nine, completely out of the blue. That was just like Marc. I asked if there was something wrong with the plane, and he said no, he'd just forgotten something he wanted to tell me."

"What?"

"Nothing really, that was the queer thing. He hemmed and hawed about some minor problems, but he never got around to anything important. And he kept looking at his watch. I remember thinking that he'd come back for some other reason and he'd just stopped in to pass some time. Now I know it was really to establish an alibi. He'd come back for Bebe, the poor cow. I should have guessed it right then, while he was here."

"Why?"

"Because he all but told me, didn't he? When he flew off the handle.

"It was my fault. I decided I had something serious to discuss, even if he didn't. I demanded that he replace Bebe. I don't want what I'm about to say to go beyond this room, Scotty. Now that she's dead it sounds so petty. But I was convinced she was going to ruin the film, with or without an assist from her gangster lover. I'd been patient long enough, I said. She had to go while there was still a chance to reshoot her scenes."

"Marcus objected?"

"My dear, he gave off sparks. He told me his backers hadn't invested their money in Lillian Lacey, that he couldn't have raised the money for a television commercial with Lillian Lacey. Not anymore. Not in 1962. This from the punter who made two fortunes and spent three selling peeks at Lillie Lacey. His new backers had put their money on Beverly Brooks's pert little ass, Marc said. And they'd get Brooks if we had to walk her around with wires."

Lacey slumped back against the sofa's ample arm. "God knows what those backers are thinking right now. I wish I had a list of them. But Marc was always so secretive. Still, his bank may know."

She looked at me over the knotty tangle of linen she was still torturing as though I might be just the gumshoe to track down her ex-husband's angels. "What do you say, Scotty? Could you trace them for me? You or that interesting boss of yours, Mr. Maguire?"

"Paddy could," I said. "I'll ask him if you like."

"Thank you. I knew I could count on you. We'll save this picture yet. We have to." I thought she'd tell me then about her financial reversals, but she held it back. "I need this picture for my nest egg, Scotty," she said delicately. "For my retirement."

I decided I owed Mabel an apology and maybe dinner. As a down payment, I made good on my promise to the reporter and mentioned to Lacey that Mabel was ready and willing to hold her hand.

Lacey wasn't listening. "And we should finish *Warrior Queen* for Marc's sake, if for no other reason. That may be the best way to present it to the backers and the press. *Warrior Queen* will be Marc's monument. His last and greatest film. That's what I'll tell them, but God knows how I'll do it, where I'll find the strength."

She was lapsing back into the basket case who'd first greeted me, perhaps because she was tired, perhaps because Ella was entering stage left with the tea.

"We'll save the picture," Lacey said from a great distance. "We'll save it together."

17

I went looking for Nicole Cararra and found her at Beverly Brooks's cottage, packing her bags. She'd answered the cottage door in her usual uninterested way, grown neither brighter nor poutier at the sight of me, and led me back—when I'd requested an interview—to a little room with closet door open and bureau drawers turned out.

"Leaving us?" I asked.

"Leaving this," Cararra said, gesturing around the cottage. "This is a star's bungalow, not a stand-in's. And who am I standing in for now? Nobody."

It was the longest speech I'd heard from her. For the first time, I detected the remnants of an accent so well hidden under the sixties American drawl that I couldn't place it. I switched to wondering who among the production staff had so much free time on his hands that he was worried about cottage allocation. It turned out the eviction notice had been self-inflicted.

"I know they'll want to move me, so I'm ready," Cararra said. "They moved Danny, so I know they'll move me. Probably to some dump in Sherwood. Or maybe they'll pay me off." Like Ella, she was dressed more for a picnic than a wake. Cararra's outfit was white pedal pushers and an untucked blue blouse, its tails knotted together in the front to show off her flat stomach.

"They gave Irwin another cabin last night," I said, "because they thought it might bother him to be back here, where his wife had been."

"Silly," Cararra said. "She will be everywhere for him. That's the way it is for Danny."

"How is it for you?"

She shrugged. "Bebe was my friend. She was the only one who was nice to me since I came to Hollywood. The only woman. Some men were nice, but not for very long. This is all I got from most of them." She held up a piece of the lingerie she'd been packing. It was black and as substantial as an *Ozzie and Harriet* plotline. "Your wife have things like this?"

"Trunks of them."

Cararra folded the garment several times without noticeably affecting its transparency. "She's a beautiful woman, your wife."

"I like her."

She signaled a change of tack with a small smile. "I thought so. You two have one of those 'till death do us part' marriages."

I was actually hoping for an even better deal than that, but it wasn't a topic I'd discuss with Cararra, even if I'd been off the clock.

"So men give you underwear," I said. "What did you get from Brooks?"

"A job on this picture. After knowing me for only a month. She was going to do more on her next film. She was going to see I had a real chance. She was generous. People took advantage of that. Men did. That's all they'll write about now that she's dead: the men who used her. They won't write about the rotten time she had growing up. Did you know about that?"

I hadn't, but I might have guessed it. It was a common theme among the golden children of Hollywood: the hard beginnings overcome, the deprivations used to justify every silly excess and indulgence the fragile survivors could lavish on themselves, including the ultimate indulgence, an early, pointless end.

"Let's talk about what happened to Brooks last night. How did she get away from you?"

"Is that it? Have you come here to blame me? You had Bebe safe and you passed her to me, and I lost her. Is that what you'll tell the newspapers?"

I had the impression Cararra wouldn't have minded that, as long as the papers spelled her name right. "I'm not here to blame anyone. I want to know how Brooks and Pioline ended up at the airstrip together."

"I don't know. After you left last night, Bebe told me she wanted to lie down. I watched her for an hour or so. She never stirred. I decided it was safe to go for a walk. My big Friday night out, a walk around the barns. The cowboys were all off somewhere, so I just talked to the horses. And I waved to a man at the cookhouse. He was sharpening knives out back in his undershirt." She added coyly, "I think he'll remember me."

"Go on."

"Go where? That's all. When I got back, Bebe was gone. I was still looking around the cottage for her when the big boom came. I knew it was Bebe dying. I blessed myself, you know." She showed me, touching her forehead, her heart, and then each of her shoulders. "I haven't done that since I was a little girl."

We were dangerously close to her own hard-luck story then. I drew us back. "Did you see Pioline that evening?"

"No."

"So you don't know how he and Brooks got together."

"Didn't I just say that?"

"Did you know they were having an affair?"

She watched me for a long time with those dark eyes, the eyes Mabel the reporter worked so hard to duplicate. Then she said, "No."

"Are you saying Brooks didn't talk about those things with you?"

"I'm saying I don't talk about those things with you."

"I'm asking for a yes or a no, not an exposé."

"So I told you: No."

"The local paper all but accused Pioline of keeping Brooks in line with tranquilizers."

The dark eyes flashed at that. "You see! It's started. Every rotten lie they can think of, they'll tell about her."

"So she wasn't using drugs?"

"No!" Defiant this time. Hopelessly so.

"They're performing an autopsy on her right now. If she took anything last night, they'll find it."

"I'll still say no to you and anyone else who asks. It's all I can do for her now. They can write what they like about Marcus Pioline. I don't give a damn. But not about Bebe. I won't join in. I don't care what they offer me. I'll sell myself before I'll sell Bebe."

Someone had felt differently about it, perhaps because he or she lacked the selling options available to Cararra. I didn't get a chance to discuss the *Herald*'s mystery source with her. Daniel Irwin banged into the cottage just then, his momentum carrying him to Cararra's door.

He only hesitated in the doorway for a tick of the clock, long enough to look from the actress to me. Then he said, "Elliott, I want to talk to you," so convincingly that I almost believed I was supposed to be there and Cararra was the surprise addition. "Outside," he added in exactly the tone you use to invite a fellow bar patron to join you in the alley for an affair of honor.

Sure enough, as he led me to the back door of the cottage, he struggled out of a natty sports coat with a phony belt in the back. When we reached the sandy stretch of bricks that served as the patio, he removed his glasses and faced me, spreading his stubby legs for balance. Yale Boxing Squad, I thought, circa 1939.

Being a Maguire Conservatory man myself, I opened my jacket wide enough to reveal my forty-five. "Where would you like it?"

Irwin was scandalized. "You'd shoot me?"

"Before I'd let you waste my time."

"I'm not armed."

"Don't worry, when they find you, you'll have one in each hand and a derringer in your shorts."

I couldn't figure out his sudden belligerence. Was it a delayed reaction to his wife's death? I couldn't believe he was upset over finding me with Cararra. I couldn't rearrange my mental filing cards that fast.

Irwin was still on the subject of his imminent demise. "You and your pal Sheriff Tyler will probably pass this off as an accident, too."

"I tried to talk Tyler into a murder investigation. Until he has more evidence, he won't budge."

"You mean *you* won't budge, you and your con-man boss. Lange told me all about Hollywood Security. How you'll go to any length to keep a fat contract alive. Well I don't care about your bank balance. You've got no right to sit on this to protect a godawful movie. Or is it even about the movie? Have you been playing some game with Remlinger with Beverly as the prize? You rescue her, so he kills her, so now you have to personally track him down. My wife will still be dead, but you can win on points."

We'd arrived at my real offense. I'd gone to Vegas after Brooks and Irwin hadn't. He could never make that up to her now, so popping me would have to do.

"Don't be so sure Tyler will go for Remlinger if he does decide the crash was murder," I said. "He might be more interested in a jealous husband who happened to be a bomber pilot during the war. You flew B-17s, didn't you? Pioline's pilot told me the first B-17 ever built crashed during takeoff because someone had left its gust lock in place. They probably told you about that your first day in flight school. And you were wandering around loose last night."

Irwin wouldn't scare. "Fine. Tell Tyler that. Tell him anything you think will get him off the pot. I know all about gust locks. Tell Tyler I still remember a training film that starred the guy who was Peter Gunn on television—"

"Craig Stevens," I said.

"Right. In this film, Stevens flew his B-24 right into a hanger because he hadn't taken his gust lock off. We laughed at that the way we laughed at most things back then, but none of us forgot it.

"Tell Tyler all about it. Tell him I'm a dangerous drunk. I don't mind being a murder suspect as long as there's a murder investigation."

"If there is an investigation," I said, "it's going to include the pill angle. You weren't so anxious for that this morning. You lied when I asked you whether you knew your wife was taking drugs."

That must have been the wrong thing to say. Irwin came at me, hands up and head down. I'd seen the tactic often from fighters with reach problems: the willingness to take a glancing blow or two on the top of the head as the price of closing with an opponent. I took a step back to set myself and smacked his raised left with an open hand. When he looked up to see what I was doing, I tagged him on the chin with a right whose length was restricted by my holster.

It was still enough to sit him down on the bricks in a movement so broken-in it had to be the way most of his bouts ended. He rubbed his jaw and looked up at me with something more than the fight knocked out of him. "Short arms, short career," he mumbled.

He got to his feet unaided and walked to the back of the cottage, to a little spigot the gardener used. He splashed some water in his face and then collapsed in a weatherproof chair whose spring steel legs bobbed him up and down for a time. "Got a cigarette?"

"No." I was in no mood for sportsmanship. "Why did you lie to me about your wife using drugs?"

"I lied because I wasn't sure Beverly was using drugs. That isn't true. I could never catch her at it, but I was sure. I didn't tell you I knew because of the next question you would have asked me: Why didn't I do something about it? I didn't want to admit how useless I'd been to Beverly."

"How long had it been going on?"

"Not long. I've been suspicious for a few weeks. Since she left Los Angeles to come up here, I've been certain. Beverly's

115

always been a handful. But suddenly I didn't seem to know her when I got her on the phone. So I came up to see for myself. At first she wasn't too bad. Then Marcus Pioline flew in on one of his inspection trips. That night Beverly was completely out of control. Before I could figure out what was going on, she'd run off to LA to the party where she met Remlinger. I went on a bender of my own after that."

"Ella said your wife was always at her worst when Pioline visited. It's what made me first suspect they were having an affair."

Irwin got to his feet. "What your wife was observing were the drugs. That crummy newspaper must be right about Pioline being the source."

It wouldn't come together. "The paper said the pills were Pioline's way of keeping Beverly in line. But they seem to have had just the opposite effect on her. Whoever was supplying her had to have another motive."

Irwin was suddenly ready for round two. "What are you saying, that Pioline was buying sex from my wife with drugs?"

I had a different candidate in mind. "Is there any chance your wife knew Remlinger before she ran off to Los Angeles?"

"I don't think so. She would have told me the night before she left for LA if she'd had a rendezvous set up. She wasn't holding anything back. Why?"

"If Remlinger was the source of the drugs, he'd have to have been in the picture before the party."

"To explain her earlier behavior," Irwin said, nodding in agreement.

"When Lange and I saw Remlinger yesterday, he told us he was here in case your wife needed him. He expected her to come to him."

"For more pills," Irwin said. "But what about the connection between Pioline's visits and Beverly's outbreaks? Are you telling me that Pioline was Remlinger's delivery boy?"

The truth caught me much harder than I'd hit the novelist. "No," I said. "Pioline only paid the freight."

18

During my drive to the airfield, I worked on the idea that Remlinger had used Pioline's plane to ferry drugs between Los Angeles and the location site. It was an idea that definitely needed work, since it brought along its own herd of questions. For example, how did the shipments get from the plane to the ranch if Pioline was a dupe and not a courier?

On the plus side, the notion that Remlinger had hidden drugs on the *Argo* shored up another favorite theory of mine, namely that Remlinger was the one who had replaced the gust lock prior to Pioline's last flight. When he'd argued against that, Sheriff Tyler had overlooked one obvious objection: How could the gangster possibly know that much about Pioline's plane? If the sheriff threw that one at me now, I'd answer that Remlinger or his man Dillon knew the *Argo* because they'd studied its comings and goings. They'd watched Clay Ford install the gust lock and remove it. They knew where the lock was kept because they'd been inside the plane, hiding their presents for Brooks.

What I never stopped to consider was Ford's part in the scheme. I'd gotten to like the guy. I admired the way he'd dug his heels in with Tyler and his reluctance to expose Pioline's relationship with Brooks. I couldn't imagine him having anything to do with shoveling pills at the starlet, but then, like the rest of me, my imagination had already had a full day.

There was a strange plane on the edge of the Sherwood runway, a twin-engine Beechcraft parked next to the big Cessna that was always there. The twin was an unadorned dull blue that said "government issue" so strongly I didn't even pause to read the emblem on the cabin door. I decided the federal crash investigators had arrived to grill Gavin and Ford.

Luckily for me, they were still working on Gavin. I could hear his droning voice through a door off the airport office, a door marked FLIGHT EXAMINATION ROOM. Ford sat in a corner of the office, looking green. He'd said earlier that Tyler scared him more than the feds, but he'd had time to reconsider. Or maybe his interview with Tyler had used up whatever he'd had left after last night. He was barely able to register surprise as I sat down.

"Here to hold my hand again?" he asked, almost managing to smile.

"Here to ask more questions."

"You'd better make them short. Charley should be just about done. I wish they'd talked to me first. I'm sick of trying to unsay everything he says."

A chair scraped in the next room, and I thought we were done before we'd started. Then Gavin's droning began again.

"I can't give you all the background," I said. "There isn't time. I need to know if the *Argo* could have been used to make deliveries between Los Angeles and the ranch."

I had specific questions ready. Was the plane ever left unlocked and unguarded in LA? Could something have been hidden aboard without Ford knowing it? Who had access to the plane at the Sherwood end? I never got to ask them.

Ford broke in with questions of his own: "You mean deliveries for Miss Brooks?"

"Yes."

"Little packages in brown paper about the size of a deck of cards?"

"You know about them?"

"I carried them myself. They were medicine."

Even Ford's naiveté had its limits. We reached them with my next question. "Who told you they were medicine?"

"Oh God," Ford said. "I knew it. I knew they had something to do with the crash. What were those packages?"

We'd arrived at a comic dance interlude. Ford had taken hold of my shoulders and I had grabbed his. I was trying to steady him while he was shaking me. At the same time, I seemed to hear Tyler's deadpan voice lecturing me about the pilot's guilty conscience. The old lawman had been right about that, but wrong in thinking the guilt was connected to any gust lock.

"Calm down," I whispered. "You'll have Gavin and the others out here."

Ford wasn't shutting up until he got his answer. "What was in those packages?"

"Drugs," I answered. "But not medicine. Narcotics maybe. I'm not sure."

Ford let me go and said "Oh God" a few more times. "I thought it was legitimate. You have to believe that."

I might have, if he'd managed to stay in one piece. "Why did you think the medicine had something to do with the crash?"

"Just a guilty feeling. I didn't like going behind Mr. Pioline's back. I knew nothing good would come of that. She said we had to do it that way because of the insurance. No company would insure the picture if they knew the star was sick. So it had to be a secret, even from Mr. Pioline."

"Brooks told you that?"

Ford hesitated. "You can't hurt her now," I said.

"No more than I already have, you mean."

"Where did the packages come from?"

"I don't know. I mean, I know how I got them, but not who put them together. I assumed it was her doctor. I had this phone number. I called it whenever Mr. Pioline told me to prep the plane for a flight up here. He never gave me much more than an hour's notice, but that was always enough time for a package to reach me."

I collected a telephone message pad and a pencil from Gavin's desk and passed them to Ford. He pulled a card from his wallet and copied a number onto the pad.

"How did the packages arrive?"

"A little runt of a guy brought them. Wore the same striped suit every time. Used cologne like a woman, but I could always smell him underneath. Wore a little gray hat with the brim turned up all around, like FDR used to do. Had a smear of moustache that was all ends and no middle."

"How were his teeth?" Ford's description had made my skin crawl in a way I thought I knew.

"Right. His teeth were brown going to black. Like he was always eating licorice, but you couldn't smell any for the cologne. Know the guy?"

"For my sins."

"Is he a messenger or something?"

"He's anything you want him to be, for a price. Speaking of which, how did Brooks pay for her medicine?"

"I don't know."

"She never passed any money back through you?"

"Never."

It was just what I'd wanted to hear. Remlinger wouldn't have been charging Brooks for the drugs. That is to say, he wouldn't have been taking her money.

"What did she pay you?" I asked.

Ford tried to bristle but couldn't work it up. "Nothing. I did it as a favor."

Several chairs scraped together in the next room. We were out of time now for sure. Ford still held the pad with the phone number. When I reached for it, he drew it back and scribbled something else.

"That's the license number of the messenger's car," he said as he handed me the slip. "A big old Packard. I copied it down one day. Guess I was starting to wonder about this deal. He didn't seem to be the kind of deliveryman a doctor would use. But I never did anything with it."

And Brooks and Pioline were dead. I could see Ford tying that noose for himself as he turned from me to the examination room. He looked like Ronald Colman marching up to the guillotine.

I got to my feet. "Don't mention this to anyone until I've had a chance to check it out."

"I can't lie to them, Elliott."

"You won't have to. They'll ask you the same questions Tyler did. Answer them the same way."

That was all the advice I had time to pass on. The inquisitors called for Ford just as I slipped out of the office. I was leaving the pilot worse off than I'd found him, but there was no help for that.

I stopped at a pay phone that hung on an outside wall of the hangar under its own corrugated tin roof. A hand-lettered sign above the phone read: "Have you closed your flight plan?"

"Never use one," I said as I dropped my coin into the slot.

Ella answered the Crowe House phone with a very combative "Well?"

"Did the doctor slip you a rabies shot, too?"

"Scotty? No. The reporters got the number of this phone. I'm ready to pull it out of the wall. Where are you?"

"At the airfield, but I'm following a lead to Los Angeles. That is, if you think you'll be okay."

"Are you kidding? Lange's got so many men around here we're using them to stake up the tomatoes."

"How about coming with me?"

"Scotty, I can't."

"Lacey isn't as bad as she's pretending to be."

"She only thinks she's pretending. But it isn't her I'm worried about. It's Jewel. There's something wrong between her and her mother. When they're in the same room together, the air is so charged the hairs on my neck stand up."

"Jewel's probably sore over her stepfather's death being used for publicity. Or maybe she was fond of Brooks. She's a lonely kid."

"I have no idea," Ella said, meaning I had none. "There's something going on. There's been an emotional dissonance on this shoot from the start. I always thought the source was Bebe. Now I'm wondering if it might be Jewel."

" 'Emotional dissonance'? Save that stuff for your novel. I'm too down-to-earth to understand it."

" 'Down-to-earth'? This from the guy who's never been able to distinguish between movie characters and the people who happen to play them. If you could, you wouldn't have spent half your life running interference for losers and louses."

I kept our string of echo patter going. " 'Losers and louses'? You've even got a title for your book. Take care of that pretty face."

Ella refused to bat that one back. Rightly so, as I'd spent too much time sparring with better opponents than Daniel Irwin. "Take care of that mug of yours," she said instead.

19

I hit the main highway—Ninety-nine—south of Fresno and made good time until Bakersfield, where I stopped for gas. On the same stop, I placed a call to Hollywood Security. I hadn't tried Paddy back at the airfield because I'd been afraid he'd tell me to stay put while he followed up the drug trail himself. If it was a trail that led to Johnny Remlinger, I wanted to be along.

Paddy didn't answer. Instead, I got the service he'd employed ever since Peggy Maguire had retired from everything but baby-sitting my kids. The operators were used to taking down odd messages for us. Today's disembodied voice didn't miss a beat as it read this one back to me: "Following lead to LA. May involve Guy De Felice. Will call at four. Elliott."

I also belatedly tried the number Ford had given me, on the off chance the deal was more legitimate than it sounded. The operator told me the number had been disconnected. I thanked her very sincerely.

I ended my drive on a street off La Brea Avenue, not far from the intersection of La Brea and San Vicente. The street was called Dockweiler, which added yet a third ethnic flavor to the street-name mix, the wrong flavor evidently, as Dockweiler was down on its luck. I cruised the low-rent properties until I came to one an architect had spent some time over. It was only a two-story storefront and walk-up, but it had lines that would have been recognized as the latest thing in, say, 1940, a year when I'd almost been in the same class. Its two columns of windows were divided by a stone pylon, fixed like an extremely long hawk nose to the center of the façade. Two shorter pylons ran up each outside edge of the building. The whole effect reminded me of the front grille of a car I'd owned around the time the building had been new, a cream-colored coupe that had probably ended its days as a hot rod for some valley teenager.

A sedan almost as old was parked next to the building. It was a Packard whose black paint was so weathered it could have passed for moss green. I didn't bother comparing its tag number with the one Ford had given me. The storefront part of the building was occupied by a baby photographer. Pictures lined the window, but they were flyblown and curled at the edges. I estimated that many of the models were now draft age.

I took a narrow staircase to the second floor, the door of De Felice Investigations, Inc. The door was locked. I knocked for form's sake. Then I opened negotiations with the tumblers. Following those, I found myself in a waiting room/hallway that was squeezed down to nothing by an unoccupied desk and a water cooler. The next door was pebbled glass, the pebbling made redundant by a healthy coating of dust. It was unlocked.

I stepped through into a large underfurnished room whose principle feature was a big black Luger being held by a cloud of cologne in a striped suit.

"Trying to discourage walk-ins?" I asked.

"Scott Elliott." The little man palmed the gun nonchalantly. "Just cleaning it."

"Do the windows next." I followed a track worn in the bottle green carpet. It led me past a swaybacked daybed.

"Thomas Scott Elliott," my host said, adding the first name I'd given up for the movies. Few people in California knew about it. I hated that one of them was Guy De Felice.

He'd arrived in town sometime while I'd been overseas, washed in on the wave of exotics and semi-exotics who had fascinated Hollywood during the war years, when a craze for all things South American had coincided with an invasion by European refugees. For a while, the town and the movies it made had taken on a genuine international flavor. Now, twenty years down the road, Simone Simon, Fritz Taber, and José Iturbi were gone, but De Felice was still here. He'd never been an actor, but he claimed to have once been an advisor to several studios on pictures with foreign locales. More believable was the rumor that he'd worked as a one-man welcome wagon for unsuspecting émigrés, finding them bad housing and low-paying jobs and even putting them in touch with worthless contacts at the studios— all for a fee.

By the time Paddy and I had run across De Felice in the fifties, he'd somehow gotten himself a private investigator's license, not an easy trick to pull off in California. Hollywood Security and De Felice Investigations had ended up as allies on a certain case, which had mortified Paddy. He hated the divorce specialists, a trade group De Felice practically headed. It had been a logical field for him, given his experience as a co-respondent. Now it seemed that De Felice was working a new field.

"My old comrade in arms," he said. His accent, always flexible, was now no more noticeable than Nicole Cararra's. "What brings you to my—what do they say nowadays?—my pad?"

I looked over the visitors' chairs and decided to stand. "I heard you were branching out, Guy."

De Felice settled back in his squeaking chair. He took what I thought was a box of matches from his jacket pocket. It turned out to be a box of the little licorice tabs, each the size of a match head and laced with nicotine, that were marketed to smokers trying to quit. De Felice had long ago decided to sacrifice his teeth for his lungs. He opened the box and held it out to me. I shook my head.

"So what if I have 'branched out'? Are you thinking I might have a place for you? I'm too much of a lone wolf for that, Thomas. But if I ever did chose a partner, it would be you. I've always liked you. You're the only one I've met in this town who's crazier for the movies than I am. Whenever I catch myself watching too many or jumbling up some memory of my own with a bit of a matinee, I always say, 'Okay, I'm bad, but I'm not so bad as Thomas Scott Elliott. Not yet.' "

He smirked at me and smoothed his fuzzy moustache. "I will tell you how bad I am, though. I took this office, this inconvenient, drafty office, because of a movie. The baby photographer downstairs reminded me of it. Baby photographer next to a detective agency, ring any bells? The photographer ends up playing detective, sort of like you, Thomas. I loved that picture. Saw it three times, I bet. Need another hint?"

"My Favorite Brunette," I said. "Paramount, 1947. Bob Hope and Dorothy Lamour. Which one are you supposed to be?"

His answering smile looked like the business end of an old drain. "Don't you recognize me? I'm the guest star, Alan Ladd."

He laughed at that with a twittery laugh. To cut it short, I said, "I met another movie fan recently. Somebody maybe in your class, Guy. Maybe in your line of work, too. Name of Johnny Remlinger."

That sobered him thoroughly. His eyes danced from the gun on his desk to the door I'd left open, to the one beyond it I'd found locked. I understood now why it had been locked.

"Expecting your business partner?" I asked. "Afraid he'll be in the mood to streamline his organization?"

"I don't know what you're talking about."

"In my oblique way, I'm talking about little brown packages the size of a deck of cards. You delivered them to the airport, to a pilot named Clay Ford. He saw they got to an actress named Beverly Brooks. You read about her death in this morning's paper. Ever since then you've been waiting for a call from the police or from someone a lot more dangerous than the police."

"You're in some movie dream now, Thomas. You're mixing it up with reality."

"The pilot will identify you."

"Okay, so he will. So what? I deliver the packages. I don't know who they're for. You think they say 'Beverly Brooks' on the front? You that naive, Thomas? Also, how am I to know what's in these packages? Do you think I put them together?"

"At one time I thought you might have. The pilot said he got them within an hour of placing a call to you. On the special line you've since had disconnected. That wouldn't leave you much time for side trips. But I don't see you as the source. I think you always had the next delivery on hand, ready and waiting. Which means you should have one here."

"You think so? You have my permission to look."

I surprised him by doing a modest amount of looking. An old tin wastepaper can stood next to the desk. It was empty, but I lifted it up anyway and ran my finger across the dented bottom. The fingertip came out black.

"Been burning your love letters?"

"Sure," De Felice said. "I do it once a month so they don't clutter up the place. What do you think?"

"I think you've been burning a brown paper wrapper and maybe a box. What was in the box went down the toilet. You did that the minute you heard Brooks was dead. So don't tell me you didn't know who the packages were for."

"No, no, no. I heard that Marcus Pioline's plane had crashed. That is why I destroyed the last delivery. Not because of Beverly Brooks. Her I only know on the screen. But I knew whose pilot had been getting the packages. I got curious one day and asked around at the airport, okay? I thought he had died, too, the pilot."

There was sincere regret in his voice over Ford's escape. "What was in the last package?"

"You're asking a lot for nothing, Thomas," he said, and I knew we'd reached the financial portion of the conversation. "You're not the police. There is only so much I will do for friendship. I have to think of myself. If I've lost one bit of business—purely legitimate for all I knew—I have to find something to replace it. That's only fair."

"When they finish the tests they're running on Brooks, I'll know what was in that box and it won't cost me a dime."

"Sure, if you feel like waiting. But will you know where the box came from? Will they run a test to tell you that?"

"How about we go to talk to the district attorney. Maybe he'll meet your price."

De Felice tapped the Luger that still lay on the desktop, leaving his hand poised above it. "We're not going anywhere together. You've seen all there is to see in my very interesting wastebasket. Step back, please. Your employer, Mr. Maguire, would blush to hear you speaking of district attorneys, Thomas. Aside from the lack of respect it shows for me, a colleague, he would hate the publicity that would surely follow. The damage to his late client's reputation and that of Miss Brooks. Say what you will about Patrick Maguire, his watchword is discretion."

"What's your price?"

"I find it convenient to go away for a time. Of course, I have friends, many invitations awaiting me wherever I might go, but travel is very expensive. It being Saturday, my banker is naturally unavailable. I'll require, perhaps, one thousand dollars."

"Paddy will pay, perhaps, one hundred."

I didn't need to convince De Felice. He knew that, if Paddy's watchword was discretion, his middle name was tight.

"You have to intercede for me, Thomas. For old times' sake. I have to have five hundred at the barest minimum."

"Before Paddy will hand me that kind of money, he'll want to know I turned over this office and shook it, gun or no gun."

De Felice called that bluff with another laugh, a less nervous one this time. "Of course. You have my permission. Turn out my pockets while you're about it. To tease you, I'll tell you that what you seek is here in black and white, directions to your goal. But you'll never find them. It's up to you to decide how much time you want to waste. As for me, I don't think I'll sleep in Los Angeles tonight. With or without your help, I really must go."

"Stay put for an hour," I said.

20

It was past three-thirty. I tried Paddy's office from a phone booth and got the service again. From the operator, I learned that Paddy had called in for his messages. He hadn't left one for me, so he was planning to be in residence for my four-o'clock call. I could plead my case in person if I hurried.

Nearly everything about Los Angeles had changed since I'd stumbled off my first sleeper in the thirties, including the way the locals pronounced the name of the place. But the only two changes people ever talked about were the traffic and the smog. The two phenomena were closely linked, although even the men in lab coats had missed the connection back when the smog had first become more than an occasional nuisance in the years right after the war. They'd blamed everything from the oil refineries to backyard barbecues, with each bad guess accompanied by angry calls from John Q. Public for the swift prosecution of the bad guys. Then the scientists had tracked the problem to the thousands of tailpipes attached to the thousands of V-8s cruising the new freeways. At that point, the local citizenry had decided to live with the stuff.

I was less philosophical about the automobile menace today, given my fear that De Felice wouldn't wait until sunset before crawling behind some baseboard where I'd never find him. The feeling I was running in sand intensified when I was snared by the leavings of a three-car accident as I headed east on Wilshire Boulevard. By the time I'd made the left onto Western, I would have happily revived the trolley system for everyone but doctors and private security operatives.

Hollywood Security's home base was a little stucco building with a tile roof on a street named Roe, not far from the intersection of Western Avenue and Sunset. For years, Paddy had talked grandly of something bigger. Then he'd quietly dropped the subject. Lately there'd been passing references to unneeded floor space and the desirability of cutting our overhead. Still we rattled around in the building with the orange roof, unwilling, like so many diehards of the movie capital, to advertise our declining fortunes with a change of address.

Paddy was paying off a cab as I pulled up. I made the mistake of showing him—by the way I parked and the trot I broke into as I followed him up the front walk—that I was in a hurry. Paddy always reacted to other people's hurries by shifting into low, from a combination of caution and cross-grainedness. I knew I was in trouble when he began patting the pockets of his green-on-green plaid sports coat for a cigar, a stall he'd used since the original Lassie was a pup.

Being somewhat cross-grained myself, I didn't break stride. "I've agreed to pay Guy De Felice five hundred dollars for the name of Beverly Brooks's drug supplier."

"Is that so?" Paddy asked, looking for a match now and deliberately not finding one. "Come inside and tell me all about it."

The storytelling ended up taking me backward through the whole long day, Paddy being unfulfilled in turn by De Felice's explanation of his courier duties, Ford's revelations about the mystery packages, Cararra's protests about Brooks's sobriety, and Lacey's plan to save the film by locating Pioline's anonymous backers. By the time I'd backtracked that far, Paddy had opened his office windows, found the correct angle for the venetian blinds, hung up his homburg and his coat, and settled himself behind his desk with his feet propped on its open file drawer. He hadn't found a match, so I pushed his silver turnip of a desk lighter across to him. He ignored it while I described the editorial from the *Heston Herald* and Doc Beard's caginess about his unnamed source. Then, because I'd given up trying to spur my employer on, I threw in my interview with Sheriff Tyler.

"A man after my own heart," Paddy said. He offered me a drink and poured one for himself. "He likes to have all his facts straight before he charges off with the posse. Must be the wisdom that comes with age. To give you one small example of my own sagacity, I'm currently wondering why I'd pay Guy De Felice five hundred dollars—or five for that matter—for whispering the address of Beverly Brooks's drugstore in my ear. You can't think the pills were the cause of the crash, unless you believe Brooks was slipping them to Pioline and they affected his depth perception."

"The drugs were Remlinger's snare for Brooks. When he found out that Pioline was beating his time, he arranged for the crash."

" 'Beating his time,' " Paddy repeated happily. "There's one you hardly ever hear anymore. I still say, who cares about the pills? We don't need them to tie Remlinger to Brooks. Their little sojourn in Las Vegas took care of that. So your formula— Remlinger loves Brooks, Brooks loves Pioline, Remlinger kills Brooks and Pioline—flimsy though it is, stands up just as well if the pills are never mentioned."

"Why not trace the person behind the pills if we can?"

"Because it will probably turn out to be Brooks herself. Most people see to their own bad habits in this life. Or it might end up being Marcus Pioline. It was his pilot playing delivery boy, after all. I don't like this Ford fellow's story. It's thin in the motivation department. Why did he agree to carry these packages? How does he come to owe Brooks a favor that might lose him his job? If Pioline was calling the shots, Ford's actions are easily explained. But the last thing we want to do is blacken Pioline's name and our own by association. He's safe enough at the moment. No Los Angeles paper will repeat those charges about the pills on the say-so of the *Hayseed Herald*. Not unless some eager beaver accidentally digs up proof for them.

"Instead of driving all the way down here to tie Remlinger to the pills, you might have done better to have figured out how Remlinger tied Brooks to Pioline. None of the people who saw them together at the camp guessed they were lovers, myself included. Are you thinking she told him about Pioline while she was in Vegas?"

"I'm thinking she told Remlinger about Pioline by running off with the guy to Palm Springs. What more did he need?"

"A crystal ball, if he was supposed to know what they were up to in time to sabotage the plane."

I'd worked out my answer to that on my drive down from the ranch. "Brooks must have promised to meet Pioline at the airstrip at eight-thirty. Or she may have agreed to ride out there with him. Either way, it would explain why he insisted on driving himself. He was jeopardizing his own production schedule for the sake of a weekend with Brooks and he didn't want Lacey or Max Froy raising hell about it in advance. But Brooks missed her ride and never showed at the airport. That's why Pioline waited and why he drove back. Brooks could have used that time to call Remlinger to tell him what she was up to. To rub his nose in it. She was high enough to pull a dumb stunt like that when I saw her earlier that evening. Or someone else from the ranch might have passed the word. Maybe Daniel Irwin did. He admitted he went looking for Remlinger that night. Maybe he actually found him and told him what his wife was planning to do.

"Remlinger beat it to the airstrip, getting there after Pioline left and while Ford and Gavin were busy at canasta. He slipped a gust lock back on, figuring nobody would see the thing in the dark. He picked the right-side lock because the cabin door is on the left side of the plane."

Paddy chewed on his cigar while I considered lighting it by force. "Pretty convenient timing," he finally said, "for it all to have happened by accident. Remlinger happening to arrive when no one's around and happening to leave just as Pioline arrives with Brooks, who'd just happened to hold him up for an hour so it would be too dark for anyone to spot the gust lock. I'd like it better if Brooks and Remlinger were in cahoots to do in Pioline, and Brooks got on the plane absentmindedly. Hell, what I'd really like is for Ford to admit he just forgot the blooming lock."

"Do you believe that's what happened?"

"No. But we're still left with the question of where your pills come in. If we're dealing with a double homicide, who got Brooks involved with drugs and when and where she was getting the stuff are all side issues."

"They would be if there was a chance we could ever prove that Remlinger is the murderer. I don't see that happening, unless he left his fingerprints on the lock or he's carrying the missing strip of red silk around in his pocket Bible."

"Both possibilities being equally likely," Paddy mused. "So you're thinking of nailing Remlinger on some charge relating to the pills? We'd be striking a blow for Marcus Pioline . . ."

He finally lit his cigar. "It might be worth five hundred—"

His phone rang then. Guy De Felice, I thought, calling to say he'd take two-fifty. But it wasn't.

Paddy had barely said hello before he followed it with "The devil take it" and then "When?" While he listened, his mouth almost lost his grip on the corona. He finished with "Thanks," leaning forward to get the word out in his hurry to hang up the phone.

"Grab your hat, Scotty. That was Lange. Clay Ford was attacked two hours ago at the Sherwood airport, worked over pretty good, too. Both legs broken." He rummaged in the desk and pulled out the twin of my automatic. "Mother of God, you don't often have to break both a man's legs before he'll tell you what you want to know."

"Remlinger?"

Paddy was heading for the door, his hat and coat in one hand and the gun in the other. "Who else? And I had him in Tijuana at least."

"What did Remlinger want from Ford?"

"Maybe a list of everything he told you, including the fact that he'd spilled the beans about De Felice," Paddy replied as he fumbled with the front-door dead bolt. "We'd best get to him in a hurry."

It was my turn to be the anchor. "We've got plenty of time. It's a three-hour drive down here from the ranch."

"Remlinger's not driving. That airport fellow, Gavin, is missing. So's his airplane. Johnny Remlinger is in Los Angeles right now."

21

I beat my earlier time on the run, spurred on by Paddy, a man
who thought traffic lights were nothing more than the city's way
of herding the tourists. The mossy Packard was still parked next
to the overdressed little building. I pointed the car out to Paddy,
but he was busy scanning the block and damning convertible
tops. Long before we reached the door of the building, he had
his hand in his coat pocket. He drew his gun as soon as we
stepped inside.

I led the way up the stairs, my own automatic out and cocked.
I was considering the dilemma posed by De Felice's front door,
the one I'd found locked and had left the same way. If we
knocked and Remlinger was inside, we might get a rude hello.
If we kicked the door down and De Felice was still fingering his
Luger, we'd get a noisy one.

It turned out to be worry wasted: The outer door was now
unlocked. We listened at it for a moment. Then Paddy motioned
me to go ahead quietly. The door did its bit, swinging open
noiselessly. I saw the water cooler, the prop receptionist desk,
and the door to the inner office, open wide. What I could see
of the room beyond was empty. Two seconds later we were
crossing the office threshold, me breaking left and Paddy right.
There was no sign of Remlinger or Dillon. Of Guy De Felice,

there were ten years' worth of signs. But the man himself was gone.

"Damn," Paddy said. "Has he flown the coop or has Remlinger snatched him?"

I found the answer on the threadbare carpet. It was a white card on which two numbers were written, one belonging to a disconnected phone and the other copied from the license plate of the car parked downstairs.

"Remlinger's been here," I said. "Clay Ford had this card in his wallet."

"Too late," Paddy said. "Too damn late." He pushed back his hat with the barrel of his gun, which reminded him he was still holding the thing. He dropped it into his pocket. "I apologize, Scotty, for laughing at your theory that Remlinger happened to come and go at the airport while Brooks was accidentally providing a diversion. I just performed the same service for the guy, with my lallygagging.

"Well, there's nothing for it now. We'll have to search this place until we find the information De Felice was going to sell us. You say he told you it was here in black-and-white?"

"Yes, but Remlinger may have taken it away."

"If he knew about it. With De Felice in the bag, he may not have bothered with secret messages. Take the reception area."

It was the easiest job Paddy had given me in years. The only piece of furniture in the narrow room was an almost square oak desk without phone or blotter or calendar. De Felice's last secretary must have taken them all in lieu of severance pay. Every drawer was empty, and there was nothing stuck to the bottom of any of them, not even a piece of gum.

While I'd been at work, Paddy had unmade the daybed. Beyond it was a door that led to a tiny bathroom. It reeked of a familiar cologne.

"Give me honest old bay rum any day," Paddy said. "Do the honors in there. If you survive, come out and help me finish up the office."

I opened the tasteful medicine cabinet, which was shaped like a scallop shell, hoping for a pill box or a bottle of cough medicine with a doctor's name on it. I found only patent medicines and toiletries, including a bottle of hair dye. There was nothing under the pedestal sink and nothing in the toilet tank except rusty water.

When I reentered the office, Paddy was standing at an open filing cabinet, folding up a good-size sheaf of mismatched papers.

"Find something?" I asked.

"Not what we're looking for. It seems that Guy might have gone in for blackmail in a minor way." He stuffed the papers into an inside pocket. "There are items here about friends of mine. Things the police shouldn't see. Too tempting for them."

I considered discussing Paddy's own resistance to temptation, but he had moved to the desk. I joined him, working the drawers on the right while he did the left.

"Say what you will about Guy De Felice," Paddy said. "He was no pack rat. There wasn't enough paper in that filing cabinet to start a decent fire. There's less in here. I wonder if he even knows how to read."

"Here's a box of shells for the Luger," I said. "But no Luger."

"Never liked them anyway." Paddy was poking around on the desktop, which was protected by a piece of well-scratched glass. It wasn't scratched enough to hide anything, though. On our side of it lay a twisted piece of paper, a crumpled drinking cup.

"Here we go," Paddy said. "Right under our noses all the time." He sniffed the paper twist and started to toss it into the empty waste can. I grabbed his wrist and then the paper. While he looked on, I worked the little cone back into a loose approximation of its original shape.

"If you're thirsty," Paddy said. "There's a whole sleeve of those things on the water cooler in the foyer. Or are you checking that for tea leaves?"

I was working with something almost as reliable as tea leaves: a memory of Guy De Felice's favorite movie. "Did you ever see a Bob Hope picture called *My Favorite Brunette*?"

"No." Paddy pushed his homburg even farther back on his head, until the brim looked like the halo on a plaster saint. "I'm partial to blonds. What exactly are we talking about here?"

"De Felice mentioned that movie to me an hour ago. Said he saw it three times."

"And?"

"Hope's a phony detective in it. He has to hide something, a map of a uranium mine, I think."

"Doesn't sound like thinking to me."

"Hope hid it inside the sleeve of cups on his office water cooler."

"Did he?" Paddy asked sarcastically, but I was already on my way across the office.

The foyer water cooler was as dusty as the rest of the room, but inside its glass tower, the full sleeve of paper cones was a pristine white. I started to pull them from the top, one by one. When that approach looked like it might kill the rest of the day, I began to pull the stack apart randomly. My second cut revealed De Felice's hole card. It literally was a card, a swanky business card, black on white, as De Felice had promised me.

"Well, I'll be." Paddy had come up behind me. I handed him my find, and he read its raised lettering aloud. "Dr. Mazar. La Habra Heights." He handed it back. "I wonder if we've time."

We didn't waste any talking it over. Not until we were in the Thunderbird and rolling. Then we had time enough to discuss *War and Peace*. La Habra Heights was out west past Whittier, in the Puente Hills, which meant it was damn near in the next county. We fought our way downtown on Pico Boulevard. There followed an interlude of driving too fast on a series of side streets called out by Paddy. Then we were outbound on Whittier Boulevard. At that point, my navigator took a break from offering free advice to the other drivers and addressed himself to me.

"Are you thinking De Felice told you about that Hope movie because he knew from the start you'd be looking for that card without his help?"

"He knew what I'd come there to ask him. He was laughing at me when he told me about the picture. He was that confident about his hiding place. He said later I could search the office before I left, for all the good it would do me."

"Lucky thing for us he got cocky."

"He must have remembered giving me the hint while Remlinger was grilling him about what I'd been after. He had the presence of mind to ask for a drink of water and to leave the cup for me to find. The presence of mind and the guts. I didn't think he had it in him."

"Didn't you? Guy De Felice has lived on nerve and not much else since you were drawing government pay." As De Felice went up in Paddy's estimation, I did a free fall. "You'll forgive me for saying so, Scotty, but you're not always the first one on your block to spot a punch line coming."

He was holding his hat on his lap, safe from the car's slipstream. That exposed his hair, what was left of it. Its silver color was making the most of the afternoon sun. I looked for a corresponding twinkle in Paddy's eyes, but didn't find any.

"Are you saying I'm slow on the uptake?"

"Neville Chamberlain was faster. Like that gentleman, you have a tendency to hold on to an idea you're fond on in the face of any amount of contradictory evidence. The latest example is this notion that Remlinger is the mastermind behind all the pill finagling."

"If he's not, why is he here in LA, covering up his tracks?"

"Who said he was covering tracks? You want to take the next left, Colima Road. Then start looking for Tarbell Canyon Road."

"You know this Mazar?"

"I know of him. I like to keep abreast of the new ways the citizens of Hollywood find for losing track of their money. It takes a deal of my time, let me tell you. Given the amount of cash involved, there's never a shortage of schemes for acquiring it. And many of our leading lights—underneath all the star trappings—are simple souls. Bebe Brooks was herself, I suspect. You could sum her up in a telegram. She just wanted to be loved. Or to be told she was beautiful."

"She wanted to be Marilyn Monroe," I said, thinking back on Irwin's diagnosis.

"Same as saying she wanted some flickering dream she'd seen on some hick town screen to be true. That's a common enough disease around here these day, God help us. It used to be the plague this town exported. In the good old days, the movies were cranked out and shipped out for the infection of the rest of the planet. They weren't taken all that seriously here, so Hollywood was spared the light-headedness and fever. Then the germs worked their way—all unseen—back into the dream factory, carried in by dreamers like Bebe Brooks. Like Monroe herself, for that matter."

"You're starting to sound like the *Heston Herald*."

Paddy ignored me. "They're made-to-order for the Dr. Mazars of this world, the dreamers. When they get here and find out this place isn't all spun sugar and goodnight kisses—not even after they've made it to the top—they go off in search of a Mazar, someone to lullaby them."

"Does he do his lullabying with pills?"

"Not that I ever heard. He must be branching out, like De Felice. It seems you have to these days if you want to survive."

I backed off the accelerator on a particularly sharp bend, my tires squealing their sarcastic thanks. "What was Mazar's original racket?"

"It's what I've been talking about: dreams. He's a dream analyst. You tell him what you're dreaming about, and he tells you what it means. Better than that, he'll tell you what to do about it, how to make what you're dreaming come true. When you come right down to it, what more does someone like Beverly Brooks want?"

"What more does anyone want?" I asked, but I asked it of myself. I knew that Paddy's portrait of Brooks was one I might have sat for, back before the war. I'd come west looking for a dream I'd seen on a hick town screen. I'd found it, too, for a time. I was sure I had, even if I couldn't always remember it clearly now. Lange had accused me of foisting that dream on Paddy, of softening him with it. I didn't want to hear the same charge from the man himself.

"The Mazar Clinic is ahead on the right," Paddy was saying.

"The building was once an observatory. I heard it was attached to Whittier College at one time. God knows how Mazar got hold of it."

I could see the place by then, a little white dome at the top of the latest hill. I couldn't see a telescope or any opening for one. Just a rounded roof as white as the water cooler cups had been, fronted by a wide low building, also white, that was pressed on all sides by the surrounding pines. In front of the place was a gravel courtyard, empty.

"Looks like another flown coop," Paddy said. Even so, he had his gun out again. His gun out and a fresh cigar in his teeth, his equivalent of hoisting a battle flag. I made do with a gun.

I didn't have to test the lock on this front door; the windowless white panel was standing slightly ajar. I reached for the door pull, a bronze casting in the shape of the sun. I hadn't pulled it very far before the smell stepped out to meet us, a mixture of spent powder and cheap cologne and something worse.

We found De Felice a few steps inside, facedown on the stone floor, a little pile that seemed to be mostly striped suit. His hands were tied behind his back, and his legs were drawn up at the knees.

"Shot while he was kneeling there," Paddy whispered. "Once behind the ear. With his own gun no less."

The Luger lay by its late owner's head, in the center of a lake of blood the polished stone floor would never drink in.

The entry area where De Felice lay was dark, but lights blazed just beyond, in the old observatory itself. The lighting was designed to do justice to the inside of the dome, which had been painted a sky blue broken up here and there by wispy white clouds highlighted in gold.

For today at least the ceiling had ceased to be the focal point of the space, its place taken by something suspended from a light fixture that hung at the very center of the room. By someone suspended there, a plump bald man with eyes that were dead but still threatened to jump from his head. A strand of wire connected him to the ceiling fixture's heavy chain, not that you could exactly see where the wire was looped around his neck.

His own weight had drawn it deep into the flesh, cutting a line as sharp as any made by a scalpel. Above the line, his skin was as white as the little temple he'd built for himself in the pines. Below the cut, everything was red.

Given all there was to draw our eyes upward, it wasn't surprising that we missed something at floor level, missed them until our shoes were grinding them into the stone. They were pills, hundreds of them, white ones and blue ones, spread out across the floor as though they—like the blood—had poured out of Mazar.

22

I picked up Mazar's phone, but didn't get further than confirming that, unlike its owner, the phone was still alive. Then Paddy touched my arm and said, "We'll talk first."

We went outside and stood on the gravel of the front drive, where the air smelled of pine and there were birds to listen to, nuthatches arguing away like neighbor dogs. Paddy tried to light the cigar he'd been chewing, but it was too pulpy to draw. He flicked it into the trees and prepped another. I collected a pipe from the glove compartment of my car, noting as I filled it that my palms were moist and that each of my fingers had taken on a twitching life of its own. Paddy noted it, too. He offered me his flask, which I waved off. He gave it a long look and then tucked it away on his hip.

"Now we know that little bedtime story Lange told us about Remlinger and the piano wire was true," he mused between launching clouds of smoke. "What in God's name have we gotten into?"

It was the question of an old man who was two seconds away from reminiscing about the days of nickel hamburgers and ten-dollar suits with two pairs of pants, days when the bad guys would draw the line at sticking each other with ice picks. A rhetorical question, you might say, but I answered it anyway, giving a summary of all I'd argued back in Paddy's office.

"Remlinger is cutting his ties to Beverly Brooks. Burying them, literally. He killed Brooks, but he knows we'll never prove it. We might have proved that he was using Mazar's setup as a way to sink his hooks into Bebe, so he eliminated the only two men who could have testified against him."

My answer yanked Paddy back to the here and now. He arrived in the mood to knock heads.

"Still on that refrain? I must have been talking to myself all the long way up here. If you think this is Remlinger's way of tidying up, you've one odd idea of housekeeping. He couldn't have tied himself any tighter to that massacre if he'd written his name in blood across Mazar's fancy ceiling. First he cripples Ford to get a line on De Felice and then he kidnaps a pilot and a plane to steal a march on you. The dullest cop in creation will finger Remlinger for De Felice's murder and throw in Mazar's for extra credit. What's more, Remlinger knows that, which makes him even more dangerous than any of us thought."

I stood my ground. "Remlinger worked Ford over to find out what he'd told me. He already knew all about De Felice."

"Says who?" Paddy left off fanning himself with his hat and ran a big hand into the stand of silver hair above his forehead. There wasn't enough left to tug on, so he scratched away instead. "You're jumping to the answer you want and then imagining a trail to get you there."

"When I mentioned Remlinger to De Felice, it scared him. He knew all about Remlinger. It had to be because he was a client."

"You're forgetting that story about the Vegas kidnapping from the *Hollywood Spy*. That was enough to introduce De Felice to Remlinger even if there wasn't such a thing as a local grapevine. As it happens, Hollywood has more grapevines than Napa Valley, and Guy De Felice was connected to most of them. I happen to be myself. The last few days, an interesting rumor has been making the rounds. Namely, that an influential underworld figure has been inquiring after the pharmacist of a certain young actress. No specifics mentioned, but the *Spy* article supplied those. So it's understandable that De Felice panicked when you dropped Remlinger's name. What's harder to figure is why he hung around waiting to be murdered. Either he thought his own trail would be impossible to follow or he really needed that grubstake he wheedled from you."

I knew all about Paddy's habit of holding things back, but that didn't make me like it any better. I countered this new angle as best I could. "Remlinger may have started that rumor as a way of distancing himself from the operation. If it's been circulating for days, he must have been planning to kill Brooks that long."

Paddy looked up to heaven but didn't actually word a prayer. "Try this on for size: Remlinger was as interested in finding Brooks's pill supplier as you were. Only he wasn't out for justice. He was after vengeance for Brooks."

"Brooks practically told me it was Remlinger feeding her the pills. The night she died, she was hinting around about what he'd done to her in Vegas. Whatever it was, she hated him for it."

Paddy had never made the acquaintance of Socrates, but he had the old Greek's teaching method down pat. "If you were pill happy, would you hate the guy who was giving them to you?"

I beat him to his next question. "Or the guy who cut you off?"

"Exactly. I've been wondering all week about that Las Vegas arrangement. Specifically about why Remlinger found it necessary to lock Bebe up and hide her clothes. Of course, it could have been she got tired of him in a hurry. She wanted out, and he wasn't having any. Or maybe he just preferred her in the altogether. Then again, it might have been exactly the way a hardcase would treat someone he was trying to dry out.

"Say it went like this. Brooks got a bellyful of these pills and skips to LA, leaving her big movie behind. At the famous party, she meets Johnny Remlinger, who happens to be as hopped up as she is, only in his case it's from being loose in Hollywood. He falls for the undeniably lovely Bebe—not just because she's a beauty, but because she's Hollywood in tight pants as far as he's concerned. Right away he spots what's wrong with her, which might have been easier for him than it was for Daniel Irwin, given the side of the tracks Remlinger lives on. And he decides to save her. Why he does I'll leave to your wife the writer to work out. Maybe he thinks it will win her over. Or maybe, being in Hollywood affected him mentally, made him decide to act like a chump from a movie. I've seen it take a guy or two that way."

"Go on," I said.

"He carried her off to Vegas to start the treatment. Only we blunder in. We snatch her and fly her back to Sherwood in the very plane that's been delivering her poison. Remlinger probably would have snatched her again, but we put the pressure on him to be good. He shows up and tells you he's there if Bebe needs him. Most everyone thinks he means he's there if Bebe gets lonely. The one or two of us who are starting to smell pills figure he's saying he's waiting around until Bebe gets desperate for a fix. But he's really saying he's hoping she's decided to turn her back on the stuff. He's there to help her if she backslides."

"Then why did he kill her?"

"That's another conclusion we shouldn't have jumped to. Take a second tour of that charnel house in there and tell me whether the technique on display has anything in common with bolting a brace to the tail of an airplane. I think we're dealing with two different killers, an incurably romantic maniac named Remlinger and a second person, a much subtler unknown."

"Could the unknown have been Mazar or De Felice? Maybe Bebe threatened to expose them. Or worse, to hand them to Remlinger. One or the other of them sabotaged the plane or arranged to have it done. Now Remlinger's closed the case before we knew it was open."

"It would be a good laugh on us," Paddy said. Then he shook his head. "Guy De Felice was a lot of nasty things, but he was no murderer. As for Mazar, you saw Brooks as late as the evening she died. Did she seem like she was ready to kick any bad habits?"

"No."

"We'll have to look elsewhere, I think."

I'd actually taken a step back toward the clinic, dumbly following Paddy's instructions to reexamine the murder room. It was only the one step backward, though. Then I was rushing forward again, toward the waiting Thunderbird. "We've got to get back to the ranch."

"What? Now? You don't think we've some loose ends to tie up here? Why the panic? Remlinger's well on his way to some hidey-hole by now."

"What if he's not? We were wrong about that before. Suppose he's on his way back to Sherwood. Suppose he knows or suspects that the crash wasn't an accident. Suppose Ford told him that, too."

"Then he'll be back to avenging Brooks," Paddy said. "He'll burn Crowe Ranch to the ground to find her killer. He'll step on anyone who gets in his way." He said "Ella" then, reading my mind. But he still wouldn't move.

"Go ahead without me, Scotty. Somebody should be here to explain things to the police. It's time we had someone in uniform on our side besides Lange."

"Call him, too," I said from the front seat of the car. "Tell him I'll be up there by nine."

"You'll have to hijack a plane . . ."

I was grinding gravel under my tires before Paddy finished the wisecrack. When his reflection appeared in my rearview mirror, it was blowing a smoke ring into the evening air.

23

Paddy was right about the timing. There was no way I could skirt the city and get as far north as Sherwood by nine. I gave it a try just the same, playing target for the highway patrol the whole way and never even drawing a wave. I rejected the LA radio stations long before I lost their signals, working the dial back and forth in search of something from the neighborhood of Sherwood or Heston, maybe an Ellington tune with a dedication from my wife: "Where the hell are you? Ella." The first five stations I found were selling the modern stuff that always made me edgier, music recorded by kids in basements to be listened to by other kids, perhaps in other basements. Then I picked up a jazz station out of Modesto and rode a Jimmie Noone retrospective toward a horizon that went from blue to purple and then to black so fast I felt I was standing still.

I reached Crowe Ranch a little before ten, almost twenty-four hours to the minute after Pioline's takeoff into the next life. I was high on nerves and roadstand coffee, ready for anything up to and including the conflagration Paddy had predicted. I found a place so quiet and ordinary that Pioline and Brooks might never have been born.

Lange had two men on the front gate, one of them Knific, my undercover agent. I asked the kid where all the reporters had gone.

"Most of them left after Miss Lacey gave her statement. That was really a show. She had them wiping their eyes, which is saying something. Those guys looked like they'd make jokes on death row."

Some of them probably had, but from the safe side of the gas chamber's door. "Where's Lange?"

Knific gave me an us-against-you look then, signaling the end of his confidences. "Asleep, I think," he said.

"Is something wrong?"

"No, sir. He's tired. He was up for forty hours. We got the word that Remlinger might be headed back this way. Everyone's ready."

If Knific could have peeked through a window of the Mazar Clinic just then, he would have gotten unready in a hurry. There was no point in scaring him, though. I told him to keep his eyes open and drove on. I thought of stopping at the bunkhouse where the security men were housed and rousting Lange, but I decided to let him sleep. I'd need him in good shape when Remlinger made his next move. No lights were visible from inside Crowe House, so I headed down to the cottage grove, where I was stopped by yet another sentry.

"Quietest Saturday night I've seen since Prohibition," he said, and yawned.

The front door to Ella's cabin was unlocked, which gave my nerves a last jangle. I found her in her bedroom, asleep. I meant to leave her that way, but she woke as I stepped back toward the door.

"Scotty, you made it. I was worried."

"My line, I think."

"I tried to wait up for you, but it was a hard day."

I sat down on the edge of the bed. Ella was still more asleep than not. I took advantage of her condition to stroke her hair, something she usually couldn't abide. Her eyes closed, but she kept talking.

"We got through it. Lillie gave the performance of her career for those reporters."

"So I heard."

"She turned her statement about Marc into a plug for keeping the movie alive. She didn't want to do that, but I talked her into it. I wanted to get rid of the craphounds," she explained, using her personal variation on newshound. "Nothing scares them off faster than a request for free publicity."

My guess was that Lacey hadn't taken much persuading, given her own hopes regarding *Warrior Queen*, but I let it pass. "Did Lacey's doctor ever show?"

"Yes. He told her to get away for a few weeks, but Lillie wouldn't hear of it. Before he left, he gave her something to make her sleep. Me, I only needed the opportunity."

"Get back to it," I said, and got up as gently as I could.

"I will when you do," Ella replied from a depth.

I squeezed her hand, something that meant as much or more to an old married couple like us than a kiss. "I'll be back. I'm going to sit up for a while and think."

"If you really mean 'drink,' the fixings are on the hearth."

They were, too: a bottle of Lamplighter Gin and another of Noilly Prat Extra Dry Vermouth, one on either side of an ice bucket. Atop the bucket was a little vial of cocktail onions, completing a Scott Elliott survival kit. I recognized the whole collection as belonging to Lacey's drink cart, which made them souvenirs from Ella's hard day. She hadn't commandeered a shaker, but she'd rinsed out a blue glass vase from somewhere that was about the right size. I poured in gin and vermouth with less than my usual precision. The ice cubes in the bucket had almost melted. I rescued a handful of tiny survivors and shook up the combination, my left hand serving first as a lid and then as a strainer as I poured myself a tall one. An especially tall one, since the only glass on hand had been designed for serving milk.

I sat down in front of the dead fireplace, after losing my jacket and holster, and drank off half the Gibson before it had a chance to warm. I was hoping the cocktail would accomplish what three hours and change in the car had failed to do, which was to shake a name loose from my head, the name of the person who had sabotaged the plane. I kept coming back to Daniel Irwin, the former pilot, the man who had wandered away from the ranch on Friday night looking for what he had called a "fruition." He'd tried to slug me for letting the crash pass as an accident, or so he'd said. Had it really been because he'd wanted to be caught and punished and I'd bungled the job? If so, he'd be happier with the service he got from Johnny Remlinger.

I stuck my gun in my belt and left the cottage, locking the front door behind me for all the good it would do. I took my refilled Gibson glass with me, inspired by the vermouth maker's slogan: "Never stir without it." The walk to Irwin's replacement cottage seemed almost as long as the drive up from the clinic. I stumbled on, guided by a light in Irwin's front window. It was being thrown by an old-fashioned reading lamp with a green glass shade. When I got as far as the cottage porch, I saw Irwin seated beside the light, an open book in his lap and a drink in his hand. He wasn't looking at the book or at the porch, though I'd made enough noise to wake him from a sound sleep. He was staring into the dark room like he was trying to commit something he'd just read to memory.

Like Ella, Irwin had left his door unlocked. I entered without knocking. Irwin didn't complain or notice me right away. When he finally did, he asked the question Ella had been too tired to word: "Did you find what you were after in LA?"

He didn't seem drunk or even particularly spent. I settled into a bentwood rocker resentfully. "How is it you're so peppy? Everyone else is keeping Boy Scout hours."

"I got more sleep last night than most of you." He added, ruefully, "More than all of you put together. Did you find out where Beverly was getting her pills?"

"Have you heard what happened to Clay Ford?"

"Of course. But not why it happened. Was Remlinger trying to get him to change his story about the gust lock?"

Leave it to Irwin to come up with a completely new angle on Ford's unfortunate meeting with Remlinger. His question made me consider Remlinger's movements all over again. Why *had* he gone to see Ford? If Paddy was right, if Remlinger had had nothing to do with the pill deliveries, how had he known to go to Ford? How had he known that the trail back to the pill source began with the pilot? Had Brooks let something slip about Ford in Las Vegas? Maybe Remlinger had simply gone to punish Ford for leaving the gust lock on. The whole revelation about De Felice was then a lucky bonus. Or an unlucky one, from De Felice's point of view. Once again, Remlinger's timing seemed too pat. It didn't seem probable that he'd happened to visit Ford just after I'd happened across the pilot's big secret.

I was too tired to work it out. And my jumbo first drink had gone right to my weary head. I made the situation worse by sipping on my jumbo second drink before I sidestepped Irwin's question. "Ford was bringing the pills to your wife. That's why her bad spells coincided with Pioline's visits. Ford thought the packages contained medicine. They were delivered to him in LA by a jack-of-all-trades named Guy De Felice. But the real source was a maybe doctor named Mazar."

"The dream analyst?" Irwin asked. He leaned forward, tossing the book he'd been reading onto the sofa beside him. It was his own first novel, *Blue Hell*.

"You know about him?"

"I knew that Beverly was seeing him. But he wasn't the source of the pills. He couldn't have been."

"Why not?"

"He warned Beverly against that stuff, against anything that would distort her subconscious visions. That's what he called her dreams. His theory is that we all have psychic ability, but in most of us it's subconscious. Instead of actual visions of the future, we have to make do with dreams. Unfortunately, those require expert interpretation. But given the right interpretation, the future becomes clear."

"You believe that stuff?"

"Of course not. It's crap, but I thought it was harmless crap. According to Mazar, any chemicals in the body introduce false messages. So alcohol and any other drugs are out. That seemed innocent enough."

"It wasn't." I distorted my next batch of psychic messages with more of the Gibson. "If he was warning his patients off pills, it was only to clear the way for his own prescriptions. How long had your wife been seeing him?"

"Not long. A month. Maybe six weeks."

"About the same length of time you told me she'd been acting up. How much was she paying him?"

"Less than she paid her drama coach. That's another reason I thought he was on the level."

"He must have been hoping for the big payoff later, when he had her good and hooked."

"What was he giving her?"

"We'll know when the lab reports come back."

"You didn't see Mazar?"

"I saw him."

"But you didn't question him."

"No." I'd come to accuse Irwin of a terrible crime, and he was cross-examining me. He didn't give me a breather so I could figure out how it had happened either.

"Did you hand Mazar over to the police?"

"Not exactly."

"Not exactly? Still covering up, aren't you? Still trying to protect your wife's damn movie. Do you know what she had Lacey tell those reporters this afternoon? 'The show must go on. Marc would have wanted it that way.' The hell he would have. He would have traded the whole picture for one more roll in the hay with a starlet."

"He did trade it for that," I said. And then, when Irwin half rose out of his seat, "Finally jealous? Or are you sticking to that double-talk about Beverly being on the *Argo* last night because it was her time to be? Forget Lacey and my wife. What did *you* tell the reporters today?"

"Me?"

"You want a murder investigation. One word to the papers and you'll get one. That never occurred to you? Or have you had second thoughts since this morning?"

"You're trying to change the subject, Elliott. Why didn't you bring in this Mazar?"

"Because he was dead when I found him."

"Dead how?"

"That's an interesting question. He was either strangled or had his throat cut or both. I don't know what they'll write on the form. Remlinger hung him from the ceiling with piano wire."

I raised my glass again and was surprised to find it empty. Before I could get over it, Irwin pulled everything together.

"Someone else doing my job for me," he said. "A gangster from Cleveland, no less. Did he know about the pills when he took Beverly to Las Vegas?"

"We think so," I said, taking credit for Paddy's brainwork. He'd taken credit for enough of mine over the years. "We think he might have been trying to dry her out. If she'd only been taking the stuff for a few weeks, he stood a decent chance."

"Then you don't think Remlinger killed her?"

"No," I said with more conviction than I actually felt. I'd grown that fond of the idea he had.

Irwin was suddenly smiling at me, crookedly. "Come to take me? I'm flattered that you brought your gun."

"I'm not a cop. I'll take you to one if you want me to. You're not safe here. We think Remlinger knows by now that the crash wasn't an accident. If he does, he'll come back here looking for the person who arranged it. He broke Ford's legs for carrying the pills and damn near decapitated the guy who rolled them. He shot the go-between through the head. God knows what he'll do to Beverly's murderer."

"My guess is, God Himself will be surprised," Irwin said, still amused. "You can't scare me into a confession, Elliott. If Remlinger wants me, he can find me right here. You'd better go look after your wife. The penalty for screwing up on that is stiff."

I climbed out of the rocker. Not because I was through with Irwin, but because it would have been ludicrous to have fallen asleep at the climax of my big scene. At the door, I turned back. "Still looking for your denouement?" I asked.

Irwin had returned to his reading. "Aren't we all?" he said.

24

Early the next morning, I slipped into Heston in a line of church-goers who seemed to consider the speed limit the eleventh commandment. For the second time in two days, I was going to the county hospital to see Clay Ford. I was fairly certain that, this time, I'd be leaving alone.

As early as it was, I'd already conducted two interviews. The first had been with Ella, in bed, and it had been a notable flop. I'd tried to persuade her to leave, to fly out to Indiana to collect the kids early or—better still—to stay out there with them for a while. My principal argument had been a detailed description of the Mazar Clinic as Paddy and I had found it, and that had been a strategically unsound choice.

"I'm not going to run off and leave everyone in that kind of danger, Scotty," her disembodied voice said. That is, I couldn't see her, as it was still dark, but I could feel her, snuggling up against me in the morning coolness. "You're not running out, are you?"

"I might, if you were clear."

"Baloney."

"Take Jewel with you," I said. "She'd like Indiana. It's quiet."

"It's not just Jewel."

"I'd say baloney back, but I don't approve of that kind of language, not even between married people."

"Speaking of being married," Ella said, "have you noticed that most of our recent talks have been in bed?"

"It's kept me going."

"We're like a movie marriage: all about the bedroom, having sex or thinking about having it."

"Not the movies I remember."

"I mean the current crop. Your old ones were more like television is today. Marriage on television is about anything but having sex. It's an odd dichotomy. You never get a view of marriage that's really like marriage. The whole package, I mean. Someday I'm going to write a script that has everything about a marriage in it, the romance, the sex, the friendship. Wait and see how hard that one is to produce."

Through all her wandering I'd held a corner of our original conversation clamped, terrier-like, in my teeth. "You'll stand a better chance of getting any new script written if you say good-bye to this place."

"I'm not afraid, Scotty. I haven't really been afraid since I met a certain ex-actor in 1947."

I know when I'm beaten, at least in retrospect. That had been the moment.

My second conference had been more profitable. It had been with Paddy, via the cookhouse phone. He'd made light of his dealings with the LA cops, saying only that there was no sign so far of Remlinger or Dillon.

"Those pills on the clinic floor," he added as an afterthought, "they were pronethalol and methaqualone."

"Not the usuals," I said.

"Nothing about this business is usual. Pronethalol is a heart medicine. But it has an interesting side effect: vivid dreams. Nightmares even. In other words, it would have produced more grist for a certain dream analyst's mill. Unfortunately, pronethalol can also cause insomnia. That's where the blue pills, the methaqualone came in. It's a new sedative they're starting to market. It could have had an additional attraction for Mazar, which is that it facilitates hypnosis."

"What about Bebe's highs? They weren't the product of any sedative."

"Maybe they were. In a certain percentage of cases, methaqualone causes restlessness and excitement instead of sleep. Some users report a high not unlike the one from heroin. I'm guessing Brooks was one of those exceptions, and Mazar didn't monitor her closely enough to spot it."

"The police lab worked awfully fast."

"The devil they did. I used a private lab. A very expensive one, I might add."

"You? How did you get samples?"

"Some of the pills got wrapped up in my handkerchief. Must have happened when I was wiping away tears for Guy De Felice. I'll call you when Remlinger surfaces."

Ford was in a new room, but he had the same deputy sheriff. That is, the doleful deputy who had been waiting the previous morning to take Ford to see Tyler was now guarding his door. That was a break for me, as it meant I got in without having to explain my visit to the old sheriff.

Ford now looked like he'd been along on Pioline's last flight. One of his legs was in plaster. The other was being supported by a board and yanked at by weights attached to wires and pulleys. The pilot's face was swollen and yellow and one eye was shut. The other eye followed me from the doorway to the side of the bed.

"Cof-fee's not here yet," Ford said with an effort that made me wince. There was cotton packed around his teeth, and it needed changing.

"I'll get by," I said. "How are you doing?"

"Swell." It was a mild enough answer to a stupid question. "I met your friend Rem-lin-ger. Nice guy. Had a nice guy with him. A bull on two legs."

"His name is Dillon."

"He did all the work," Ford said, speaking with less effort as his jaw loosened up.

"Sorry," I said.

Ford moved his head slightly on his pillow. "Had it coming."

"When did it happen?"

"After feds left. Gavin and I talking . . . office . . . they came in. Charley okay?"

"I haven't heard yet." I was afraid he'd ask about De Felice next, so I moved on to business. "I need to know what you told Remlinger."

"Everything," he said, getting the whole word out in one go. He shut his good eye. "The packages. The little man in LA. The phone number. And I told him I'd told you, Elliott. Sorry."

He was sorry, too. Sorry to the point of losing his grip again. I wondered if his guard had told him of De Felice and Mazar.

"Take it easy," I said. "I'm okay."

"Glad," Ford said without cheering up any.

"What else did you tell Remlinger?"

"Else?" Ford asked, his eye open again and wide.

"What did you tell him about the crash?"

"The crash? He asked why I wasn't on the plane. I told him about Mr. P's . . . trips. That pissed him off." Ford tried to smile at the memory but couldn't get it done.

I was trying not to smile, although I suddenly felt like laughing out loud. Or cheering. I kept it all out of my voice as I asked, "Was that all?"

"Yes."

I moved gingerly, afraid Ford would disappoint me yet. "What about the gust lock?"

"What about it?"

"Did you tell Remlinger that you'd taken it off? That someone else must have put it back on?"

"Hell no. He never asked. Why would he? He put it back on himself, right?"

"He never asked about it?"

"No. I would have told him if he had. Hell, I would have handed him the plans for the Polaris submarine if I'd had them. Can't take it. Know that now."

I glanced at his legs before I caught myself. "I'd say you took plenty."

This time Ford shook his head emphatically. "They did that *after* I talked."

He shut his eye again, holding in something that shook him. I put my hand on his shoulder, hating myself for what I was putting him through. When he'd quieted down, I asked, "Did you confront Remlinger about the crash?"

"What?"

"Did you accuse him of being responsible for it?"

"Hell no. Didn't want to let on that I knew. Thought he'd kill me then for sure."

I squeezed his shoulder again and let it go. "You may have saved some lives over at the ranch."

Ford wasn't buying. "I was looking to my own neck. Nothing else. No one else. No one."

"Promise me you won't talk to any reporters about the crash."

"What good's my word on that?" Ford asked, and began to cry.

25

It was still dewy as I left the hospital, but Ford was about to get his second visitor. Sheriff Tyler was coming up the front walk as I descended the hospital steps. I waited at the bottom of the steps, wondering if the deputy guarding Ford's room had slipped away to call his boss after I'd arrived. That would make Tyler my visitor, not Ford's.

I would have guessed that the sheriff had a bowlegged, where'd-I-leave-my-horse gait, but the old-timer was as light on his feet as Cassius Clay. And almost as natty today in an ice-cream suit and a tan Stetson with a stingy brim. He needed a string tie to finish the outfit off. Instead he wore a narrow blue one as prim as any banker's.

"Morning, Elliott," he said when he'd joined me in the shade of a linden tree. "This is a bad business. Young man just misses getting killed in a plane wreck and ends up in the hospital anyway because he was a delivery boy for a pretty girl. Bad business. From what I read on the Teletype, Mr. Remlinger did a lot worse down in Los Angeles. So maybe that Ford boy's luck is holding after all."

"Any word on Charley Gavin?"

"Yep. He was found early this morning tied up in his plane at an airfield near Van Nuys. He'd been there all night, so he was plenty mad. I expect he'll feel a lot luckier, too, when he hears how his passengers treated those two fellows at the clinic."

He took a breather then to examine his fancy boots. I was hoping he'd roll himself a cigarette so I could bum it from him, but he left his thumbs in his belt. "Seems like I owe you an apology, Elliott," he finally said. "None of this might have happened if I'd followed up better yesterday."

I had to make a decision then: bring Tyler in on the story to date or let him wander. Ford had given me my first glimpse of daylight since the smoker Paddy and I had held in front of Mazar's clinic. Remlinger didn't know the crash had been deliberately planned. Which meant he had no reason to come back to the San Ignacio Valley and wouldn't have until some newspaper blew the story wide open. I had until that happened to find Brooks's murderer. I had considerably less time now to decide whether Tyler would be a help or a hindrance.

In the end, I decided I had to tell him. If he now believed that Remlinger had caused the crash, he might give Ford's gustlock testimony to the papers, slamming my window of opportunity right across my neck.

"If you'd followed up the way I wanted you to," I said, "the cops down in LA might be reading about Sherwood on the Teletype this morning."

Tyler gave me a look that knocked some of the road dust off my shoulders. "How long a story is this going to be?" he asked.

"Long enough."

"We might as well be comfortable, then. Come on."

He led me back toward the little park that kept his offices and the Herald Building at a safe distance from one another. Just shy of the grass and trees, Tyler made a left into a storefront diner, the Morning Café. He'd been nodded to by several people during our walk, but that was nothing compared with the greeting he got when he entered the crowded restaurant. It was like the arrival of the guest of honor at a surprise party.

Tyler headed for the back of the place, pausing at the counter long enough to order two "special coffees." The last booth in the row of booths was taken, but the occupants got up, dishes and mugs in hand, when Tyler was still ten feet away.

"Thanks, boys," he called out, managing to sound surprised and even touched.

A waitress was wiping the table down before we'd settled. Another delivered the coffee. I could tell what made it special without tasting it. The aroma of heated whiskey was strong enough to open sinuses as far away as the park. I thought of Paddy again. The Tyler experience was definitely wasted on me.

The local Annette Funicello stopped by next to ask Tyler if he cared for a sweet roll. He didn't. Neither did I, but I began to reconsider a career in small-town law enforcement. "Doesn't seem like you have much to worry about come election time," I said.

"Don't take all this glad-handing too seriously. I don't. They'll be just as friendly to the new sheriff if Doc Beard has his way. Now how about showing me your cards?"

I passed along Hollywood Security's latest thinking on the crash, keeping my voice low, though everyone in the place seemed to be making an effort not to listen in.

"This boss of yours, Maguire, seems like the genuine article," Tyler said when I'd finished. "I'd like to meet him. So now Remlinger didn't fritz up the plane. And you're expecting him to find out who did and take up where he left off down south."

"I was until I spoke to Ford just now. He didn't tell Remlinger the plane was sabotaged, because he still thought Remlinger was the saboteur. That means Remlinger has no reason to come back here."

"Whereas," Tyler said, "if I'd launched a full-blown murder investigation yesterday the way you wanted me to, Remlinger would still be on the warpath. Well, it's nice to do something right, even if it's by accident. The question is, what do we do now?"

"Find the real saboteur before Remlinger goes back to cutting throats."

"Still so sure there was a saboteur, now that you've let Remlinger off? Your feelings about him were nine-tenths of the proof you had."

"There's still one-tenth left: the gust lock."

Tyler took a drink, pursing his lips together afterward contentedly. "I'd say it's still six, two, and even whether the crash was an accident, Remlinger's work, or murder by an unknown party. I agree with Maguire that subtlety doesn't seem to be Remlinger's style. Still, just because he ran amok at the clinic doesn't mean he couldn't have acted more circumspectly up here. He was killing vermin down there—to his way of thinking. Up here he was passing judgment on a woman he loved.

"Think of it this way. He could have suspected that Brooks was going to run off with Pioline, because someone tipped him off or she called him herself to taunt him with it. His opinion of his own charms is such that he's not sure she'll actually go through with it. So he slips the gust lock on the plane. Now it's up to her. If she doesn't go with Pioline, she doesn't get hurt. If she does, she gets what she deserves."

"Remlinger would have to have been willing to kill Pioline just to test Brooks," I said.

"And Ford," Tyler said, nodding. "He has no way of knowing Ford wouldn't be on that plane. Well, you've seen Remlinger's handiwork. Do you think he would have cared about that one way or the other?"

"No."

"No. So I'd still be looking for a John Remlinger, if I was looking for a murderer. I take it you have another name in mind."

I did—Daniel Irwin—but that wasn't something I was ready to share with Tyler. "What I have in mind is a favor. I'd like you to keep Ford's story about the gust lock quiet a while longer."

"That's easy enough, since I've been doing it all along. It will mean keeping the press away from Ford, but that shouldn't be too hard. I suppose you want me to stay clear of the ranch, too, so the papers don't get the idea there's something new to interest them there."

"Yes."

"Well now, that's a different order of favor. If one of your movie crowd is a murderer, someone's got to look into it."

"I will," I said. "Lange and I will. We can come and go at the ranch without drawing attention."

"Isn't that a conflict of interest? You two are working to protect the very people you suspect."

I looked him in the eye, hoping mine were less raw than they felt. "My wife's at that ranch, Sheriff. I'm not going to put anything ahead of getting her clear of this. There's only one way to protect anyone from Remlinger. That's to find Brooks's murderer before Remlinger realizes there's one to find."

Tyler finished his coffee and thought about it. "I'll give you a couple of days," he said. "If you're on the wrong scent, and I think you are, it won't hurt anything. And sitting on the information about the gust lock a while longer won't affect the manhunt for Remlinger one way or the other, given what he did yesterday. But you're wrong about there only being one way to protect folks from him. The sure way is to hunt him down. The law will work on that while you question your people at the ranch. Just be sure to let me know if any of them decides to leave the county."

"I will," I said. "Thanks."

I reached out to shake his hand as I stood. Tyler's grip closed on mine and held me there, halfway out of the booth. "How well do you know this Lange?" he asked.

"We go back a ways. He's never let me down."

"Was he in charge back then?"

"No," I said.

Tyler nodded and released my hand. "You might want to keep an eye on him. He seemed to me yesterday to be straining under his load. Giving orders is a lot harder than taking them. You might recall that from the service."

"Not me," I said. "I never got past my second stripe."

26

Sometime while I'd been gone from Crowe Ranch, a circus had come to town. That was my first thought, when I hit the traffic jam at the ranch gate. There were representatives of the press lining up to get in, though fewer than the day before. Their ranks were filled out by the buses Pioline had hired to run the crew and the bit players between Sherwood and the shooting site. Whatever they'd gathered for today, it wasn't shooting. I couldn't see a toga or a tunic in the crowd milling around the main house.

When I finally made it through the gate, I spotted Lange. He was directing traffic, mostly by glaring at it. He glared at me, too, but I pulled up next to him anyway and climbed out.

"What's going on?"

"Lacey's giving another speech. This one's for the cast and crew. She's got some kind of announcement to make. I hope to God it's that we're packing up and getting out of here. Where the hell did you get off to this time?"

With Tyler's warning about Lange still tickling my ear, I stepped up for a closer look. He seemed as buttoned-down as ever, though he'd had a little trouble with his razor that morning. So had I, as I'd been bothered by memories of Mazar's last shave. I was about to give Lange a pass when I caught a whiff of something that reminded me of the sheriff's coffee.

"You okay?" I asked.

"Of course," he said, and the way he said it told me that he wasn't, that Tyler had been right.

"You haven't answered my question. Where have you been?"

"To Heston," I said. "To see Ford. You weren't up when I left."

He looked away. "I was all in last night." I thought he'd tell me then that he still was all in, but he didn't. "I took the call from Maguire about Guy De Felice. The little grafter was the original roach, but he didn't deserve what he got."

"Have you told anyone else about the murders?"

"Who was I going to tell?" Lange asked, stating his dilemma succinctly. Somehow, in the midst of his little army, he was more isolated than I was. Command was hell, as Tyler had said. With or without the sweet rolls.

"I spread the word that Remlinger might be headed our way," he said. "That was all."

He paused to chew out the driver of the last bus, which had gotten a little close to the Thunderbird. Lange laid into him like the car belonged to his mother. Or was his mother.

When he turned back to me, his cheeks were pink and sweaty. "Maguire's three minutes ran out before he got around to telling me why Remlinger was coming back to slaughter us. Are we all supposed to be drug dealers?"

"No," I said, "but one of us is a murderer."

I told him about Paddy's insight into Remlinger's motives and then the part Paddy didn't know himself, our big break, that Remlinger still thought the crash had been an accident. Lange took this good news the same way he'd taken the preceding bad news, which was like he'd been drafted again.

"A fucking bomb," he said. "That's what we're sitting on."

"Again," I said, trying to stir his old belligerence, but he'd used it all on the bus driver. "Have you seen any of the papers? How are they handling the clinic murders?"

"It was just a news flash in the papers we've gotten so far. Two men found dead, no mention of Brooks. Today the crash is the big story, and Remlinger is mentioned in that, in the background on Brooks. By tomorrow, they'll have tied it all together.

The radio and television geniuses will get the word out even sooner."

"We can't help that," I said. Lange's men were herding the extras and the crew and the few faithful reporters toward the rise on which Crowe House stood. "It just means we have to find the murderer that much faster."

"Today it's 'we,'" Lange said bitterly. "Yesterday it was me and my shadow. Hell, it's show time."

Lacey had emerged from the house, escorted by Max Froy. Following the star and her director were Jewel and Ella and Nicole Cararra. The stand-in was the odd woman in that grouping, but she didn't act it. Cararra was beaming like she'd just taken title to the ranch. The feeling I'd been enjoying since my talk with Ford—that I was ahead of events for once—did a quick fade.

Froy called the cast and crew to order, as he'd often done before, with and without megaphone. He didn't need one today. His armor-plated German accent easily carried to the edge of the crowd, where Lange and I had placed ourselves.

"Okay, kids," Froy said one last time. "Thank you for coming. I know you are all as shocked and saddened as we are by what happened Friday night when we lost our producer and good friend, Marcus Pioline, friend to us all, even those of us working with him for the first time, and one of the bright talents of our cast, Beverly Brooks. And I know you are wondering what will happen now, what will happen to *Warrior Queen*, this important film that we've all worked so hard on.

"Today, we have some answers for you. To tell you about them, I give you our star, Lillian Lacey."

I had time during the hopeful applause that followed to consider that Froy had boomed out the word "star" during his introduction of Lacey but had omitted it entirely from his very brief eulogy of Brooks.

Lange had noticed, too. "You can't back a dead horse," he side-mouthed.

Lacey was sporting a variation on the housewife-at-the-supermarket disguise she'd worn to the airport the day I'd delivered Brooks to her fate. Her red hair was held in check again by a scarf, and the green eyes were hidden behind dark glasses. It wasn't the costume of a star reclaiming her throne, but then this star was supposed to be struggling out of a mourning bed.

"Thank you all," she said. She had the lung power to top Froy, but she'd chosen to speak under him, forcing the crowd to surge forward to hear her. "Yesterday I told the press that I felt I had to finish this picture as a tribute to Marc. Today I'm able to tell you that we *will* finish *Warrior Queen*. The distributors of Marc's films, Universal International, have come forward to guarantee the funds we need to finish shooting." More applause, more genuine this time.

"And we've made another decision we'd like to share with you," Lacey continued, stepping with an old hand's timing on the last of the ovation. "A decision with which we know you'll agree heartily. *Warrior Queen* will be a tribute to both Marc and Beverly Brooks. Max has decided that enough of Beverly's very fine performance exists to allow us to complete the film without recasting her part."

The hand that followed was as much, I thought, for Lacey's generosity as it was for the news that the world would get one more dose of Brooks. Lacey was forgiving the woman who had almost wrecked the movie and who had died running off with Lacey's onetime husband. I knew how much of the decision had been dictated by Lacey's finances, and I still almost clapped myself. Almost.

"For any additional footage we need," Lacey continued, "we will be calling on the services of Beverly's good friend Nicole Cararra."

Applause a fourth time—hesitant now and scattered, barely enough to cover Cararra's short walk downstage on Froy's arm. She was wearing a short embroidered jacket that was very padded in the shoulders and tight white pants, very unpadded everywhere.

"Here is the lady," the director boomed, "who with the help

of all of you will save this film. I predict it will be the first of many films for her."

Lange tapped my arm like the pro he was, without appearing to move. I followed his gaze and saw Daniel Irwin shouldering his way into the crowd to our right. His round face was livid, and he wasn't bothering to look at the people he was pushing aside. All four of his eyes were fixed on Nicole Cararra. I decided right away that he intended to do what I'd taunted him for not doing yesterday. He was going to use a Lillian Lacey press conference to tell the world his wife had been murdered.

I was moving though the crowd before the thought had cleared my head. Luckily the next person Irwin chose to shove was an employee of Lange Limited. The guard pushed back, hard. Before the startled Irwin could react, we were there, Lange beside him with a death grip on his arm and me blocking his way. When Irwin drew a breath to protest, Lange forced it out of him by giving the arm he held a twist.

"Not a word," I said. "Not until you've talked to us. Not unless you're planning to confess."

"The hell I am," Irwin squeezed out through gaps in his teeth.

Behind me Froy was still extolling the new life Universal had breathed into *Warrior Queen*, overlaying my whispering nicely.

"You can walk away with us right now," I said, "or I'll make a citizen's arrest for murder. You can wait for Remlinger and his bone cracker in Tyler's jug."

Irwin didn't reply, so I chose for him. "We'll walk down to his cottage," I said to Lange.

He yanked Irwin around, and I stepped up to take the novelist's free arm. The guard Irwin had shoved fell in behind us. The operation had been noticed by several extras and at least one of the reporters. There was nothing for it but to hope that the witnesses put the whole thing down to Irwin's resentment over his wife's being used to plug the movie, posthumously.

As it turned out, that was part of Irwin's beef, the last prod that had gotten him out of the stands and onto the field. When we were safely inside his cottage with a sentry posted outside, the novelist rounded on Lange. "Gone over to their side, have you? You were full of warnings about Hollywood Security yesterday. Now it's the picture first and to hell with the truth."

"We just use 'to hell with the truth' on our business cards," I said. "The rest won't fit."

"Damn," Lange said, "it's hot already." He sank into the rocker I'd used the night before. "What's all this?" he asked, kicking at fragments of paper that littered the floor. "Looks like somebody tore a book apart. Is everybody nuts around here?"

Irwin didn't acknowledge the question. Neither did I, beyond wishing that Lange had ended it with "except me."

The novelist turned on me next. "How can you think of letting them go on filming until Remlinger is caught? Don't you care about your wife or Lacey or her daughter? You said last night that Remlinger was on his way back here to avenge Beverly's death. What if he just starts shooting people on the theory he'll get the killer sooner or later?"

"He's not coming back. Not unless you send him an invitation. That's what I had to tell you." I went on to describe my interview with Ford and the deal I'd struck with Tyler.

At the end of it, Irwin asked, "Why didn't you just hand me over? Then you were covered either way."

"Don't tempt us," Lange snapped.

"I want to be sure," I said. "I have to be sure, with Remlinger in the mix. Let's go back to the night of the crash. You said you went to the San Ignacio Inn. How did you get there?"

"I bummed a ride with some of the ranch hands. They took me as far as Sherwood. The fare was listening to them tell me over and over again what a lucky guy I was. You can ask them if you don't believe me."

"We will, brother," Lange said.

"What time did you get there?"

"Eight o'clock. A little after."

"Then what?"

"I walked to the inn. I went to Remlinger's room. He wasn't there."

"Did you ask for his room number at the desk?"

"I didn't have to. It was part of the message he passed to Beverly that morning. And the extras were all buzzing about the suite he'd commandeered."

"Somebody at the inn must have seen you," I prompted.

"I don't know."

"Hell of an alibi," Lange said. "How about we figure how long it takes to walk from downtown Sherwood to the airstrip."

Irwin considered him for a while, so I did, too, seeing a tired guy in a gaudy uniform sitting among the scattered remains of a novel.

Then Irwin asked, "How about if I saw someone at the inn? Would that count as an alibi?"

"Whom did you see?" I asked, but I knew the answer. Lange had told me by sinking farther into the rocker.

"Him," Irwin said, nodding toward Lange. "He showed up just as I was starting back toward town. Would have been almost eight-thirty."

I remembered then that Lange had been among the missing on Friday night when Beverly Brooks had been giving her recitation at the smoking stump. I started to ask him about it and didn't. The look on his face told me that being questioned in front of Irwin was more than he could take. I owed him better than that anyway.

I turned to Irwin. "We're putting you on ice. If anyone asks, we'll say you're upset over not being consulted on the Universal deal. If a reporter should find his way in here, you say the same thing. No mention of gust locks or murders."

Irwin had the same idea about that as Lange had voiced earlier. "The papers will work it out for themselves soon enough."

I shrugged and then jerked my head toward the door for Lange's benefit. He got up slowly.

"We'll leave a man here to see that no one gets in. No reporters," I added, but Irwin knew whom I meant.

"What am I suppose to do to pass the time while I'm playing sitting duck for you?" he demanded.

I slid a fragment of *Blue Hell* toward him with the toe of my shoe. "Try putting that back together."

27

Lange's man was waiting outside the cottage, keeping an especially straight face. How much he'd heard of what we'd said and what he'd made of it was anybody's guess. He certainly acted strangely, his gaze bouncing between Lange and me like we had a game of Ping-Pong going. But that may only have been because we'd almost caught him smoking.

I thought I'd have to give the guard his orders. Then Lange kicked in. "Mr. Irwin is indisposed. Nobody gets in to bother him. And he doesn't get out."

"Yes, sir," the guy said. Now that it was a matter of orders, he could shut his brain down happily. I'd seen the operation often enough before, in other foot soldiers. As I watched it again, I wondered if he would have balked at an order to loosen Irwin's teeth.

Lange and I walked away from the main house. Without discussing it, we chose an open space below the cottage grove, a fenced pasture. The horse contingent hadn't used it recently judging by the grass, which was almost long enough to ripple in the hot breeze.

"We've got more important things to talk about than this," Lange said, just as I was thinking I'd have to prod him to speak.

"Make it short then," I said. "What were you doing at the San Ignacio Inn on Friday night?"

"Same as Irwin. I went to see Remlinger."

"Why?"

"To deliver the message Pioline would have given him if we'd found him at home that afternoon. That he should make himself scarce. Or else."

"Pioline took me and you along when he made that visit. You went alone. Why?"

"Because I had to," Lange said, his voice iron hard. "Because that was the point of the exercise."

"You're losing me." I got the look again, the one that said don't push me. I didn't have a choice now. "Why did you go there by yourself?"

"Because I was afraid to, damn you. Because the idea of going scared the crap out of me. Because I hadn't gone out there that morning by myself. I'd come looking for you to hold my hand."

"So what? You've covered my back often enough."

"You weren't along as an extra pair of eyes. You were supplying the nerve. You knew that."

The hell I had, I would have said if Lange had passed me the ball. But he was charging on.

"I've gone up against guys who thought they were tough and guys who were. Thugs like Dillon, dangerous because they don't think as far ahead as their next breath. I know them and I can handle them. I can handle the small stomach and the sweats that are part of dealing with dirt like that. But Remlinger's come over me a whole new way."

"You told me Remlinger was a whole new animal," I said.

Lange nodded. "When I was warning you about Maguire going soft. There's a laugh, me worrying about him. I bet he strolled into that clinic with his hat pushed back and a damn cigar in his mouth, like a guy walking off his Sunday dinner."

"You hadn't even met Remlinger when you were passing on that warning. Or when we went out to the inn that first time. Or had you met him?"

"Relax. I'd never laid eyes on the guy before you and I went to the inn. But I'd found out all about him. It might have been better if I had met him before the Cleveland cops bent my ear with his record. Or maybe not. Maybe it didn't have anything to do with anything I heard. Maybe it was something I just knew."

"Don't tell me *you've* been having dreams."

"Not dreams. I don't know what you'd call them. Your wife might know the name for the feelings I've had. I've thought of asking her.

"I told myself I was reacting differently this time because of Lange Limited, because I'd built it up and made it something good. For the first time in my life, I had something to lose, and Johnny Remlinger was just the guy who could knock it all down."

"That's a natural enough worry."

"Natural enough, but not true. Remlinger isn't a threat to my company—don't ask me how I know—he's my own personal hoodoo."

"Keep going," I said. "I'm feeling better and better."

"I know it's crazy, Elliott. That's why I went out to the inn, to prove to myself that it was crazy. At least I think that's why I went. Maybe I just wanted to get it over with. I didn't find Remlinger or Dillon. I don't know how I missed Irwin. I gave the place a thorough shaking down."

"You can't have been too spooked if you got that done."

Lange shook his head. "That was before my real willies started. Ever since the crash, I've been feeling myself slipping. Last night when Maguire called, it was more than I could take. I drank myself to sleep last night. Me. I wouldn't have heard Remlinger arrive if he'd come through the bunkhouse wall in a tank."

He let out a long breath. "I'm glad I told you, Elliott, Even though saying it out loud washes me up. You had a right to know. If it comes to a showdown with Remlinger, you can't count on me."

"I know better," I said.

As pep talks went, mine had brevity going for it and not much else. Still, Lange drew himself up. "What's our next move?"

"We check on Irwin's alibi for Friday night. He ended up in a saloon, drinking with a bunch of the ranch hands, maybe the same ones who delivered him to Sherwood. If you find those guys, you can verify both ends of Irwin's story. See if there's a gap in the middle long enough to cover his visit to the inn and a side trip to the airport."

"I don't know about Irwin," Lange said. "He's acting so guilty, he's got to be innocent."

"I'll pass that one on to Paddy," I said. "He'll stick it into that detective manual he's always threatening to write."

Lange knew the mythical manual, Paddy's imaginary repository for all the stupid moves his employees had made over the years. Remembering it got a grimace out of Lange, the twisted one he used as a smile.

"Irwin's all we've got at the moment," I said. "If anyone else had left the ranch that night, the men you had on the gate would have reported it."

Lange pointed to the wire fence that bordered the pasture. "We could step through that right now and who would be the wiser? The men I've had patrolling are mostly for show. Maybe your murderer walked to the airport. It's only three or four miles if you cut straight across. Half hour there maybe and a half hour back."

"Half an hour to walk four miles cross country?"

"We've done it at double time with a full pack."

"Speak for yourself," I said. "The artillery had chauffeurs."

"We should be checking everybody for an hour gap between nine and ten o'clock, if we're figuring the gust lock was replaced sometime while Pioline was back here collecting Brooks."

I did the smiling this time, with undisguised relief. "I thought you weren't going to be any help."

"I'll be fine till the loud noises start. You check with the actors. I'll talk to the ranch hands about Irwin."

"Yes, sir," I said, saluting.

"Stick it in your ear, Elliott," Lange said, and marched off.

28

Lange skirted the cottage grove on his climb up to the main compound. I walked straight into the trees, hoping to find Ella at our cottage. I wanted to get her views on Froy's plan to finish *Warrior Queen* using Cararra's body and no one's head. Instead, I came across the body itself. That is, as I emerged from not finding my wife, I heard Cararra kicking up a fuss somewhere nearby. I followed the sound to Irwin's plush cell, where I found the former stand-in in a heated conversation with the doorman. I looked for Irwin to join the fray, but the cottage door never opened.

"Hey!" Cararra called to me. "Hey you, Elliott! This pig won't let me in to see Danny."

A lot had happened since I'd last seen Cararra, but none of it was more remarkable than her transformation from displaced person to junior queen of the lot. It made me dizzy all over again, a condition I palmed off on Irwin.

"Danny's not up to company right now," I said.

"Did you hit him again?" Cararra demanded. "I saw you hit him yesterday. I told Max what you were up to."

"Mr. Froy, you mean?"

"I call him Max now, since he's signed me to a personal contract. He sees big things for me. He thinks I'll be a star."

Cararra wasn't the only one stepping up a rank. It sounded

like Froy was happily picking up where Pioline had left off, without taking into account the producer's sorry end. "Maybe you should call him Uncle Max," I said.

"You have an evil mind, Elliott," Cararra said, purring the line as though the idea pleased her.

"Shouldn't you be talking to the press?"

"All that is over for today. Max didn't want me to be over-exposed. He sent me down here to rest."

"Good idea."

"No good idea. First I want to see Danny. I must explain to him that I mean no disrespect to Bebe. I'm not taking her place. I'm trying to save her last film, like Max said."

She was addressing the cottage now, not me. It was another opportunity for Irwin to step out. He declined.

I took Cararra by her elbow and led her toward Brooks's cottage. "Why don't you give Irwin a day to get used to the idea? His wife isn't even buried yet."

"She never will be buried," Cararra said. "Not really. Because she never really died. That's what being a star means."

"Thanks," I said, "I've always wondered."

"Thanks yourself for letting go of my arm. I can walk without you pawing me. And I can find my own way."

"Before you do, I'd like to ask you again about Friday night. I'm going to be checking your story. Care to make any changes first?"

Cararra stopped and turned to face me, smiling her pleased smile again. "You're not just a big lug like you look. Ella said you weren't, but I wasn't sure. You knew all along I wasn't telling you the truth yesterday."

I kept my mouth shut and waited, not wanting to drop back into the big lug category prematurely.

"What I said, I said for Bebe. For her reputation. As though one woman could guard that with so many lying newspapers in the world. Bebe was a married woman. So she and Danny were having troubles, so what? They were still married. She should have still acted married. If she didn't it was up to me to keep it quiet. That's how I felt about it yesterday."

"How are you feeling today?"

"That I should tell the truth about Bebe always. That I can't fight lies with more lies. Her friends will understand the truth. Even Danny will understand. Nobody else matters."

"So let's have it."

"I told you yesterday that Bebe and that awful Marcus Pioline weren't having an affair. Well, they were. There."

"For how long?"

"That I don't know. Not long, I think. She only told me about it the day before the accident. And she made me promise not to tell anyone. That was another reason why I lied to you. Sorry."

"What did Brooks see in Pioline, if he was so awful?"

Cararra shrugged with her face, the gesture overbroad, as though I'd asked her why the sun comes up in the east. "Who knows with these things?" She started down the path again, walking slowly while she thought it through. "Maybe she was grateful to him for rescuing her from Las Vegas. Or for giving her work. Maybe she was looking for a father. I think that was it, maybe. I think Bebe wanted someone to tell her what to do always, to take care of her. She wasn't ready for a partner, for an equal. For a Danny."

"Is that the trouble she and Danny were having?"

"Sure. Bebe believed she was getting some genius who could answer all her questions. Instead she got a man who was all questions and no answers. And who wanted her all to himself. Wanted her—you know—physically that way. Like my contract with Max: exclusive."

"Got you," I said, before she could draw a picture for me in the dirt of the path.

We arrived at Cararra's new home, assuming, as she seemed to be, that she would inherit Brooks's perks along with her part. Given Froy's interest, I wouldn't have bet against it.

"Sorry I can't ask you in," she said, blocking me from even the little porch. "I have to think of appearances now. And I don't want to make your wife jealous. She's rewriting Bebe's part for me. Max said so."

He'd meant that Ella would be busy cutting every one of

Brooks's lines and close-ups that hadn't already been filmed, but I didn't mention that. As irritating as Cararra was in her glory, I didn't want any part in toppling her. I could remember my own glorified, puffed-up period too clearly.

"We'll talk here then," I said.

"What talk? I told you the truth. We're friends now, okay?"

"How did Pioline and Brooks get together that last night? You told me you left Brooks asleep."

"Okay, that was a lie, too. Bebe wouldn't lay down that night. She wouldn't even sit down. You remember how she was. You saw her. First she changed out of her bathing suit and into that peach dress. She made herself up like she had a big date. I thought to myself, watch out, she's up to something.

"She paced around the cottage for a while. Then she said she was going for a walk. I could come if I liked, but I couldn't stop her. Why should I have?"

I pictured the answer, a basement morgue in Heston, but didn't bring it up.

"We'd just started up the hill to the main house when we met Pioline coming down. He was angry or pretending to be angry. Where had Bebe been, he wanted to know. Why hadn't she come out to the airport as they'd arranged?"

Cararra was suddenly fidgety. Specifically, she was fascinated by one of my lapels, the right one from my point of view. As lapels went, it was okay. A little narrow for my taste, but I was getting used to that. To Cararra, it seemed to be a genuine thing of beauty.

"I change my mind," she said. "It's too hot to stand out here. Come inside."

She found it hot inside as well, or so it seemed. Two steps through the door, she lost the little orange bullfighter's jacket that had made her filmy, spaghetti-strapped blouse suitable for wearing out of doors. Then she lounged on a sofa that had been upholstered in Indian blankets, rich ones in dark reds and blues.

"Sit down." She indicated the free cushion with a sandaled foot. Then she kicked the sandal off. "I'm resting now, Max!" she called out, laughing throatily. "Uncle Max, I'm resting!"

I hadn't acted on her invitation, so she repeated it. "Sit down. Give your flat feet a rest. Do you secret policemen have flat feet like regular policemen?"

"If we do, we keep it to ourselves." I dropped my hat on the coffee table. Like every other coffee table I'd seen at the ranch, it was a whimsical one. This time, a wooden barrel had been sawed in half and topped with a faded checkerboard.

I sat a safe distance from Cararra, if not from her legs in their perfectly creased white pants. She countered the move by pivoting around, so the legs were out of sight, my view filled instead with dark eyes and very full, very orange lips. I found myself agreeing with Froy's professional judgment. Cararra was a one-in-a-thousand beauty, with skin that could laugh at the tightest close-up.

"So?" she asked.

"So Pioline showed up mad. What did Brooks do?"

If my devotion to duty bothered her, she didn't let on. "What do you think?" she breathed. "Bebe pouted and called him Marc Baby and stroked him." She demonstrated on my killer lapel. "He forgot he was mad soon enough. They jumped in his car and woosh! Off they went."

There it was, the last piece I needed in my reconstruction of Pioline and Brooks's movements on Friday night. It was exactly how I'd imagined it happening. Then I remembered something I hadn't imagined, a piece I'd been handed that wouldn't fit.

"Did Bebe get a call that night? Maybe half an hour before she met Pioline?" Cararra was still so close I felt I was questioning the tip of her upturned nose.

"A call? A telephone call? There's no phone here, you know that. You have to go up to the palace where Queen Boudica lives to make a call. And then Her Majesty's maid won't let you in. So then you go to the cookhouse, where the men stare at you. It isn't very pleasant."

"No one came down to tell Brooks she had a call?"

"No."

"Let's get back to the cookhouse where men stare at you. You told me you saw someone there after Brooks left. Is that part of today's story?"

"The man with the knives saw me."

"Who saw you after the crash?"

"Excuse me?"

"The big boom came, you blessed yourself. Then what happened? You didn't go out to the crash site with the others."

"No. I came back here. I wanted to be alone."

"To wait for Irwin?"

"No." Cararra didn't take offense at the question. She told me so by kissing me. It was a light kiss, light and one-sided. "What's the matter, Elliott? Afraid your wife will find out you kissed me?"

"Technically I haven't."

"What a Jesuit you are. So if I make love to you right now and you can sit through it without moving, you won't technically be an adulterer?"

"The philosophy boys are still batting that one around."

"Let's risk it." Her right hand began to descend my lapel yet again. Then it slipped beneath it.

"We've one more lie to deal with first," I said. "The one about Brooks not using drugs."

Cararra froze, perhaps because of what I'd said, perhaps because the tips of her wandering fingers had touched my holster.

She drew herself back, bringing her whole head and her shoulders into the frame. "That was not a lie. You knew the truth. I knew the truth. I wouldn't say it out loud because I didn't want to hurt Bebe."

"So you knew all along?"

"Yes. Just that she was suffering that way. Nothing more. Nothing that could have helped you. Nothing the police would want to know. I looked for the pills, but I never found them. I asked her once—once only—why she did it. That made her so angry, she almost sent me away. I decided that being a friend meant keeping my mouth shut."

Being a kept friend certainly did. "How about her source? Did you know where she was getting the stuff?"

Cararra settled wearily against her arm of the sofa. "No. Just that there were many deliveries and they were always small. That is why—I think—I never found anything when I searched. And why Bebe was anxious so often. I don't know why they treated her that way, whoever was giving it to her."

Maybe to minimize the side effects. If so, the deliveries hadn't been small enough. That brought us to the subject of Dr. Mazar. I asked Cararra if she knew the name.

"The dream doctor, yes, Bebe spoke of him. She met him before she and I got together. She was going to take me to see him when we were done shooting here."

She hadn't read today's paper, but then, she'd had a busy day. She conveyed that by slowing closing her big brown eyes. "Mazar was another of the men Bebe searched out to tell her what to do. To guide her. Always the same with her. It was her weakness. Her fatal weakness.

"I'll rest now for real, Elliott. I have an early call tomorrow. You go quietly."

29

This time I didn't stop looking for Ella until I found her. She and Max Froy were having a conference in the screened dining room. They sat on opposite sides of one of the long tables, loose pages from Ella's script spread between them. I thought of Irwin and his disassembled novel. The job facing Ella looked no less rugged.

They were both happy to see me, Ella on general principle and Froy because he was in high spirits and wanted to spread them around.

"Hello, Scotty!" he said while the screen door was still drawing out its cymbal crash. "Have you come to watch our phoenix rise from its—" He cut the question off one word short of a complete faux pas. It didn't slow him much. "Your wife will be a busy woman. You must forgive her in advance for that. We all must stay busy if we are to carry this off."

"Busy may not be enough," I said. "You can't have shot more than a handful of scenes with Brooks."

"We haven't," Ella said, looking down at the pages with their red marginal notes, enough for a whole new script. "Even if she hadn't taken French leave last week, we wouldn't have much."

"We have enough," Froy said. "We have enough. Don't forget the costume and makeup tests I shot in the studio. We'll work some magic with those, you wait and see. I'm already in touch with some photographic effects geniuses, the best around. You'll see Bebe at the head of Boudica's army, and it will take your breath away. You will believe she was really there."

"Are they going to put words in her mouth, too?" I asked. "Or are you calling in Mel Blanc?"

"We're having to reevaluate the dialogue, of course. Many of Bebe's lines will now be Jewel's. She's a trooper in the making, that one. She can handle it. Other scenes we will just cut. We are restoring the script more than changing it. As Ella originally conceived it, it was Boudica's picture, Lillie's picture. Marcus made us shift the focus to Bebe to satisfy his bankers. Now we have the best of both worlds: Beverly Brooks's name and drawing power but a picture built around Lillie's more substantial talents."

Froy was so pleased with the way things had fallen out I considered adding him to my short list of suspects. The thought reminded me that I should be taking care of business. I asked Froy where he'd been between nine and ten o'clock on Friday evening, explaining my interest by saying that I was looking for witnesses to Brooks's movements.

"Can't help you there, Scotty. I was out at the shooting site with Lyle, my assistant, and Greg Polack, our cameraman. We're camping out there, as you know. Like gypsies in our little trailers. We went out after dinner and worked until we heard the crash.

"Poor Marcus," he said. "I still can't believe he's gone. If he were here, he would be so excited about our ideas."

"Only then they'd be his ideas," Ella said.

Froy didn't hear her. He was fixing me with the basilisk look he used to quiet a soundstage full of actors. "Still not convinced we'll succeed, are you?" he asked. "Tell me, do you remember a movie called *Saratoga*? It was a piece of MGM fluff from 1937, a horse-racing comedy. Being a Metro picture, it had a great cast, fluff or not. Clark Gable, Jean Harlow, Walter Pidgeon, and on and on. Well, it happened that poor Jean Harlow died while they were filming it. Uremic poisoning—most unfortunate—I won't go into that. MGM decided to finish the picture. They did a little rewriting, as we are doing, filmed some scenes using a double, as we will do, and there you are. They had a motion picture."

"I remember *Saratoga*," I said. "The ending was a mess. They paraded the double around in a big picture hat so you couldn't see her face. They might as well have used Larry Fine."

Froy laughed affably. "You've a great memory for movies, Scotty. The best maybe. But you're forgetting one little detail regarding *Saratoga*. It grossed two million dollars, far and away the biggest hit of the year. You know why, of course."

Ella paused in the process of gathering up the pages of her mortally wounded script. "Everyone wanted to see a dead star," she said.

"Let's say rather that they wanted to say good-bye to a beloved actress. Allow me to make a wager with you, Ella, Scotty. *Warrior Queen* will be Beverly Brooks's most successful film, just as *Saratoga* was Harlow's."

"Harlow's and Mary Dees's," I said, justifying Froy's high opinion of my memory. "Dees was the stand-in they used for Harlow. It wasn't the start of a brilliant career for her."

"That's how these things go, Scotty. You know that better than any of us. You're only given a chance to make it, no more. There are no sure things."

"Speaking of long shots," I said. "I hear you've taken a piece of the action on Nicole Cararra. She told me you signed her to a personal contract."

"Correct, I have. It's as you say, a long-shot bet. Or a flyer on the market. A broker chap tried to get me to buy stock in a company called International Business Machines back in the thirties. I turned him down. The crash was too recent a memory. Now I'm paying through the nose for IBM shares. This is the same thing. I'm taking a chance on a stock called Nicole Cararra. Getting in at the ground floor. You won't be able to tell she's in *Warrior Queen*, not if we do our job right. But she will get publicity. I'll arrange that. And then a little part in another picture, and we'll see. Maybe boom, maybe bust.

"I'll tell you both—not to speak ill of the dead—Beverly Brooks's future was not so rosy. Her timing was not so good.

Blonds were a fifties thing. It's now the sixties. I'm seeing exotic brunettes as the trend. Picture a wave of Sophia Lorens."

"I'd prefer Scotty didn't," Ella said. "Not at his time of life."

One of the cookhouse hands arrived to ask if we were interested in lunch. Ella was, and so was I, though for once I hadn't even been thinking about food. Froy demurred.

"I must go out to the shooting site and prepare for tomorrow. Ella, you have enough to keep you busy, yes? Good. We'll talk on the set tomorrow. Scotty, keep your fingers crossed for us."

Froy left and we were served coffee and Ella still didn't say much. "Don't take the news about blonds so hard," I said. "You girls have had a nice run."

"While we're on the subject of my worries," Ella rejoined, "you're wearing a lot of Shalimar today. I'm guessing you've been spending time with someone who applies the stuff with a garden hose. Was it Bebe's ghost or Nicole Cararra?"

"There's a difference?" I asked.

"Not from the neck down, not from what I've heard. Care to offer any expert testimony?"

She was smiling, finally, though her pale eyes were looking plain washed out and the lines around them appeared less like detailing today and more like wear.

"You know what my job is like," I said. "So many beautiful women throw themselves at my feet it keeps my shoes polished."

"I knew you weren't in it for the money."

The main course, chili con carne and sourdough bread, arrived and Ella's mood went south again. "Nicole Cararra. I almost feel sorry for her. The way Max is leading her on with that personal contract. You can bet he'll be collecting little dividends on that investment. Getting in on the ground floor my hat. More like getting in at the mezzanine, if I know Max."

"I'm eating," I said.

"And it's a cheap way of keeping her in line while he's working out his plan for the movie."

"Will his scheme work?"

"Sure, one way or the other. We'll either have a movie or a

wax museum. Lillie will get her screen time back, which is fine by me. But I'm worried about Jewel."

"Because she can't act?"

Ella pushed her chili away. "This is a movie, Scotty. She doesn't have to act. She has to project something from the screen. The part calls for her to be a beautiful young daughter of privilege who's misused. I've seen her test. She gets that across fine. She hates being forced to do this picture so much, her self-pity and resentment jump right off the screen at you."

"What's the problem then?"

"Jewel is the problem. I told you before, something's not right about that girl."

"Emotional dissonance, I remember. I've been meaning to look it up."

"I'm not sure she's ready for more responsibility, Scotty. I'm not sure she'll hold together. And I'm not convinced we have the right to ask it of her."

I still thought that Jewel was reacting very naturally to her stepfather's death and that the rest of the cast and crew, who seemed content to let Pioline and Brooks bury themselves, were the ones with the problem. But I'd tried that objection earlier, and Ella hadn't bitten. So I traded my empty bowl for her nearly full one and dug in.

"I want you to talk to her, Scotty."

"Me?"

"We have to find out what's bothering her. I told you before, it's critical. More important than any photographic tricks Max comes up with."

"If she hasn't confided in you, what makes you think she'll tell me anything?"

"You're Jimmy Stewart from *Vertigo*. She's in awe of you. I've been careful not to say anything that might wise her up."

"Thanks."

"Will you talk to her?"

"Yes. I have to anyway. I have to check her alibi for the night of the crash." I told Ella what Lange and I were up to and why.

"So that's why you asked Max where he'd been on Friday night. But that's crazy, Scotty. What motive would any of us have for wrecking that plane?"

"Froy gets to be producer and director both. Lillie Lacey has her screen time back. Jewel's been bumped up to first princess. Cararra has a new career. You've got your script back to its original shape, more or less. Luckily you have a great alibi for the time in question."

"Those are movie motives, Scotty. Detective movie motives. Real people don't kill for reasons like that."

"Lange's talking to the real people," I said as I stood. "I'm covering the actors."

30

Ella went ahead to Crowe House to prep Jewel for Jimmy Stewart's entrance. I used a different screen door to exit the dining room, my route taking me into the kitchen. It was a building unto itself, its single space divided lengthwise by a central counter, a wooden one stained like the floor of a garage. Long steel sinks flanked the doorway I'd come through. On the opposite wall, unfinished on the inside, were stoves and ovens, black as rolling stock. The air of the place was heavy with grease and smelled of fried beef and onions. I could feel my second-hand Shalimar smacking the canvas with its chin.

Next to the doorway where I stood was the old black wall phone the sensitive Cararra didn't care for. A pencil hung from a bit of string tacked next to the phone, and the board wall was covered with doodles and notes, most of them phone numbers. The number I was interested in was printed on a paper circle pasted to the center of the phone's dial. I verified that it wasn't the number I'd memorized for Crowe House, which meant that this phone was a separate line, not an extension.

The waiter who had served us was washing dishes at one of the galvanized sinks. I asked him who had been on duty Friday night around eight-thirty, and he nodded toward a man who was standing near the stoves, stirring a large pot.

The man didn't look like a chuck-wagon driver, being slender and fair-skinned with short gray hair parted down the middle. But he had the dialogue down.

"Don't tell me," he began with no more smile than the pot was wearing, "you came to say something nice about the chili. Let's hear it. And make it original."

"I spilled some on my tie," I said, "and it only burned a small hole."

"Haven't heard that one word for word," the cook conceded. "But only because I don't get many customers who wear ties. Or who carry guns under their arms. What do you want?"

"Were you working last Friday night?"

"Yep."

"Did a telephone call come in about nine o'clock?"

He paid me the compliment of actually thinking about it. "No. Can't recall the phone ringing at all that evening."

"You were in here around nine?"

"No. I was out back, sharpening knives. But I can hear the phone out there. I'm not deaf yet, but I am looking forward to it."

So he was the guy Cararra had seen during her walk, the walk she'd originally claimed to have taken while Brooks slept. She had to have actually wandered by after Brooks and Pioline left. I asked the cook whether he'd noticed her.

"I'm not blind either," he said, seeing her again in memory. Inspired by the mental image, he added, "Thank the Lord."

"What time was that?"

"Dunno. Don't wear a watch." He held up a bony wrist that had no telltale tan lines. "Dropped my last one in the stew and never got it back. Guy who found it must have thought it was a premium."

"Must have." I started to add my good-byes, but he wasn't through yet.

"Miss Cararra didn't look like herself that night. She wasn't happy. She looked like her last friend had asked for the loan of a suitcase." He paused and assumed a look himself. If I read it right, he was deliberately placing a chip on his shoulder. "I thought about going over and talking to her." Go ahead, he was really saying, tell me I don't have a snowball's chance in hell with her. When I didn't, he added, "I thought she needed someone to cheer her up."

"She did," I said. "But the position's been filled."

Ella was waiting for me on the front step of the main house. The guard who had been shooting the breeze with her stepped away deferentially as I approached.

"Forget the password?" I asked.

"No. The last of the reporters is still in there. I've had it with Lillie's noble widow routine. You won't be able to interview Jewel right now. Lillie has her handcuffed, figuratively speaking. I asked Jewel to come by the cottage tonight to go over some new dialogue. You can talk to her privately then."

"I was looking forward to us getting handcuffed tonight."

"Figuratively speaking?"

"Up to you."

"Don't think I don't like it when you come on like a sailor on shore leave," Ella said, her voice as flat as tap water. "What woman wouldn't? But talking to Jewel is important."

"Aye aye, ma'am," I said, and we parted.

I was admitted by Hilly, Lacey's maid, who was also her cook and dresser as the occasion demanded. Her real name was Hilbery, but I'd never heard anyone but Pioline use it, which meant I wouldn't be hearing it again. She'd been with Lacey forever and hadn't been a young woman when she'd applied for the job. Or so I judged by her wrinkles, which were as deep and convoluted as a Bergman film. Hilly and I had a nodding acquaintance. I nodded to her now, being careful to keep all thoughts of shore leave out of my mind.

A nod was all I had time for, as Lacey was in the main room, a few steps beyond the front door, wrapping up her interview. Her greeting to me was a single raised finger, which I took to mean, "Don't interrupt this thought or go away."

The precious thought concerned what a fine memorial *Warrior Queen* would make for Pioline. I had that one down by heart, so I shifted my attention to Lacey's audience. It was Mabel, the San Francisco reporter who had given me a lift from Heston. Today's white hat was a pillbox number. With it Mabel wore a neat pink suit, but her eyes were still in deep mourning. They never left Lacey's face as the actress transitioned smoothly from Pioline to Jewel.

"It was Mark's dream that this picture be a vehicle for launching his stepdaughter's career. Although he never called her his stepdaughter. He always called you daughter, didn't he, dear?"

Jewel was seated on the big leather sofa next to her mother. Ella had joked about handcuffs. I saw now that it hadn't really been a joke. Lacey had a death grip on Jewel's wrist, as though she expected her fey child to bolt at any second.

"Yes," Jewel replied after a ten-second pause. The answer had the advantage of being difficult to misquote. Otherwise it wasn't the stuff of great interviews. Lacey dove into the breach.

"It means so much to me to be able to guide Jewel through her first film. I remember how lost I was after the war, a widow with a little baby trying to make it in pictures. I feel a little that way now, with Marc gone. Thank heavens I have friends around me." Here Lacey actually patted Mabel's hand. "Friends who will help me look after Jewel just as Marc always did."

Mabel gushed something affirmative. I was sure that in her finished article Jewel would come across as eloquent and poised as Grace Kelly circa 1955.

Lacey then pretended to notice me all over again, giving the reporter her signal to withdraw. When the hugs were over and Hilly had shown Mabel out, Lacey lit into Jewel.

"What on earth is the matter with you? Can't you even try to help me? Must I always feel as though I'm still lugging you about in my arms? Do you know what this chance is worth? Have you the slightest idea? Can't you imagine what that Cararra woman would make of the opportunity to be interviewed by an important newspaper? How she would put herself out and put herself over?"

To all these questions, Jewel hadn't a single answer. Lacey

was still holding her daughter's arm. She tossed it away now with something like despair. "You're damned lucky Max Froy has decided to save the footage of Bebe. If he had opted to replace her, even with a rank amateur like Cararra, you'd be shoved right off the screen. It will happen yet, if you're not careful. You'll be upstaged by long shots of Cararra's bloody backside."

Jewel continued to sit impassively, without any of the blushing and fussing I'd seen when she and her mother had last done their act for me. I chalked up another one for Ella. Something wasn't right with Jewel. A reaction to the events of the past two days, maybe. Something akin to shell shock.

"Scotty, I'm sorry," Lacey said, turning her back on her daughter without rising from the sofa. "Have you any news of our Mr. Remlinger? We heard what he did to Clay Ford. Horrible. Which of us is next, do you know?"

"No," I said. I was looking past the actress, looking for some reaction out of Jewel—fear, revulsion, curiosity—but there was nothing. "We may have seen the last of him for a while. He's a police matter now. If he's still in California, they'll get him. In the meantime, I need to know everyone's whereabouts on Friday night."

"Whatever for, Scotty?" Lacey asked, confused.

"I'm trying to verify Brooks's movements," I said, "to see if she may have had some contact with Remlinger." It sounded thin to me. To Lacey, who still considered Remlinger the answer to all questions, it seemed to be plausible enough.

"I never saw Bebe after we returned to the ranch that evening. She didn't come to dinner, as you know. After dinner, I came back here. I was here until Marc came in on his mysterious return trip."

"Which was about twenty past nine?"

"I suppose. Yes, about then. He only stayed a very few minutes. Establishing his alibi, the old rogue."

"How few?"

"Ten minutes, no more."

"You didn't happen to see him or Brooks after that?"

"I couldn't have, could I? I was out back on the patio, trying to equal your expertise with a cocktail shaker. It had been one hell of a day, and it hadn't bottomed."

I turned to Jewel of the monosyllabic answer. "Were you here when your stepfather stopped in?"

"No. I mean, I was, but I was taking a bath." She finally gave out with her trademark blush. The confirmation that there was still blood in her system so comforted me I smiled.

"It's always been Jewel's way of relaxing," Lacey said, patting her daughter's hand. It was the same gesture she'd extended to Mabel, but now it was unstudied.

"So you didn't see your stepfather or Miss Brooks after dinner?"

"No. I was up there for an hour. From nine until about ten." She glanced at the ceiling, indicating some bathroom that hadn't been included on my earlier tour. "I was just coming downstairs when I heard that horrible noise. I rushed outside. The horses were making a din and men were rushing around." She added, unnecessarily, "It frightened me."

Lacey drew her close. "You've been frightened since you came here. If you could only see how much your fear is taking from you."

Jewel escaped the embrace by standing. "I'd like to go to my room. Did you want to ask me anything else?"

I had one more question, but it was for Lacey. "Marcus made a phone call from the airport office around nine. Did he call you?"

"Me? No. The phone may have rung, though. Do you remember, dear?"

"I think I heard it," Jewel said.

"Hilly! Hilly, where are you? Hilly, did a call come in on Friday evening?"

"A call from Gabriel," the old woman muttered as she shuffled in. "A telephone call? Mr. P's call?"

"Yes," Lacey said, exasperated. "Why didn't you bring the phone out to me?"

" 'Cause first, the phone doesn't reach to the patio. The bleeding antique doesn't reach to the other end of the sofa. And second, the call wasn't for you."

I stepped between the boxers. "Who was it for?"

"For Miss Brooks, except it wasn't exactly for her either. Mr. P asked whether Miss Brooks was here, but he knew good and well she wasn't. When did she ever trouble herself to pay a visit to us? He was really looking for somebody to go after her, to walk down the hill in the heat and the dust and bring her back so he could talk with her.

"I played dumb. I said no she wasn't here and goodnight and then he came right out and asked if I'd go get her. He had something to say to her about the movie, which I knew was a lie. Imagine him thinking that he could knit a scarf for me, who's known him close to twenty years. If I had a pound note for every Bebe Brooks—"

"Hilly!"

"Beg pardon." She made a movement that was either a curtsy or a shifting of her undergarments. "I said I'd be delighted to go after Her Highness, but first I'd have to get my mistress's leave. That fixed him. He told me not to bother and rang off. When he showed up himself half an hour later, all sweaty and dusty from the road, he wouldn't even give me a civil hello."

So much for Pioline's last mystery. Or his last but one. I thanked them and left.

31

Ella was in the shower when I finally got to the cottage at the end of a hot, frustrating afternoon. I stuck my head into the bathroom and whistled the whistle we used, so she'd know it was me banging around and not Dillon. That was my excuse for looking in, anyway.

I mixed myself a drink and sat down on the front porch to await Jewel. Based on the way my day had gone, I wasn't expecting much from the interview. I'd gone down to the corral after leaving Crowe House, looking for Lange. I'd found him questioning the ranch hands and I'd joined in, trying to find someone who had seen Cararra after she'd inspired tender sentiments in the knife-sharpening cook. If her story was true, I had all the alibi I needed for her. She'd seen Pioline and Brooks off, so she couldn't possibly have beaten them to the airport. But another witness—especially one who wore a watch—would have made me that much happier. Unfortunately, I never found anyone who'd seen her near the stables. The two hands who hadn't been off boozing with Irwin in Sherwood had been holed up in the ranch's tack room, listening to baseball on the radio. They'd alternated innings between the league-leading Dodgers, who'd been hosting the Cubs, and the second-place Giants, who'd been playing Pittsburgh.

When Lange finished, we compared notes. He seemed more his old self, perhaps because he was fed up.

"Irwin's story checks out. At least there's no hour gap in it. No one on the whole damn spread seems to have been alone that night."

"Lucky for us," I said, "or we'd have to figure out why any of the hands would want to bring down a plane." I wasn't feeling lucky, though, or particularly sharp. I passed on Cararra's story about the rendezvous between the producer and his star and the testimony of Lacey and her maid. "About the only one unaccounted for for a full hour is Jewel. She was in the tub."

"Any witnesses?" Lange asked, attempting a leer.

"Forgot to ask. Are you still sure we're talking about an hour?"

"I've sent a man to walk the route. If he doesn't get lost, we'll know exactly how long it takes. That will pretty much kill today. What do we do tomorrow?"

Tomorrow. I hadn't considered it. On my drive up from Los Angeles, the possibility of a single day with no surprises from Remlinger had seemed too much to hope for. Now it was just possible that we had shaken him for good.

"We start working Sherwood," I said. "The rest of the crew and the extras."

"The extras? What motive are we talking about now? They didn't like the box lunches Pioline was serving? Or the spiked heels Brooks wore when she walked all over them? And why stop at our people? Why not the locals? Why not everybody this side of Fresno for Christ's sake?"

Ella took up the same theme as we walked up to dinner, Jewel having failed to appear. "This is anything but a well-constructed plot, Scotty. You need this all to be happening on a desert island or some estate where they lock the gates at dusk. There's just no way to limit the suspects to the people on this ranch."

I'd had time to think about it since Lange had lined that same ball my way. Time and a couple of restorative Gibsons. I'd seen that Lange had been right, that we'd been working backward. "You limit your suspects by motive," I said now, "not geography.

If Remlinger didn't sabotage that plane, it has to be someone at this ranch. Someone who knew Brooks and Pioline."

"Only Danny Irwin has even half a real motive, and he has the best alibi."

"Then his alibi has a hole we haven't found or someone else has a motive we haven't tripped over. Period."

"I love a man with the courage of his convictions. Or is that gin I smell?"

Lange saved me, double-timing up just then, the sweat on his cheeks cutting channels through the dust. "My man found it between here and the airstrip," he panted. "Closer to here."

So far as I could tell, he was referring to his fist, which he was holding out for us. When he was sure of our attention, he relaxed his fingers. A strip of faded red cloth was curled on his palm. I took one end of it and raised it from his hand. There was white lettering on it, or lettering that had once been white, before the red dye of the fabric had bled into it, turning it pink. Clay Ford hadn't mentioned the warning message when he'd described the streamer, but he'd imparted the sense of it: "Remove before flight."

I held it up for Ella to see. "We're on a desert island after all. This was attached to the gust lock. Whoever put the lock on the plane tore this off. And then dropped it on the way back here."

Lange snatched the ribbon away from me and rolled it up again. "Don't wave that thing around. For all we know, Remlinger has someone here on his payroll."

"Maybe one of the horses," Ella said, but her delivery was uninspired. She was staring at Lange, and it occurred to me that I hadn't told her of the change in him.

"How long did it take your man to walk there and back?"

"That's the bad news. It's forty-five minutes each way. Twice as long as it takes to drive it on that dog's hind leg of a road, an hour and a half round trip."

"We don't have anyone with that much loose time," Ella said.

"We have Jewel Lacey," Lange replied. "If she slipped out of the cottage right after her bath was run, she would have reached the airfield just as Pioline was starting back with Brooks."

"You can't be serious," Ella said. "Not Jewel."

She was addressing me, so I answered her. "You said yourself she hasn't been right since the crash. And that she's at the center of whatever's been wrong with this production."

"At the center of the production's problems, yes, but she can't be a murderer. There has to be some other explanation."

Lange was still working out the time table. "Jewel couldn't have gotten back before ten-thirty. That's a good fifteen minutes after we got organized and headed for the crash site. She didn't go out there with us. And I don't recall seeing her before we left."

"It was mass confusion," Ella said. "I didn't find Lillie for ten minutes or more."

"She wasn't out on her patio?" I asked.

"No, she was . . ."

"What?"

Ella looked frightened. "She was out looking for Jewel."

We talked it over while Ella and I ate and Lange pushed his food around on his plate. We shared the dining room with ranch hands who sat as far from us as possible. I couldn't blame them.

Lange left well before the dessert cart came by—had there been one—saying he had to see about Irwin's dinner.

Ella contemplated his empty place for some time. "What's eating him?" she finally asked.

"Remlinger is. And the idea that his number may be up."

"Have you ever felt that way, Scotty? Like you were standing in someone's crosshairs?"

"Not since the reviews for my last picture came out."

"I'm serious."

"No. Not even during the war. I was always more worried for the other guys. I figured I was the star of the picture. The star never gets it."

"They didn't used to," Ella said. "Times have changed."

I thought of saying that it didn't matter, as I hadn't turned out to be the star of my own life anyway. I didn't say it. I know Ella didn't approve of that style of humor.

We weren't back at the cottage long enough for Duke Ellington and company to finish one pass through "Things Ain't What They Used To Be" before Jewel showed up. She approached as warily as a fawn coming up to a salt lick at dusk. We watched through the front window as she paused a few yards shy of the door, took a step, and paused again. I don't think she would have finished the trip if Ella hadn't stepped out to greet her. Even then she wouldn't come inside. We settled in on the front porch, Jewel and I in the Adirondack chairs and Ella sitting between us on the single step.

Jewel was wearing a shapeless smock of a sundress, one worn from washing and marked here and there with spots of dried paint that no amount of washing would get out. She'd dressed up as the art student she was wishing she could be again. I took it to be her way of dispelling *Warrior Queen* for an evening at least, the equivalent of Lange's drinking and my interrupted session with Ellington.

I listened wistfully to the last bars of the recording while Ella explained to Jewel that the business about going over changes to the script had been a ruse, that we knew something was bothering her, that we wanted to help if we could. Every time Ella said "we," Jewel looked at me. But she didn't speak. I tried to think of what Jimmy Stewart would say.

It came out weak: "If there's anything I can do, you only have to ask."

"Get them to stop the picture," she said.

If she had asked me to arrest her, it wouldn't have surprised me more. Not that everyone from the grips on up didn't know she hated being in the picture. What surprised me was the conviction she seemed to have that I had any say in what Froy and her mother did.

"If you want out, you have to speak up," I said. "Now, before the shooting starts again."

"I don't want to quit," Jewel said. "That's not enough. That would still leave everyone else in danger. My mother, you two . . ."

There was another name on her lips, but it wouldn't take the plunge. "Everyone would still be in danger. The only way to end the danger is to end the movie. I'm sorry, Ella. I know how hard you've worked on this. I know what it means to give up a dream. Believe me, I do. But it's the only way. And it may not be enough. Stopping the filming, getting us all away from here, may not be enough. But we've got to try."

Her words were urgent, but she herself seemed sleepy. I asked, "Have you talked to your mother about this?"

"I've tried. She'll only say that the show goes on no matter what, that I'd know that if I were a professional. I'm not a professional. I don't want to be one, not if it means not feeling anything."

That would never be her problem. "If you know something that's frightening you, tell us what it is."

"I don't know anything. I mean, I don't have any information." Her fatigue was almost trancelike. It was a temptation I couldn't pass up.

"You couldn't know anything, could you?" I said. "You were in the tub when everything was happening." At my feet, Ella stirred.

"Yes," Jewel said.

"Hilly draw it for you?"

"No. Getting her to do anything is always more trouble than doing it yourself."

"She look in on you?"

"No."

Ella was reaching a hand around behind her back. I lifted the foot nearest her and crossed my legs. "How about after the crash?" I asked. "You said you went outside. Did you speak to anyone?"

"No," Jewel said.

"You didn't go to the crash site."

"No, I couldn't."

"What did you do?"

"I don't know. I was confused. I don't remember."

Ella came to her aid then. "Tell us about your feelings."

"You'll laugh at me."

"No we won't," Ella said, as much warning me as reassuring the girl.

"I knew it was all going to happen," Jewel said, so dreamy now that her head was moving back and forth by itself. "I mean, I knew something was going to happen. I've known since the night we filmed Mother's—Boudica's—speech at the bonfire. When she was calling on Andrasta to let loose a chaos on the land. I remember thinking that we could be doing that same thing accidentally: wishing down a terrible storm that could destroy us all."

"That was just a speech in a script," Ella said.

"You got it from a history book," Jewel said, murmuring more than speaking. "You told me so. Those were Boudica's exact words, as far as the Romans knew. I know it's crazy, but I thought, 'We could be casting an ancient spell. Letting loose some curse none of us can control.' And the very next day, the evil showed up."

"It wasn't a curse or a demon that showed up," I said. "It was thug named Remlinger."

Jewel's big eyes were closing. "That may just be a name it happens to have."

I listened as Ella tried to talk her out of it, thinking that, if I'd been a little more bushed or there'd been a campfire handy to throw moving shadows about, she might have had two believers on her hands.

That was all we got from Jewel. We walked her back to the main house, Ella not trusting me to lay off the questioning if I was alone with her ward for even the length of the walk.

On our return trip, I began to wonder if there might be enough evening left for us to enjoy, there being other ways to forget one's troubles besides listening to phonograph records. I approached the subject obliquely, asking my wife if there was anything I could do for her.

"Yes," she said. "Hold me."

I shelved my plans and held her for the rest of the night. We held each other, and made it safely through to daylight.

32

Ella the writer had often told me that she could go to bed worrying over some problem with a scene or a line of dialogue and awake the next morning with the answer in the forefront of her mind, delivered by some shoemaker's elves of her subconscious, who had been busy toiling over it while she slept. She demonstrated this faculty for me on Monday morning, the morning of what turned out to be the last day of the *Warrior Queen* shoot. She was going over her hair with a handheld dryer that would have looked exactly like a Buck Rogers ray pistol if not for the big chrome engine housing jutting out from one side. I was sitting behind her on the edge of the bed, watching her reflection in the mirror, reluctant to admit that the day had started and I should be at work.

"Suppose," she said over the noise of the dryer, "that Marcus drove the murderer out to the airstrip that night when he made his last trip."

The proposition drew me back from a nostalgic reverie over how high her breasts rode when her arms were over her head. "Lange's men at the ranch gate would have seen a third person in the car."

"Not if the murderer had been hidden in the backseat. Marcus could have missed him or her and the guards could have, too."

I thought about it. A Plymouth Fury was no Sedan de Ville. It would have been difficult for anyone to have ridden in the back out of sight. The trunk would have been a better place, but that left the problem of getting in and out unassisted. "Go on," I said.

"It was dark by the time they got to the field. While everyone was in the office, the murderer could have slipped out of the car, installed the gust lock, and then walked back to the ranch, dropping that streamer along the way."

I searched back through Clay Ford's testimony, trying to remember whether there'd been any delay between the lovers' arrival in the Fury and their departure in the *Argo*. I couldn't remember one, but that might just have been the way Ford had told the story. It would have been natural enough for Pioline and his pilot to have consulted for a few minutes, since the producer was proposing a completely new flight plan. But how could the murderer have counted on that? The last thing I needed was another scenario in which events just happened to fall into place. I needed one in which things happened because the murderer made them happen. When I objected, though, it was on more general grounds.

"What do we gain with this?"

Ella switched off the death ray, and her reflection in the mirror caught my wandering gaze and held it. "It gives us a way of getting Nicole Cararra back in the picture. I'm not saying I think she did it. Just that she could have. It scared me last night to hear you and Lange talking about Jewel. I know you're wrong there. I'm just trying to show you there are still other suspects. Ones with better motives. You think Cararra is off the short list because she waved good-bye to Marcus and Bebe and she was seen afterward by the cook. She couldn't have walked to the field and gotten there soon enough."

"Something like that," I said.

"Well, we only have her word for what happened and the order in which it happened. Suppose she was telling you the truth the first time you questioned her, when she said she left Bebe in the cottage that night and went for a walk. She went up to the main camp so she could be seen by someone who'd remember her later. Then she waited for Pioline to show up."

"She knew he was coming back?"

"Yes. Bebe told her. When he arrived, Cararra slipped into the car, either while he was in Crowe House with Lillie or after that, while he was collecting Bebe. Marcus delivered her to the airport, and she sabotaged the plane. Then she walked here across country, taking her time. Nobody saw her until we all got back from the crash site hours later."

While I thought about it, she dressed, perhaps as an aid to my thinking. When she was putting the finishing touches on a wisp of scarf tied around her neck, I said, "You mentioned Cararra having a better motive than Jewel. Yesterday you didn't think she'd gotten enough out of Brooks's death."

"As I recall, you were suggesting she might have killed Bebe to get her part. That's nonsense and you know it."

"So what was her motive?"

"Danny Irwin. She's interested in the guy, or haven't you noticed?"

"She killed two people on the off chance of landing Irwin?"

Ella didn't answer me. She knew I was just trying to see how far she'd go to protect Jewel, that I knew the answer already. She been hesitant to implicate Cararra. Now I was asking her to do the same thing to a man she liked, a writer she respected. I felt bad about that, but not bad enough to pack my tent.

I stood up. "You're saying that Cararra and Irwin were in it together. That would explain how Cararra knew the ins and outs of sabotaging a plane. She had a former pilot coaching her. It also accounts for his trip to Sherwood. He wasn't really looking for Remlinger or even a drink. He wanted a cast-iron alibi. He knew we'd suspect the jealous husband. That was part of his cover. He pretended to go berserk at the press conference yesterday to stay in character and to give the impression he didn't like Cararra's ascension. Somewhere down the road, they'll reconcile. Irwin will end up with whatever money Brooks didn't squander and a new woman to spend it on."

"Not just a new one," Ella said, scared now and quiet. "A woman who could double for his wife physically but- unlike Bebe—happens to be nuts about him."

"I guess I should talk to Cararra again."

"Not this morning, Scotty. She's got an early call. Max wants to hit the ground running. You'll have to wait till the lunch break or this evening." She added, pointedly, "Max will be using Jewel today, too, if she's up to it."

If we all left Jewel alone, she meant. I kissed Ella and headed out to punch the clock. If Cararra was unavailable, I still had Irwin, who was starting day two of his house arrest. But I didn't visit him either. I climbed into the Thunderbird and left the ranch, after notifying the front-gate guard of my destination.

The name I'd whispered in his unshell-like ear was Heston. I'd decided to visit Clay Ford, both to see how he was getting on and to find out if there really had been an opportunity for Cararra—or anyone else—to tinker with the gust lock after Pioline and Brooks arrived at the field. While I was in Heston, I planned to stop in and talk to Tyler, to see if Remlinger had turned up anywhere.

That was the program, but I never got it done. I made the dusty drive to Heston with the top down, putting up with the dust for the sake of the morning air. I got as far as the front desk of the hospital and the hallway just beyond it. A Rose Marie impersonator left the desk to chase me, waving a yellow slip of paper and calling out, "Scott Elliott! Scott Elliott!"

I had a flashback to the days when I'd been asked to sign the occasional autograph. The woman was old enough to remember that time, unfortunately for her. I toyed for a second with the vain idea that she'd been chasing me with that piece of paper since 1941. Then I accepted it for what it was: a telephone message slip.

"You are Mr. Elliott, are you not? They described you perfectly."

I didn't ask whether the image of John Payne had been invoked again. I thanked her and took the slip. Before I could read it, she rattled off the message.

"You're to call that number immediately. It's most urgent. You can use the phone on my desk."

I did, recognizing the Crowe House number as I dialed it. Lillie Lacey answered.

"Scotty? Good, very good. You're needed, Scotty. That Cararra woman's run off. Can you believe it? She's supposed to be out on the shooting site right now. Jewel is going to fill in, but we must have Cararra back. If she wants more money, promise it to her. Promise her anything."

"Mind if I find her first?"

"Find her? We know where she's gone. Lange spoke to the ranch hand who smuggled her out. The former ranch hand, if I have anything to say about it. He took her to Sherwood. She's catching a bus to somewhere. Lange's gone to talk with her, but I don't trust him to handle it. You go, Scotty, and fetch her. If you should meet a bus on the way, stop it."

I started to suggest shooting out the tires, but she'd already hung up. I scribbled a note to Ford containing the question I'd come to ask, and entrusted it to my one-woman fan club. She promised it would get to the pilot, cross her heart and hope to die.

I didn't meet a bus on the road to Sherwood or pass one. No Greyhounds passed me, either, but then they would have needed jet engines to have gotten it done. Even so, I arrived in Sherwood after Lange. I spotted his Fury parked in front of the little general store, the one with the memorial to Hemingway in its front window. There were also advertisements in the window, one of them for bus service between LA and San Francisco.

Just inside the door, a gentleman in a worn white coat was stacking tin flasks of hand soap on a shelf. The back of the store held a little lunch counter. Cararra was seated there, and Lange was just beyond her, talking in a low voice. Describing his brass knuckles maybe. She was turned a little away from him, either to watch me or to show that she had absolutely no interest in what he was saying.

"What time's her bus?" I asked the grocer.

"Thirty minutes," he said, "if she decides she likes that one."

I took the stool on Cararra's free side. She was no longer turned that way. She was facing the near wall, her gloved hands placed before her and drawn into fists. The grocer had followed me. He stepped behind the counter, becoming a waiter just that easily.

"I don't suppose you'll be having anything either," he said to me, glancing at the bare wood in front of the two love birds.

"Coffee," I said. He gave me a better-than-nothing shrug and placed a full mug on the counter.

When he'd gone, I said to Cararra, "You have until I finish this to get used to the idea that you're coming back."

"I won't come back."

Her voice was so dead it stayed the mug that I'd been raising nonchalantly to my lips. I looked her over again. She was dressed in a beautiful black suit—Brooks's surely—with beige lapels that matched her beige blouse. The suit only had three-quarter-length sleeves, but its wearer's forearms were protected by gauntlet-length gloves, also beige. Her hat was a back lampshade with a broad black band. Her makeup—what I could see of it—was perfect. But for the more formal attire, she looked exactly as she had when she'd greeted her new public the day before. Exactly the same and completely different. As lifeless somehow as Beverly Brooks had been on the burning hillside when I'd covered her face.

"What are you after?" I asked. And then, when the echoes of that had faded, "Is it more money?"

"She won't say," Lange put in. "This is a waste of our time. They could wire Brooks's measurements down to Hollywood and get half a dozen stand-ins up here by lunch time. They'd have their own blond hair, too. Let's just take her and go. This is Froy's lookout and Lacey's."

Cararra found her voice. "You put a hand on me, and I'll yell for the police."

"That wouldn't be smart," I said. "You're wearing borrowed clothes. If we report them as stolen, Froy and Lacey will be able to interview you during visiting hours at the county jail. Those reporters from yesterday may stop by, too."

Cararra's face darkened, but she said nothing. I was glad the only silverware on the counter was my coffee spoon.

I drained my mug. "Let's go. You escort the lady. I'll collect her bag."

The grocer and waiter and stationmaster handed me a calfskin case with the initials BB under its handle. Outside, Lange was shutting the Fury's door behind his charge.

"Your girlfriend get cold feet?"

I paid him for the coffee. "You said something just now about her having to like the next bus. What did you mean by that?"

"Just that she got here plenty early for the Los Angeles bus, bought a ticket, and waited. The bus came on time, but she wouldn't get on. Traded her ticket for one on the Frisco bus. I'm not sure she wanted to take that bus either. She acted like she didn't want to stay but couldn't bring herself to leave. So I'm guessing cold feet."

I asked myself if the answer could be as simple as that, if Cararra had just turned camera shy now that her big moment was at hand. I'd heard of it happening once or twice, to people who had waited a lot longer for their big breaks than Cararra. Or had Ella been right after all? Was Cararra a secret player in all that had happened and coming apart now under the pressure?

I thought it over as I trailed the Plymouth back to the ranch, staying well back to avoid the dust barrage. Lange delivered the runaway to Crowe House, presumably so Lacey could reopen contract negotiations. I drove down to the cottage grove, to Daniel Irwin's most recent address. I found him out back with the man who was supposed to be keeping an eye on him. They were playing cards, and the guard was winning, to judge from the piles of toothpicks they were using for chips.

I asked Lange's man to give us ten minutes and sat down in his vacated chair. Irwin was looking more collected this morning, at least emotionally. Externally, he looked like the widower he'd recently become: unshaven, uncombed, his white tennis shirt and shorts straight from the bottom of a suitcase. I selected a toothpick from the novelist's pile and stuck it in my teeth.

"You owe me a dollar," he said. "And an apology."

"Which do you think you're more likely to get?"

"You all but promised me that Remlinger would come by last night to see me. He never showed."

"Sorry."

"You will be. I'm planning to have you and Lange charged with unlawful confinement."

"I'll pass that on to Lange, when he gets a free minute. Right now, he's interrogating Nicole Cararra," I added, though I thought it more likely that he'd dumped her and run. "She panicked this morning and skipped. She could be telling all she knows about what really happened on Friday night. Or she may be able to hold it in for another day or even two."

Irwin smiled at me. "She can tell it live on *I've Got a Secret* for all I care."

"You're not interested in what happens to her, a woman in love with you?"

Irwin looked like I'd socked him again. "You're a real bastard, Elliott. That's the inside story on you. You play this detached, dreamy character who never gets ruffled because he's never really there mentally. Part of him is always back at the plantation the Yankees burned or with some regiment that got wiped out or watching all over again while a lost love waves a handkerchief from a pier. That's the role you like, but it's just a role. People feel sorry for you or cut you a break because they know you used to be an actor and now you're not. They think—I did— 'He doesn't really want to be doing this. It hurts him as much as it hurts me.' Only it doesn't hurt you. That's the payoff. The war twisted you that way. You didn't fall into a dirty job. You sought it out. You may not even know you did; you're no powerhouse upstairs. All you may know is, deep down inside, being a bastard feels better than anything."

We sat for a time admiring Irwin's handiwork. The mood was broken by the sound of someone coming toward us through the cottage, someone who was slamming every door he passed through, just as Carson Drury had in the famous scene at the end of *First Citizen*.

It was Lange. "They just phoned from the shooting site. Jewel's car never got there. It left here an hour ago."

For a second I thought he was saying that Jewel had gone AWOL, a la Cararra. Then he blurted out, "Ella's with her."

33

I drove us out along the road to the shooting site, Lange in the front seat next to me and Irwin in back. I wasn't sure how Irwin had gotten invited, but it didn't matter. Nothing mattered except making time.

I gave the car its head until I came to the dip in the road that Ella had warned me about on the evening I'd driven her and the Daniel Irwins from the shoot to the ranch. I slowed, planning to take the gully as fast as I could. Then I saw the car parked at the bottom and braked, seriously.

The car was one of our rented Plymouths, and both its front doors were standing open. It was off to the side of the road, door handle deep in dry weeds. The Thunderbird came to rest beside it, slewed across the right-of-way.

I reached the Fury first. The front bench seat was empty. The rear one was occupied by one of Lange's men, his hands tied behind his back. It was Harris, the man I'd almost run down on my dash to the airport on Friday night. He looked now like he *had* been run over, only more recently. His eyes were swollen and his nose and mouth were bloody. His face had been slammed against something, probably the hood of the car. He said, "Remlinger," using as much blood as air. That was it.

While Irwin cradled him and I untied his hands, Lange made

a discovery: a folded piece of paper tucked into Harris's shirt pocket. "It's addressed to you," Lange said, handing it over.

Sure enough, my name was printed on the outside of the fold, next to a smear of blood. The message inside was written in a surprisingly immature hand, a copybook style that would have passed any fourth-grade teacher's inspection.

"We have to talk," it said. "I'll send word to you where if you can't figure it out. No uniforms and the ladies won't be hurt."

There was no signature, unless that was what the blood was meant to represent. I passed the note to Lange. Irwin, who had propped Harris up against the side of the sedan, read it over his shoulder. The paper twitched in Lange's hand, which somehow steadied me a little.

"It's what I told you yesterday," Lange said. "Remlinger's bought somebody inside the ranch. That's how he knew that Jewel and Ella would be out here with only one guard. The spy called Remlinger and tipped him off."

"Called him where?" I asked. "Where could he have been that he could have gotten here in time to stop the car? They must just have been waiting out here, hoping for their chance."

"There's a third alternative," Irwin said. He was turned away from us, looking toward the old mission. It seemed very close now, looming above us almost on its wrinkled hill. "You remember me telling you about the photographers who were watching us? I saw those flashes of light again this morning."

Lange grabbed his arm. "What flashes of light?"

"Reflections on a telephoto lens, I thought. I thought it was how the local paper was keeping an eye on us. Sorry, Elliott."

"Remlinger's been up there all this time?" Lange asked. "Watching us?" He turned his attention to me without letting go of the novelist. "Why the hell didn't you tell me about this so I could have had the place searched?"

Because I was no powerhouse upstairs, as Irwin had recently put it. Irwin's guess about the mission explained one mystery that had bothered me on and off since yesterday. Namely, why had Remlinger gone to question Clay Ford? If Remlinger hadn't known the crash was a setup, why had he bothered with the pilot? I'd decided that it had to have been because Brooks had dropped some hint about Ford's role in the drug deliveries. It suddenly seemed just as likely that I'd led Remlinger to Ford when I'd driven to the airport on Saturday and not come back. Remlinger had gotten curious and lucked onto Ford's guilty secret.

"What do we do now?" Lange was asking.

"I go talk to him. He said I was welcome to drop in early if I could figure out where."

Lange released Irwin and faced me. "He doesn't want talk, Elliott. He wants you. You're the next guy on his hit list, the one who brought Brooks back here to die." He was working himself into a sweat. And me with him.

"He could have gotten me anytime. If he's been watching the ranch, he's seen me come and go. He's after something else."

"What?"

I shrugged. "One way to find out."

Lange stepped forward then, in more ways than one. "I'm going with you."

I looked him over. He was paler than Harris and a muscle in his left cheek was twitching away like Carmen Miranda's better hip. He was thinking of a drink, ten to one. Or he had been until that very moment. Now he was thinking of Ella.

"Thanks," I said, putting a hand on his shoulder. "But Remlinger said no uniforms. He probably had you in mind."

"Yeah," Lange said hollowly. "He's scared of me."

"Take your man back to the ranch and call Tyler. Tell him to cover the roads out of here, but not to move in until you hear from me."

"Suppose we don't hear from you."

"Give me an hour. After that, you can come after me."

That took care of Lange. Next up was Irwin. "I haven't worn a uniform in years," he said. "I'll go with you."

"What for?" Lange demanded. "To hand Remlinger another hostage? He's got plenty right now."

"Suppose you're right and Remlinger only wants to trade the women for Elliott. They may need help getting back."

Here Lange and Irwin looked toward the moaning Harris, and I didn't. "There's no time to argue," I said. "If you want to come, come. But you follow orders."

"Agreed," Irwin said.

We helped Lange get his man into the Plymouth. Then we drove in tandem until we reached the first cutoff to the north. I waved to Lange and turned left.

Irwin got chatty almost at once. "What if this isn't the road to the mission?"

"We hunt around until we find it."

From there he jumped to the war. It was never very far away for some guys. "I always wondered how you ground sloggers found your way around in France. On clear days, I used to look down at the roads. None of the ones I could see ran straight for very long. I figured you were lost about half the time."

"So did we." I asked myself whether Irwin was windier than he'd acted in front of Lange or if he was trying to help me, to give my nerves a break. I resented that possibility, even as I fell in with the plan. "I remember looking up at the bomber formations and wondering how you guys found your way."

"Not much to it. Just take your compass heading, figure in magnetic variation, wind deflection, calculate your true airspeed based on the wind again and your density altitude, and you're all set. Or you could do what I always did, which was to call down to the navigator and ask him."

He sounded genuinely nostalgic, but whether it was for the war or for a time when he'd had someone to ask directions of I couldn't tell.

Then, out of the blue, he said, "You have to hand me over, Elliott. To Remlinger."

"What?"

"He's not after you. That was Lange's imagination running away with him. I only agreed with it so you'd bring me along. You were closer to the truth. Remlinger is after something else. Or rather, someone else. He's finally put it all together. He knows his dream girl—my wife—was murdered. He's figuring you can tell him who did it. He'll kill your wife and Jewel if you don't. Kill them and not bat an eye. So you have to hand me over."

I brought the Thunderbird to a halt. "Is this a confession?"

Irwin thought about it. "No," he finally said. "It's an out for you and those women."

"Are you involved in your wife's death? Did you put Nicole Cararra up to it?"

"Make up anything you want, but leave Cararra out of it. Leave everyone else out. You mention another name, any name, and Remlinger will take another life. Tell him I went out to the airport that night from Sherwood after the ranch hands dropped me off. If he asks how, tell him I hot-wired a car."

"What about your hike up to the San Ignacio Inn and back?"

"Never made it."

"You saw Lange there."

"Say I didn't. Say one of the bit players who're staying there saw Lange and happened to mention it later that night in the bar where I was drinking."

"Is that the truth?"

"The truth is your wife is in a bad spot. I can help you get her out of it. Then we'll be even."

"The hell we will," I said. "I didn't jump on any grenades for your wife. I'm not going to help you commit suicide. Get out. You can walk back to the ranch."

Irwin never moved. "Have it your way. Forget I said anything. Let me come along. I promise I'll follow orders."

Of all he'd said, that was the first thing I believed. It was a bad place to start.

34

We were on the right road, as it happened. I wasn't sure for most of the drive. I had the mission's hill in sight the whole way and I couldn't see anything like a road up it, either on its brown face or in the deeply eroded clefts where thick stands of pine were sheltered from the wind. Then the tract we were following turned west and circled the base of the hill. When we'd reached the western slope, the road began to climb in a series of sharp switchbacks, invisible from below. We zigzagged upward until—by my rough calculation—we were very near the top. I pulled over next to trees that had sprouted from cracks in some exposed rock like big-city dandelions coming up through a sidewalk.

"What gives?" Irwin asked.

"You're waiting here with the car. I'll finish the trip on foot. Remlinger will be more likely to let you go if he never actually has you. I'll send Ella and Jewel down if I can. Wait for an hour. If no one's come by then, go down and hurry Tyler along."

The way Irwin was eyeing me made me think of the old sheriff's warning about the pressures of command. I said, "Need any of that in writing?"

"No." He looked at his watch. "I have thirteen oh seven."

"Close enough," I said and got out of the car. As an afterthought, I drew my gun and handed it to him. It was the same model handgun he'd been trained to use by the Army Air Corps, by a lucky chance. Maybe even the same gun. Irwin cycled the action expertly and placed it on the dashboard.

"Listen, Elliott, about what I said back at the ranch."

"The bit about me being a bastard?"

"Yeah."

"Keep it in mind," I said.

I started up what turned out to be the last switchback, wishing before I'd scared my third lizard that I'd left my jacket and tie and hat behind. There was no open ground to cross at the top of the hill. The mission's gate was right there, or what was left of it, a gap in stone walls next to the remains of a campanario, its bells long gone. Beyond the gate was a courtyard, and standing in the middle of that was Johnny Remlinger.

He didn't look like a man who had, within the past forty-eight hours, killed two men, crippled a third, and smashed the face of a fourth. He wasn't bloodied, but I hadn't expected him to be. He'd probably never laid a hand on any of his victims. But he wasn't ruffled or foaming, either, the way I'd been picturing him since the evening of the crash. And he didn't look like he'd been camping out under the stars, the guest of some long-dead monks. He was bareheaded but not informal in a khaki suit and a gold silk tie with black diamonds. The tie shone in the full sun, as did his shirt and shoes and the nickel plating of the snub-nosed revolver he raised as I neared him.

"Welcome to my castle, Elliott," he said, taking up where we'd left off days ago, with his favorite movie, *The Adventures of Robin Hood*. "You didn't waste any time finding it. Nothing like my suite in Vegas for amenities, but lots of privacy." He didn't have his guidebook today, but he had memorized parts of it. "This place is an *asistencia*. You probably thought it was a mission, but it's not. The missions were all built along the old royal road, the El Camino. But they set up branch operations in the hills to keep tabs on friendly Indian tribes. That's what San Ignacio started life as, an *asistencia*."

He was inviting me to look around, so I did, seeing more crumbling walls, adobe brick ones within the protection of the stone perimeter. Only one of the original structures was more or less intact. It was the chapel, and it stood to my left, on the highest ground within the compound. The planks of a dead door were propped across its entrance.

When I looked back to Remlinger, he was gesturing with his gun. "Hands," he said. "Grab some air with them."

I did, and he patted me down. Up close I could see that he wasn't really commuting from the St. Francis Hotel after all. His thick black hair was a little matted, and the shave he'd given himself—or gotten from Dillon—was as choppy as Lange's recent efforts.

"Holster but no gun?" he asked.

"I'm one book of green stamps shy." It sounded—as Lacey had said of an earlier wisecrack—like the line of an actor playing a detective. That may have been why Remlinger liked it.

He showed me his capped teeth for the first time. "Guess I don't need this," he said, waving the revolver under my nose. "You won't try anything, the stakes being what they are. Still . . ."

He hit me in the face with the gun, snapping his wrist so quickly I never saw the blow coming. I staggered backward, blinded by fireworks.

"You weren't kidding back in Vegas about being a boxer, were you, Elliott? I can tell by the way you crouched a little just then to keep your balance. That was for covering up about Beverly's murder. You knew the truth all along and you kept quiet. Why did you do that, Elliott? Why did you dummy up when you should have been raising hell?"

I tasted blood. It was running down from my right cheekbone, though I couldn't feel the cut. I couldn't feel the cheekbone. "I thought I knew who killed her," I said, bracing myself for the next blow.

Remlinger slipped the pistol into his jacket pocket and left his hand in there with it. "Me, you mean? Why would I hurt her? I loved her. I was her protector. I am her protector."

Robin Hood to a dead Maid Marian. Paddy had been right about everything. Remlinger suddenly seemed less substantial than the sunlight flooding the courtyard. I almost staggered again. "Sorry," I said. "I didn't realize that at the time. I didn't have the Vegas deal figured right."

"And now you do?"

"You were trying to wean Brooks from the pills she was taking."

"Not trying, big brain. I did it. I got her off that poison. I knew the night I met her that it was up to me to do it. Her prickless husband was never going to get the job done. So I did it. And I executed the quack who thought poisoning her was an easy way into her bank account. You heard about what I did to him?"

"I saw it. While his blood was still draining."

"No kidding. Was Maguire there, too?"

I nodded.

"Damn. I wish I'd known you were that close. I would have hung around. You and your boss deserved to be guests at that party, for taking Beverly away from me.

"You know, I never saw her again after you snatched her from my suite. I mean really saw her. I caught a glimpse of her the evening we scouted this place. She was parading around in a bathing suit—with you part of the time. But that was just a few seconds through field glasses, not a real look. I never got a last look thanks to you. Never even really said good-bye to her. Just locked her in her room one day and went off to play cards. Thought I'd see her again a thousand times.

"Tell me something, Elliott. Did you say good-bye to your wife this morning? Watch yourself." He raised his gun without taking it from his jacket pocket. "Come at me again like that, and I'll have to make a hole in my suit. Your suit, too."

"I'd like to see my wife now."

"I bet you would. I know how much I'd like to see Beverly one more time. It's never going to happen for me. It's twisting the knife in my gut just to talk about it. I should give you the Mazar treatment for that alone. But I'm not going to. I'm going to give you a chance to redeem yourself instead. Interested?"

"Let the women go, and I'll listen to any proposition you want to make."

He showed me his teeth again, but not with a smile. "You're not giving any orders around here, smalltime. The women stay. And you're going to do more than listen to my proposition. You're going to jump on board. That's why the women are staying put, so you'll do as you're told."

"What do you want me to do?"

"Better. Much better. I'm glad that big brain of yours is kicking in. You'd be worthless to me without it. I need a detective, and you're the only one handy. You're going to solve a mystery for me. I'm going to give you a piece of information I've come across. You're going to put it into that big brain of yours and give out with the name of Beverly's killer."

"You saw something the night of the crash, when you were up here watching the ranch?"

"That isn't what I'm talking about. The only thing I saw that night was Beverly acting like a tramp. I knew right away that she was sick again, that she was back on those damned pills. We packed up here and headed down to the ranch. I was going to take Beverly away that night and to hell with Gus Graffino's orders and everyone else's. So I missed what happened after you took Beverly back to her cabin.

"I decided to wait until dark to take her. That was the biggest mistake I ever made. Before we could move in, we saw the explosion at the airport. I knew it was that damn plane. And I knew who they'd blame for it."

He was sweating finally, and I realized that I was, too, that my face was streaming. I didn't dare raise a hand to wipe my eyes.

"I didn't know Beverly was on the plane, or I would have gone to her. Ten of you wouldn't have kept me away. But I didn't go far either. The next day we got a paper. I found out they were calling the crash an accident, that I was in the clear. But I also found out that Beverly was dead."

His eyes went into soft focus. After a little of that, he said, "That pilot guy, the old one, Gavin. He told me he found her. That he folded her hands. That true?"

"Yes," I said.

"He told me you covered her with your coat. True?"

I nodded.

"And that you kept some creep from taking her picture."

"Lange did."

Remlinger nodded and drifted off again to reverie land. I stole a glance at the chapel. There was no way of telling whether Ella and Jewel were inside and, if they were, whether Dillon was with them. Without knowing, I couldn't make a move. So I was stuck with Remlinger as a client. Once I admitted that to myself, I was anxious to get to work.

"If you didn't see anything that night, how did you come across this information? Is it something you've seen since?"

"No. It's better than anything you can see through binoculars."

"Who's the source? The same person who told you the crash wasn't an accident?"

"Yeah, but that's more than you need to know. You worry about your own probation. If you want to get through it, you do exactly as I tell you. You listen to what I'm going to say. Then you go back and work it through and bring me the killer. Tonight."

"Tonight?"

"Don't worry. That'll be plenty of time for an experienced man like you. I'd do the job myself, but Lange's made that ranch a little Alcatraz. Just don't get any ideas about turning anyone over to the police. You do all your turning over to me. Understand?"

"Yes," I said.

"And if I see anything like a cop before you come back, there'll be no point in you coming."

Mentioning the police was bad luck for Remlinger and me both. I had a second to picture Sheriff Tyler and wonder how I'd handle him. Then two shots rang out, the first almost covered by the second. I knew before the second shot sounded that the truce we'd worked out was dead and I was next.

The gunfire had come from behind the mission. Remlinger turned his head that way before he could catch himself, and I was on him, my left hand finding his wrist as he tried to pull the gun from his pocket. At the same time, he was falling backward. I expected to land on top of him and pin him, but that wasn't how it happened. He seemed to collapse under me like he wasn't really there. Then he used his legs and my momentum to throw me forward like the apprentice half of a tumbling act. I landed clear of him or almost clear. I still had a death grip on his wrist, which I'd yanked free of his pocket as I'd sailed over his head. I had a second's glimpse of his manicured gun hand as we scrambled to our feet. It was empty.

Remlinger struck first, landing a knee that would have knocked the wind out of me if I'd had any left. I threw a right that snapped his head back. I was setting my weight for another when I spotted the revolver. It was on the ground behind him.

I dove for it first, Remlinger following a half second late and tangling himself in my legs. I kicked him clear as I came up with the gun, and that was a mistake. He'd been shielding me from Dillon, who'd entered the courtyard through a gap in the back wall with his own pistol drawn. He fired at a range of thirty yards and missed.

I fired a wild shot, lying there on my back like a sunbather. Then I dove to my right, rolled once, and came up ready to fire again. All the while, Dillon was blazing away, but the muzzle of his big automatic was still pointing to where I'd been lying when he'd first staggered in.

Even when I fired a second shot—a forlorn hope at that range from a two-inch barrel—he didn't look my way. He pulled his trigger until his gun was empty. Then he fell forward, open-eyed, onto the packed earth.

35

Remlinger was gone. I did an unsteady three-sixty in the center of the courtyard, the revolver cocked and ready. There was nothing to shoot at. I could see that the boards stood undisturbed across the door of the ruined chapel, but I was still torn between going there right away and making sure of Dillon. In the end, I crossed to him, kicked the gun from his hand, and rolled him over. He was still as dead as he'd looked when he'd fallen. It would be up to a coroner to say, but my guess was he hadn't died of a lucky shot from me.

I collected his empty gun—a Browning Hi-Power—and sprinted for the chapel. The dried out old boards blocking the entrance were weightless, or felt that way. Beyond them, the roofless single room was as bright as the courtyard. Sunlight was most of what the room contained, sunlight and rubble and the two women I'd come to find, who were seated on the raised portion of the stone floor where the altar had once stood. They were back to back, tied and gagged.

I removed their gags first. I needn't have bothered as far as Jewel was concerned. Not so Ella.

"Scotty, you okay? It sounded like a battle out there."

"Our side won." I didn't have to ask how she was doing. I'd heard her more worked up over one of the kids' scraped knees.

"Did you get Remlinger?"

Jewel, still tied with her back to Ella, strained to look at me then—imploringly, I thought. I knew I was about to set a personal record for the downhill from hero to goat. "One of the roadblocks will."

"That's how they got us," Ella said as I untied knots I recognized from my work on Harris. "I can't believe we fell for it, Scotty. Not a roadblock exactly. Their car was parked in the middle of the road with the hood up. We stopped to help and that was it."

They got to their feet, Jewel massaging her wrists and my less demure wife her backside. "They didn't hurt you?" I asked.

In reply, Ella took the wispy scarf from her neck and began daubing at my cheek. "Can't you get them to hit you someplace besides your face?"

"I always forget to ask," I said, squeezing her arms. Her eyes started to fill up. It wasn't time for that part of the scene. I gave her a gentle shake. "Will you be okay in here for a while? I'll leave you the gun. We may have a man down out there."

Jewel had turned away to give us some privacy. She crowded in now. "Don't leave us."

"She's right, Scotty. Let's stay together."

"Dillon's out there, dead."

Ella spoke for both of them. "Good."

I led the way out, the gaudy revolver in my hand. I gave the dead gunman a wide berth. As wide a one as I could, anyway, since my goal was the gap in the perimeter wall through which he'd entered. I checked Jewel as we passed the body, expecting to see her averting her eyes. She was examining Dillon, curiously.

Beyond the wall was a stretch of level ground that might once have been anything from a garden to a graveyard. Trees were growing there now, wind-stunted pines as tangled as brambles. On the far side of the little forest we found a car, a Chrysler Imperial. Not far from it, we found Daniel Irwin.

He was seated on the ground, his back against a boulder. My gun lay next to him. His face was as white as his tennis shirt had once been. It was stained now with red, the wound looking like a clown's boutonniere pinned to his left shoulder.

Irwin was still conscious. "Did a little recon," he said when I crouched over him. "Thought I'd come up behind them. Walked right into one of them. Dillon, I guess. I think I got him, too."

"You did," I said.

There was someone beside me, holding Irwin's hand. I assumed it was Ella, but when I got around to looking, I saw Jewel. That freed my wife for more important work. I handed her the revolver.

"We have to get him down in a hurry. Keep watch."

I checked the Imperial for keys, but I'd used up all my breaks for the moment. I reentered the compound and searched Irwin's dueling partner. In one coat pocket, I found a heavy metal cylinder, threaded at one end. A noise suppressor for the Browning. The car keys were in his hip pocket.

We loaded Irwin into the sedan, me carrying his body and Jewel cradling his head. I shut her in the back with him, and we started out, crawling at first along a stony ledge that led around to the front of the mission and the start of the switchback road.

I drove us down it was fast as I safely could, slowing only for the hairpin turns. I didn't give the turn where I'd left the Thunderbird any special treatment. I expected the T-Bird to be gone, and it was.

"Remlinger stole my car," I said to Ella, who was riding shotgun.

"Let me guess," she said. "Now you're *really* mad."

Lange and two of his finest were waiting at the bottom of the hill next to one of the production company's cars. Nearby were two sheriff's deputies, ruefully examining their own car, which was nose down in a ditch.

"We were just about to start up when we saw you coming down," Lange said, smiling at Ella in spite of himself. "Remlinger ran Tyler's men off the road just before we got here. They thought it was you in the T-Bird until it was too late. Now he's halfway to who knows where."

Sirens were approaching and we waited for them, figuring a black-and-white would be Irwin's fastest ticket to help. I told Lange the news about Dillon, which he took as well as Ella had. And I described the trade Remlinger had tried to make—the killer for the women—and how the gunfight had broken it up before Remlinger could pass on his information.

"Amateurs," Lange said in disgust as the reinforcements pulled up.

While he was supervising the transfer of the amateur in question to the squad car, Ella took me aside.

"You think Remlinger just wanted us as hostages?"

I recognize a feint every once in a while. I thought I did now, so I didn't answer.

"I think he wanted to question Jewel," Ella said. "She was the one he was after. He was happy enough to get me, I guess because I guaranteed your cooperation. But I was just a bonus. I decided to ride along with Jewel at the last minute. Remlinger can't have known I was going to be there to kidnap."

Only an hour earlier, I would have borrowed Irwin's answer and told Ella that Remlinger had spotted her joining Jewel from his mountain observation post. I'd since driven the route backward, from the dip in the road to the mission, and I knew Remlinger couldn't have made it in time, not if he'd waited to leave until Jewel and Ella and Harris were moving. Either the gangster had staked out the road and taken whomever he got, or Lange was right after all, and we had a spy inside the ranch.

My wife had come over to the same way of thinking. "Someone on our side isn't, Scotty."

"What did Remlinger ask Jewel?"

"I don't know. Dillon took me outside while she was being questioned. I could hear him talking, but I couldn't make out what he was asking her."

At that moment, Jewel was being dissuaded—almost forcibly—from accompanying Irwin to the hospital. When he'd been dispatched, we rode back to Crowe Ranch, Jewel between Ella and me in the backseat of Lange's car. I should have pumped her there and then, but I didn't, not trusting Lange's driver. Not even trusting Lange completely, though I knew the feeling was crazy.

It was the only chance I'd get to question her, at least for a while. Lillian Lacey was waiting at the ranch gate when we pulled in. She looked like a touring company Medea, with her makeup smeared and her red hair streaming down uncombed.

She fussed over Jewel, embracing her, thanking God and Ella and me for her safe deliverance. For once, Jewel returned the hugs. When they'd gotten that out of their systems, Lacey passed her daughter to the waiting Hilly, who was standing nearby, looking about as natural out-of-doors as a commode.

"Take her upstairs, Hilly," Lacey said. "See that she lies down."

"I'd like to talk to her first," I said.

I saw Jewel draw away. Then Lacey was standing between us. "What, now? Are you mad, Scotty? You know what she's been through, what you've all been through. There'll be time enough later, when we're sure she's all right."

I looked to Ella for help and didn't get any. "Later would be better, Scotty." She took off after the departing maid and Jewel.

Lacey lingered. "It's not that I'm ungrateful," she said. "I'll be grateful forever for what you've done. I was a fool to think we could carry on with that monster on the loose. They'll get him now, won't they?"

"Yes," I said.

She took that slight consolation away with her, leaving me alone. Or almost alone. Lange was nearby, redeploying his forces. I interrupted.

"I need a car."

"For what?"

"I'm going to Heston."

"Wait a minute, and I may be able to save you the trip. The hospital called with an answer to that note you left for Ford. I forgot all about it. He said Pioline didn't do anything when he got back to the airfield with Brooks except climb in the plane."

That sank Ella's attempt to draw Cararra back in. There'd been no time for anyone hidden in Pioline's car to tinker with the *Argo*.

"Is that what you were going after?" Lange asked. "Or were you looking to get your cheek stitched up?"

"Neither," I said, holding out my hand. "I'm going to shoot up a newspaper."

Lange dropped his keys into my open palm. "Have fun," he said.

36

It was my second drive to Heston that day, but it felt as though years had passed. It wasn't just that I was driving a borrowed sedan, that I was sweat-stained and dirty, that my hands smelled of gunpowder and my left cheek and the eye above it both ached. I felt older, more than a few hours older. Older and wiser.

Questioning Jewel being out for the moment, I'd decided to track down Remlinger's spy. I might have done it by searching everyone for carrier pigeons or keeping watch on the cookhouse phone or starting some hot rumor going and waiting to see who waved signal flags at the mission. But I didn't have that much time to spend. So I'd decided on a shortcut. A grandstand play. A big scene.

I'd tried to track a ranch informant down once before, but not very hard. On the morning after the crash, when the *Heston Herald* had told the world that Beverly Brooks was using drugs supplied by Marcus Pioline, I'd gone to see the paper's editor, Doc Beard. He'd declined to tell me who had sold him the story, and I'd left it at that.

Now I'd stumbled across another secret informant, and I was figuring the odds of two of them operating in so small a place as Crowe Ranch to be long in the extreme. Those odds suggested that what we really had was one informant, one opportunist, selling to all comers. So I was on my way to readdress my question to Beard.

There might have been more going on. I'd been in an ugly mood ever since I'd let Remlinger slip away with no more than a sore jaw after all he'd done and all he'd threatened to do. I may have been planning to take a little of my frustration out on Beard, a man who'd rubbed my nose in it once, to put it mildly. If so, I was every bit the bastard that Irwin had pegged me for. Well, novelists were paid to be perceptive.

I found a parking space in front of the Herald Building, a shady space. I sat in it long enough to examine Dillon's Browning. Ella had handed Remlinger's revolver over to one of Tyler's men like the responsible citizen she was, but I'd somehow forgotten the Hi-Power. I verified now that it was truly empty, clip and chamber. Then I put it back in my pocket and went inside.

The newsroom was quieter today. I actually heard the bell on the front door tinkle as I shut it behind me. The room's two occupants looked up, and one of them kept looking, the cub reporter whose coffee I'd stolen. He even smiled, though whether that was because he was happy to see me or because I looked like I'd been in a train wreck, I couldn't say.

"Where is everybody?" I asked. "Siesta?"

"They're on their way to the old mission. There was a shooting out there, in case you haven't heard."

"I heard the shots," I said to get the kid's full attention. "And it's an *asistencia*, not a mission. Your boss in?"

"Yes," he said, properly pop-eyed.

"Alone?"

"Yes."

"This place have a back stairs?"

"Yes."

"A back door, too?"

"Yeah," he said, but his eyes were narrowing fast. "Why do you want to know?"

"I think I'm being followed. What's out back? Paint me a word picture."

"It's just an alley. There's our loading dock. And the back of the hardware store on the next street. The hardware guys set up a horseshoe pitch. They're always in the way of our delivery trucks."

"Thanks," I said. "I feel like I've been there. Keep a lookout for me. If you see a one-legged man in a slouch hat, ring Beard's phone once and hang up."

I climbed the rickety stairs to the second floor, feeling my climb to the mission again in my calves and shins. Beard's office was easy to find. I just followed the sound of his voice. He was speaking on the phone, maybe to a deaf person, demanding news of the wounded man who had been rushed to the county hospital. I waited in the hallway until he hung up in disgust. Then I stepped into his office and shut the door behind me.

The room was bigger than the supply closet where we'd had our last chat. Otherwise, it didn't have much going for it. The walls lacked the newspaperman's usual collection of grainy photographs, but I did spot an explanation for Beard's nickname: a framed diploma from a school in Missouri certifying his doctorate in journalism.

"Elliott," Beard said. "The man himself. The man of the hour. Talk about the mountain coming to Mohammed. Don't tell me you're actually going to be of some use to me."

"Not if I can help it."

"You're not here about the shooting at the mission?"

"Not to talk about it."

"What do you want then?" He didn't know, but he was already scared. A vein in one of the hollows of his forehead was throbbing. The look of me had gotten it going, the burned-out, used-up look. You can't beat typecasting.

"I want the same thing I wanted the last time I was here, the name of the source for the slander story on Marcus Pioline."

He stretched himself out in his chair, all phony nonchalance. "I'll give you the same answer. Take a hike. That name is privileged information. Protected by the Constitution of the United States. Like I told you, you can't win a wrestling match with a newspaper."

"I wasn't figuring on wrestling." I produced the Browning, slowly.

"What the hell is that?"

"My court order. Ready to laugh at it?"

He gave it a try. "You've got to be crazy. You think you can bluff me with that?"

"I am feeling a little crazy this evening." I backtracked to the office door and locked it. "My wife was held hostage this afternoon, up at old San Ignacio. She could have been the one they rushed to the hospital. Or she could have died up there, like a gunman named Dillon did. This belonged to Dillon, by the way."

I thought about drawing the blinds, but the only witnesses were the trees in Heston Park. I sat down on the edge of the desk instead.

"My wife is still in danger. We all are until Johnny Remlinger is caught. He has a spy at the ranch. I think it's the same one you have. When you tell me who it is, I'll be that much closer to Remlinger."

"You're that much closer to jail, buddy. I'm going to turn you in for this. And I don't mean to your pal Tyler."

"After you tell me the name of your source, you can call J. Edgar Hoover for all I care."

"I'm sorry, Elliott," Beard said, his concern undercut by a nervous licking of his lips. "I understand your problem. I'd like to help you. But there are principles at stake."

"Lives, too," I said.

"Who's going to protect your wife when you're in jail? You think you can just murder me and walk away? You were seen coming in here."

"Actually, I wasn't. I came in through the alley. The hardware clerks weren't pitching horseshoes today."

Beard swallowed, elaborately. "They'll see you leave. Somebody will hear the shot."

"Thanks for reminding me." I pulled out the suppressor and threaded it onto the Browning's barrel. I'd forgotten to rehearse that in the car. It would have been a good joke on me if it hadn't fit. It screwed on almost effortlessly.

"Like I said, I got this toy from Dillon. After he was dead, naturally. When they autopsy you, they'll find a bullet that matches the one they're digging out of Daniel Irwin right now. He's the guy they rushed to the hospital. You'll be another victim of the gangster crime spree. Unless you talk."

I had to give Beard credit. A lot of people in his spot would have been babbling. His brain was still in gear. "Dillon's been dead for hours. No one will believe he shot me. Not even Tyler."

"Didn't I tell you? Johnny Remlinger picked this up as he escaped. That's the way I remember it; and I was the only witness."

I yanked back the slide on the automatic for something to do. "Last chance," I said, thinking that it was mine, that Beard spilled now or I tossed in my cards.

"Her name is Cararra. Nicole Cararra. She called me here the night of the crash. I mean early the next morning, two or three A.M. She sold me the Pioline drug angle."

"How'd you pay her?"

"One of my guys slipped her an envelope during Lacey's press conference. Cararra was supposed to give us a follow-up, but she hasn't."

"She's been a busy girl," I said. I unthreaded the silencer and tucked it and the Browning away.

The pale was coming back into Beard's sunken cheeks. By the time I reached his door, he felt safe enough to threaten me. "I'll be sending the cops out to see you," he said.

"Thanks. We'll need them tonight."

37

I'd last seen Cararra entering Crowe House on Lange's arm, way back before the day's excitement had started, but I didn't go to the main house to find her. I drove to the cottage grove, to Beverly Brooks's little bungalow. It was the logical place to look for her ghost.

Cararra was lounging behind the cottage, on the sandy patio where I'd knocked Daniel Irwin on his artistic pretensions. A place I remembered fondly, to be honest. Despite the concentrated heat of the long day, she was wearing the same black and beige suit Lange and I had found her in earlier. She'd lost her hat and gauntlets, though. She might have traded them for the wine bottles on the little table beside her and the stemmed glass in her hand. She'd been using the latter to empty the former, or so I inferred from her greeting.

"Not dead yet, Elliott? That's a shame."

"No fault of yours," I said, sitting in a second chair and tossing my hat onto a third.

"I don't know what you're talking about, as usual."

I wasn't exactly sure myself, also as usual. A dozen possibilities had been dancing around in my head since I'd left Beard, each one more fantastic than the last. Now, facing Cararra, I wondered if any of them was fantastic enough. She looked that changed, that transformed. Not by the wine. By something like the shock that turns a person's hair white overnight in story-books. Her hair was still as dark as a bijou balcony, but the rest of her had aged. The youth that had been threatening to burst her skin, which had been nine-tenths of her beauty, was gone, leaving her whole being oddly slack. I was reminded—as I'd been at the Sherwood lunch counter—of the dead Brooks. Cararra's resemblance to her had been her fortune, but the link seemed to have continued after Brooks's death. In some twist out of Poe, Cararra was keeping pace with the body in the morgue.

To shake that morbid chain of thought, I grabbed at its only tangible link—the memory of the lunch counter—and used it as my starting point.

"What was that stunt this morning all about?"

"What stunt? I changed my mind about the movie. It's not the best vehicle for me. It's going to be a disaster, and I don't want to be in a disaster. So I decided to go away."

"You weren't very certain about where you were going."

"What do you mean now? Talk simpler."

I checked the level of the last bottle and decided I'd have to. "You bought a ticket to LA but wouldn't get on the bus."

"I changed my mind again. I've been to Los Angeles. Los Angeles stinks, and I don't mean the oil refineries. City of Angels. City of Angles is more like it."

"Mind if I use that one?"

"Use the door, Elliott. Use your flat feet." She used her wine-glass again.

"So you were going to get onto the San Francisco bus when it came?"

"Of course. Yes. What do you think?"

"I think you were going to make another excuse. I think you were going to trade tickets all day if you had to. I don't think you were waiting for any bus. I think you were waiting for me."

The death's-head leered at me. "Because I'm in love with you?"

"Because Johnny Remlinger told you to wait. He told you to go there in the first place. He wanted to get his hands on Jewel.

You told him how he could do it. You knew she'd be rushed to the shooting site if you took a powder. And you knew that Lange or I or both of us would be sent after you, making Remlinger's job that much easier."

"I didn't know it," Cararra said quietly. "He knew it. It was all his idea. He thought of everything. Then he made me do it."

"Remlinger?"

She nodded, but wouldn't look at me. "He came here last night. I woke up, and he was standing next to my bed. He'd come to kill me. He was mad over me taking Bebe's part. Like Danny, he thought I was replacing her. He didn't see that I was helping her.

"He pulled the sheet off me. I was naked. I thought he might rape me before he murdered me. He didn't. He looked at me like I was unclean. The way you're looking at me now."

I wasted a few seconds wondering whether Remlinger had been struck like me by the impression that Cararra was decomposing. Then I concentrated on the lie Cararra was telling me.

"Why didn't he kill you?"

"He had a use for me. He wanted to talk to Jewel, but he didn't dare enter Crowe House. There were too many guards. I don't know why he wanted to see her. He made me tell him about this morning's call sheet. I didn't want to, but I was frightened to death, naked and alone with him. So I told him that I had the early call, and Jewel would come out to the site later. Remlinger told me I shouldn't go to the site. I should pretend to run away. So I did. I did it to save my life. I'm sorry for Jewel, but I was frightened."

"Being naked and alone," I added, comfortingly. "What else did you tell him?"

"What? Nothing. That's all."

"Nothing about the night Brooks died?"

"No."

"Let me put it another way. Why did Remlinger come back here?"

It was the question I should have asked as soon as Harris the guard had gotten the word Remlinger past his bloody lips. Why had the gangster come back? He hadn't known about the gust lock. He hadn't known Brooks's death was murder. He'd punished the men who were poisoning her with drugs. Why then had he come back?

I hadn't thought to ask the question until after my tête-à-tête with Beard, and what I'd learned from the editor had contributed to the answer I'd come up with.

Cararra hadn't come up with anything, not even a convincing blank look. So I said, "Let's start with another subplot. Why did you sell the local paper that story about Pioline giving Brooks her pills?"

"Me? I tried to protect Bebe's reputation. I wouldn't even tell you the truth about the pills."

"I remember that performance. It was nice work. All those speeches about lying newspapers. Turns out you knew they were lying because you were the one selling them the lies. Don't say you weren't. Your editor friend gave me your name, under duress. And the reporter who made the payoff can identify you."

Cararra switched to defiance, her old standby. "So I called them, so what?"

"Why did you do that to the friend who'd given you so much?"

"Because she hadn't given me enough. That's what I realized when I knew she was dead. It was all promises, nothing in hand." She held one limp hand out, palm up, and slapped it with the back of the other. "I couldn't even pay my way back to Los Angeles. So I got myself some traveling money. A stake. You understand? Bebe was dead. Nothing I said could hurt her."

"How about Pioline? You hurt his reputation with the story about the pills."

"Newspapers don't pay for nothing. They pay for dirt. Bebe was getting drugs from somewhere. Why not from Pioline, the old pig? So he wasn't the one after all. So I'm sorry."

"Pretty neat package. I'm tying up a different one myself. I think you named Pioline as the provider of Brooks's pills so no one would spend much time looking for the real source. Namely you."

Cararra leered again. "I have my explanation, you have yours."

"Mine's better than yours. It explains how the *Herald*'s source knew the pills were tranquilizers, even though they had anything but a tranquilizing effect on Brooks. It also answers the question I asked you just now: Why did Remlinger come back? I was assuming all along that he'd only show himself around here again if he found out that Brooks was murdered. I never even thought of another possibility, that there might be a person unaccounted for in the drug scheme, someone Remlinger would want to punish.

"I'm figuring it like this. I led Remlinger to Clay Ford, who gave him enough information to track down Guy De Felice, who led him to Dr. Mazar. That was the end of the line, I thought, but suppose that, while he was tearing around Mazar's temple, Remlinger found some mention of another Mazar employee. You."

Cararra was still smiling. "What did he find, my time card? My pay stub? My social security number?"

I'd taken a misstep, but I had an alternate route as a backup. "Clay Ford is pretty depressed—despondent you'd say—and not over his legs being broken. He's acting like he handed his mother to Remlinger, and that's puzzled me. Okay, two men are dead who might not have been if he'd kept quiet, but they were nothing to Ford and pill pushers into the bargain. So why is he being so hard on himself?"

I'd managed to wipe the grin off the skull across from me. No easy trick.

"Suppose he gave Remlinger another name, one he hadn't shared with me. He spoke of the woman who had set up the pill transfer, and I jumped to the conclusion that he meant Brooks, a conclusion he was careful not to correct. And he never explained why he'd risk a soft job to pass Brooks her medicine. It's the kind of boneheaded thing a man in love will do. So Ford might have been in love with Brooks. There's a lot of that going around. Only he never went near her on the hillside where the plane crashed.

"So I'm thinking it was you he was in love with. That you were using him and letting him use you in exchange. He'd have risked his job to keep you happy and swallowed any explanation you gave him.

"Then Remlinger got hold of him, and Ford gave you up. That's what's killing him now, the sap. He'd be better off mourning De Felice."

The skull's dark eyes flashed at that. "What do you know, Elliott? You know everything and nothing. You don't know how I felt about Clay. How I still feel about him. I know what he went through with Remlinger and Dillon. I went through the same thing last night. They came here—right under your nose—to kill me."

She reached into the pocket of her suit coat. I slid my hand inside my own jacket, even though it was obvious from the cut of hers that the tailor hadn't allowed room for firearms. What Cararra produced was a bottle full of blue and white pills, identical to the ones that had been scattered across Mazar's floor.

"He was going to force these down my throat. Remlinger. He said he hoped I had nightmares I never woke from."

"Because you were working for Mazar."

"No, damn you. Because I set it up with Clay to carry Bebe's medicine from Los Angeles. Bebe asked me to. I did it because I was her friend."

"Sorry to keep coming up with variations on your themes," I said, "but I can't help wondering about the timing. You only knew Brooks for a few weeks, the same few weeks she was involved with Mazar. It could be a coincidence, or it could be you steered Brooks Mazar's way. Or it could have been just the reverse. Mazar could have told her that some dream she'd had meant that she was going to meet a new friend. Maybe a best friend, a sister. A dark sister. Which way did it happen?"

"You'll never know."

She was probably right. With Mazar and Brooks both dead, I probably would never know for sure. "Answer a hypothetical question for me. Why were the pill shipments so small?"

"I'd only be guessing," she said, uninterested.

"So guess."

"It could have been because the drugs were so dangerous, the pills to make you dream and the ones to let you sleep through the dreams. Dangerous in big numbers. A dead patient would be bad for business. Or it could have been Mazar's way of staying in control."

"Of Brooks or his staff?"

"Both. What did you say the other guy's name was?"

"De Felice."

"Mazar might not have trusted him."

"What was Mazar after from Brooks? Irwin said she didn't pay him much."

"More guessing you want? Anyone can guess that. If he was explaining her dreams to her he could influence her, persuade her to invest in phony deals he set up. Schemes Danny never heard of. That's what I would guess."

"Let's get back to what you know, like what you told Remlinger to save your life."

She tried to wait me out, but her attention span wasn't up to it. "I told him his precious Bebe had been murdered. I'd heard you and Danny yelling about the gust lock before you hit him, but I wasn't sure what you meant until I phoned Clay at the airfield. He told me all about it. It was all he could talk about, how the crash had been no accident and that no one would believe him. It saved me, knowing that. When I told Remlinger that last night, he forgot about everything else."

"Why didn't you come to me after he'd gone?"

She held up the pill bottle. "Why didn't I just take these and get it over with? He left these as a reminder of what he could still do to me."

"What else did you tell him?"

"That I'd lied to you about Bebe and Pioline being lovers. And about them planning to run away together. She couldn't stand the sight of him, not when she was herself. When she was using the pills, she didn't care. Any man was fine. Remlinger never saw the joke in that, the—what do you call it?—the irony. When he met Bebe she was as high as the price of a decent life. She went with him because she was high. But he had to get noble and cure her. So she leaves him. If he had left well enough alone, they would have lived happily ever after."

"Why did you change your story about Brooks and Pioline?"

"For this," Cararra said, gesturing toward the cottage. That she gestured with the pill bottle was an irony *she* failed to see. "For my chance. Now I won't live long enough to make good on it."

"Who told you to lie to me?"

The stillborn star was looking around at the trappings she'd inherited. As frightened as she was, she wasn't handing anything back. "I didn't tell Remlinger that. I'm not telling you."

I got to my feet. I thought about going through my routine with the Browning again, but I decided not to bother. Cararra had already stood up under worse. "You told Remlinger something else. You must have. He promised me a clue that would lead me to the murderer. What else did he shake out of you?"

"Just something I heard Pioline say that last night. Nothing that will help you."

"Tell me."

"Bebe had gotten away from me. She ran up to the main house with me following. Pioline was there on the front steps, talking to that awful maid, the little dried-up woman."

"Hilly?"

"She had hold of his arm. He pulled away from her and ran right into Bebe. She begged him to take her away with him. I thought Pioline would help me get her back down here, but he didn't. He acted like he knew he would be dead in an hour and didn't give a damn. And he said something strange, like, 'You're Jewel's sister, right? The other princess. That makes me your stepfather.'

"Bebe said he could be anything he wanted to be if he'd take her away. Then he shrugged and said, 'They can only hang me once.' "

38

I left Cararra to finish her wine or pills or both in peace. Anyone watching me go would have thought that I'd been the one hitting the bottle. I was dead-footed, shuffling, unseeing. I should say I was finally seeing, that I was blinded by the light of a revelation. This dawn came with a sound track. It was Ella doing a voice-over, explaining again that she couldn't have been the target of Remlinger's kidnapping because she'd only joined the expedition at the last minute.

The gist of my brainstorm was this: I'd spent nearly three days trying to solve the wrong murder, Beverly Brooks's murder. I'd concentrated on her from the start, the woman with all the lovers and all the woes. I'd only considered Pioline in the context of Brooks, certain he'd died because he'd made the mistake of keeping the wrong company.

Cararra's latest story had stood all that on its head. Brooks couldn't have been the murderer's intended victim any more than Ella had been Remlinger's. Like Ella, Brooks had been a last-second addition to the passenger list. She'd had no secret arrangement with Pioline for the murderer to discover, no long-running affair to drive someone like Daniel Irwin nuts with jealousy. All she'd had was enough methaqualone in her system to make Pioline look good. She'd picked a condemned man, and taken his last walk with him.

If Brooks's reasons for tagging along had ended up being simpler than I'd imagined, Pioline's motives for taking her had tangled themselves like old Christmas lights. The move had been about more than a roll in the hay. It had somehow involved Jewel—the cause of everything, as Ella had said from the start.

And there they were, Jewel and Ella, coming down the hill toward me under the watchful eye of Knific, junior member of Lange's crumbling firm.

"Mr. Lange asked me to walk the ladies down," he said. Then he looked to the west, toward the sun's feeble good-bye wave, a rosy glow over the hills. The edgy Lange must have looked in the same direction when he'd given Knific his assignment.

"Sheriff Tyler's up there with him," Knific added. "The sheriff's plenty steamed over Remlinger getting away. He says you and Mr. Irwin shouldn't have gone up to the mission until all the roadblocks were set."

"Any word on Irwin?"

Jewel started to answer. Ella shut her up with a hand on her arm. Knific said: "We heard he's out of danger. Except from Sheriff Tyler."

"Thanks," I said. "I'll take it from here." I would have liked to have kept the kid—and his sidearm—around, but I didn't want him overhearing my interview with Jewel. "Tell your boss and the sheriff that Remlinger got onto the ranch last night."

I didn't have to pass on the rest of the warning. Knific glanced toward the west again. "I'll tell him."

As soon as he'd gone, Jewel blurted out the speech she'd had corked up. "I'd like to go to the hospital to see Danny. To thank him. Ella said you'd take me."

I looked to my wife for confirmation. "I had to get her someplace where you could talk to her, Scotty. In private. Maybe on the way to the hospital."

"How'd you persuade Lacey to let her go?"

"I didn't. Lillie's in conference with Max. Jewel and I left her a note and walked out." She then downshifted into the slow, careful speech she used with our kids when she meant business.

"You have to talk with her, Scotty. Jewel's been hinting around about what Remlinger asked her. I think it's important."

"I know it is," I said. "I just spoke with Remlinger's dialogue coach. We'll go down to the cottage."

"What about the hospital?" Jewel asked.

"Let's talk first. Then we'll see."

I searched our little rooms for hidden gangsters while Ella and Jewel settled in by the cold fireplace. When I'd finished with the bedroom, I collected the thirty-two I'd hidden under the mattress, the gun I'd taped to the doorframe in Vegas a hundred years earlier. I slipped it into my belt, my pockets being laden with the Browning and its silencer and my shoulder holster full of Colt. Three-gun Elliott, they call me, the paranoid operative.

For once Ella and Jewel weren't side by side. My wife was on the little love seat, while her secondhand daughter had chosen an old morris chair across from her. I was happy enough to claim the empty spot on the couch. Ella could pat my hand if Jewel no longer required the treatment.

At the moment, Jewel was watching us both, uneasily. She might have been thinking that we needed to clean up a bit. She had, maybe in one of her restorative baths. She was wearing her artist's smock again. It seemed to me now less a tenuous connection to her past life than a clever disguise.

"Tell Scotty what Remlinger asked you," Ella said.

"No," Jewel said flatly. "I shouldn't have mentioned it to you. I shouldn't have trusted you."

"You've never trusted us," I said. "If you had, you and Ella wouldn't have ended up bound and gagged today." That didn't get a reaction, so I added, "And Irwin wouldn't have gotten himself shot."

"I never meant for him to get hurt," Jewel said. "Or anyone else. But it keeps happening. I keep making it happen."

"You?" Ella asked. "How?"

Jewel only had eyes for me. It was as though her bond with Ella had been transferred to me. Or to some movie-inspired hope I represented.

"Remlinger asked you about your relationship with your step-father, didn't he?" I said.

Beside me, Ella stirred, wanting to ask me how I knew. Jewel showed no such curiosity. So far, I was still an Alfred Hitchcock hero. *The Man Who Knew Too Much.* Oddly, I was starting to feel as though I did.

"He didn't call it a relationship," Jewel said.

"What did he call it?"

She shuddered. "I didn't tell him anything. I didn't tell anyone who could have told him. But he *knew.* You didn't believe me last night when I said that Remlinger might be more than a criminal. More than a man. But he knew things without me telling him."

I cut in before she could really spook herself. "He knew because your stepfather told him. Not directly. But not from beyond the grave, either. Did Remlinger ask you whether you were having sex with your stepfather?"

"Scotty," Ella whispered.

"Sorry," I said to the room in general. "We haven't time to talk around it. We're almost out of time."

"Remlinger didn't talk around it," Jewel said. "He whispered in my ear, but they weren't words it helps to whisper. He asked if I was fucking my stepdaddy. Fucking him behind my old mother's back. I told him no," she said, her unnatural calm cracking. "I told him *no!*"

"What did happen between you and Pioline?"

"What Remlinger already knew. What everybody who looks at me knows." She glanced one last time toward Ella. "My step-daddy fucked *me!* I didn't have right words for it until today. I always thought he raped me. I thought that was the worst way you could say it. Even that's too polite. Too worn out. He fucked me. Fucked me. Fucked me!"

She was on her feet, and Ella was beside her. My wife might have stayed with me for all the comfort she was to Jewel, who drew away at her touch, as I'd seen her draw away from her mother's.

"You knew," Jewel spat at her. "You all knew. You knew there was something wrong with me. That's why you pitied me. Why everyone else treated me like I didn't matter. Everyone who looks at me can tell!"

"Sit down," I said, just loud enough for Jewel to hear me. She towered over me for a second, a youthful re-creation of her mother's performance as mad Boudica, all burning eyes and wild hair. Then she sat mechanically, Ella kneeling beside her.

"When did it happen?" I was still underplaying and doing it easily. I felt as cold and dead as the blackened stones in the hearth.

"Five years ago. I was fifteen. Marcus and my mother were still married then. They'd fight sometimes, over his women, but they hadn't had their big fight yet.

"I'd just gotten home from school. Marcus was there. My mother was away on tour. He came into my room. He talked to me about my classes. He didn't often do that. I should have suspected something, but I didn't. I should have known from the way he'd been looking at me for months before that, when he'd barely noticed me all my life.

"He told me how pretty I was. How tall and beautiful I'd become. Then he was touching me, pawing my breasts and pulling him down to me, the little man. I was dizzy, faint, ashamed before it even happened. Burning with the shame of it. I still feel that heat. It's the only part I can feel."

"It wasn't your fault," Ella said.

"He said it was. He said I'd forced it on him by being beautiful and acting like I wanted him. I never wanted him. I'd never thought of him that way. Hadn't had thoughts like that about boys even. Since then, I haven't been able to think of any boy— of any man—without thinking of him. He never came near me again, but that hasn't helped."

They can only hang me once. That's what Pioline had said to Brooks, Jewel's fairy-tale sister, as he'd carried her off. Cararra had been telling the truth for once. "You told your mother."

"Not right away. Not for years. But not because I believed it really had been my fault. Marcus said if I told her it would be the end of their marriage, that my mother would never forgive him or me. So I kept quiet. It didn't save their marriage. Not for very long. After they'd divorced, I let it out. I was having trouble at school. Trouble at everything. I broke down one day and told her."

"What did she do?"

"Nothing at first. She was afraid of what the scandal would do . . . what it would do to me. Then *Warrior Queen* came along, and everything changed. Mother told me it was Marcus's way of trying to make amends. That he was going to give me this wonderful gift: stardom. I didn't want it, but I couldn't make her understand that. I couldn't make her see that this was the rape all over again: tearing me out of my school, dressing me up like a whore, showing me off that way to every man with the price of a ticket. She couldn't understand why I wouldn't jump at the chance to strip for her beloved camera. She thought I was just embarrassed, shy. Even when I made her understand that it was the fucking I'd taken that made me feel this way, she wouldn't back down.

"She's like that—blunt, direct. It may be the war that did it to her. She had to carry on back then, never mind what she felt when my father was killed. That's her solution for everything. Carry on and you'll get through it. She was the same when she was trying to teach me to ride. Riding came naturally to her, so it had to come naturally to me. If you fall off a horse, you just get back on. If I was ashamed of myself, ashamed of my body and what it could do to men, I should parade around in CinemaScope for every man in the world to see. Then I'd get over it. She might as well have put me to work in a brothel."

Jewel was crying finally, crying on Ella's shoulder. It was the moment to fade to black, but I still had some lines. "Did Remlinger ask you if you'd killed your stepfather?"

Jewel looked up, frightened all over again. "Yes," she said.

"What did you tell him?"

"That I couldn't have, not even if I'd wanted to. I don't know anything about airplanes."

"Daniel Irwin does. He could have told you all you needed to know, after you'd described what Pioline had done to you."

"No," Jewel said, her barometric skin suddenly white. "I've never told him what happened to me. Never talked to him really. But I think he's someone I can tell. He's someone I want to tell."

"I didn't do anything to Marcus but wish him dead. You've got to believe me."

Remlinger must have. He was ready to send me out to find the killer when he'd already had Jewel safely locked away. For once the gangster and I were in sync.

"The night of the crash, after you heard the explosion and rushed outside, where did you go?"

"Nowhere," Jewel said. "I told you before I don't know. I was frightened."

Not half as frightened as she was now. I got up, drawing Ella to her feet in the same motion. I handed her the thirty-two.

"Other wives get flowers," she said. "I keep getting guns."

"I'm leaving you in a bad spot," I said. "But you're as safe here as anywhere on the ranch. Keep your eyes open until I get back. Shoot anyone who isn't whistling 'Take the "A" Train.' "

"What about Danny?" Jewel asked. "You were going to take me to see him." She was less beaten up by our talk than I was. There was no substitute for youth.

"I'll take you tomorrow if you still want to go. When it's light again." Even a middle-aged guy could hope.

39

Tyler was still in the main yard near the cookhouse when I got there. And he was still, as Knific had delicately put it, steamed. If anything, he'd gotten steamier, thanks to Lange. The two were going at each other, standing toe to toe in a pool of light cast by a bug-proof bulb on the corner of the building. Their argument—about me and the roadblocks—had put some starch back into Lange. I silently thanked the sheriff for that as I stepped into the ring.

"There you are," Tyler said, making my arrival official. "You bollixed that business this afternoon. Bollixed it good. I trusted you, but you wouldn't trust me. You bollixed it up, and Remlinger got away. Any murders he commits from now on will be on your head."

"Whose head would it have been on if his wife had gotten killed this afternoon?" Lange demanded, taking the words out of my mouth. That is, those would have been my words if I'd had any interest in Tyler's lament.

I spotted Knific waiting just outside the yellow circle, and I called to him. "Do me a favor. Find Bud for me. He's the foreman."

"I know Bud," the big kid said. "We're practically sleeping together." He waited for a nod from Lange, which was only right. Then he trotted off.

Tyler showed his age then by pushing on with a topic that everyone else had left behind, as an old man will. "You're damn lucky your wife didn't get hit in that shooting gallery you and Irwin set up."

"I feel the same way about it." The shooting-gallery crack reminded me that it was time for a little disarmament.

As I reached for the Browning, Tyler gave me an even better lead-in. "You still owe me an official statement of what went on up there."

"Here's something on account," I said, and handed him the gun and silencer. "I took those from Dillon. After he was dead. It's the gun he used to shoot Irwin and God knows who else."

"Any fingerprints left on it besides yours?" Tyler asked.

I shrugged. I was one big shrug on the subject of Dillon. "Maybe on the clip. It's empty, by the way."

The sheriff stepped closer and spoke softer. "I heard a rumor that someone waved a gun like this under the nose of one of our leading citizens earlier this evening."

I caught a hint of a smile in the shadows underneath the Stetson. The old man was close to forgiving me for spoiling his roadblocks. He was that tickled. If I'd winged Beard, I would have been free and clear.

"News to me," I said.

"His word against yours, huh? It's been my experience that that defense doesn't work so well when one of the parties runs a newspaper. I may have to haul you in yet."

I almost said that he was welcome to lock me up and throw away the key if he gave me an hour to tie up loose ends. It was the moment for a cryptic gibe like that, something to let the boys know I'd solved the murder. They could ask admiring questions, questions I'd put off with a promise to explain all later. That would have been sweet, after all the stumbling around I'd done. It would have been a kindness to Lange, too, to have told him we were close to making Johnny Remlinger someone else's albatross.

But I didn't say it. I wasn't ready to share Jewel's confidences. Which meant that, wherever they led me, I had to go alone.

I was saved from replying by the approach of Bud. I spotted him and Knific passing through the light spilling from the open back door of the kitchen. I told Tyler and Lange I'd be right back and crossed to meet the foreman.

Knific stood nearby during the interview, which was fine by me. We all have to learn sometime. Bud was wearing a gun tonight like the rest of us. His was a big Wild West revolver strapped to his hip. If Remlinger did show up, there was going to be one hell of a cross fire.

"You wanted to see me?"

"Friday morning at breakfast you were grilling your men about a horse that had been put away wet. Did anyone ever own up to that?"

"Nope. They stuck to the story that it must have happened sometime during the night, when the horses were fussing. Only they weren't fussing on Thursday night. On Friday night now, after the crash, it was a different story. We liked to never get them settled down."

"You saw to the horses after the crash?"

"Not directly after. Didn't have the men or the time. I'm talking about when we got back from the airfield."

"Was there one horse more spooked than the others on Friday night? One that looked like it had been sweating?"

"Yep. Same horse as Thursday night. So I guess I was wrong to blame the hands. It wasn't a horse I'd have guessed would ever be that skittish, an old mare with a big heart. She was still bug-eyed at midnight when we got back."

If I was guessing right, the horse had had plenty to be bug-eyed about. She had been a witness to a murder.

Down by the corral, someone called out. I could hear horses moving around and men's voices calming them.

"What a night this is going to be," Bud said.

He clearly wanted to go, but I wasn't through stalling. "Was there any sign that the mare had been ridden that night?"

"What night? Friday?"

"And Thursday."

"Ridden you say? No. There was no saddle or bridle."

"A bridle would be easy enough to get and get rid of."

"But not a saddle. Two of my men were glued to the tack-room radio on Friday night."

"No saddle," I said.

"You're thinking someone rode the mare bareback?" Bud pulled at his chin. "She'd be the horse to pick for that kind of riding. She's docile but game."

"Does she have enough in her to canter to the airfield and back?"

"That's not much of a run cross country. She could gallop it, if she only had to do it once."

The sound of men shouting came out of the darkness then. I picked the word "fire" out of the jumble of voices, an instant after I smelled the smoke.

"The horses!" Bud yelled. "God damn it, the horses!"

He and Knific ran off toward the fracas. I turned back toward the yellow circle. Tyler had disappeared. Lange was standing there alone.

"Step out of that light," I called. "You're a target."

That snapped Lange out of his trance. "Come on then," he said as he trotted past me.

"I've got business at the main house," I said.

I saw him turn in the last of the light from the kitchen. He was nodding to me. Did he know? Had he known all along? I didn't get a chance to ask.

"Good luck," he said. Then he was gone.

40

Hilly was standing on the front steps of Crowe House, staring down the hill toward the corral. I joined her there, being a guy with all the time in the world. I could still smell smoke, but the actual fire had yet to show itself.

"Our guard's run off to see the show," Hilly said. "What kind of protection is that?"

"I'll cover for him."

"I'd do as well myself," she replied, her tone less ungrateful than her words.

"This is like the old days," I said.

"What?" Hilly asked. She was frightened and distracted, which I hadn't expected.

"Like the war."

"The war? Londoners lit their cigarettes on bigger fires than this whole place would make. The war."

"Were you in London then?"

"Only once," she said, not taking her eyes off the invisible blaze. "Once on leave. I wouldn't go back. It was like trying to get away from the fighting by visiting a bloody battlefield. I took my leave in the country after that. Milked cows."

"You were in the service like Miss Lacey?"

"Like her? I was with her. Same outfit. Coastal Command. RAF. Only I wasn't working for her then. She was working for me. Ordnance. You wouldn't guess it from looking at her now, but she could take apart a Vickers gun with her eyes closed."

"Did you ever serve as ground crew for the planes?"

"We all of us served as everything—" She turned and looked at me for the first time. "Damn you," she said.

I stepped into the house with Hilly at my heels. Lacey was pacing the living room, her open robe trailing behind her. It wasn't the terry cloth robe she used for her weepy widow part. This one was silk and dark green. Beneath it she wore a white chiffon negligee. Not exactly meeting attire, but then there was no sign of the man she'd been meeting with—Max Froy. That was just as well, as it meant there was one less person to get rid of.

"Where's my daughter?" Lacey demanded.

"With Ella," I said. "At our cottage."

"Pretty high-handed of her, taking Jewel away without telling me. Whatever got into her? And what's going on outside? Are they having a rodeo?"

"No," I said. "A fire. Like the one they used for your big scene, the one where you called up the bogeymen. Jewel thinks you might actually have worked a spell that night."

"Impressionable child. She would have to have an artistic temperament, the very last thing you need in Hollywood. I think she'd be safer up here, don't you?"

"No," I said, "I don't. If you're worried, send Hilly down to sit with her."

Lacey stopped her pacing and stared at me. "Do you really think that's best?"

"Yes," I said.

"Go on then, Hilly. When the excitement's died down, you can bring her back."

"I'm staying," Hilly replied.

Lacey gave the mutiny no mind. "Go on, I said. I'll be fine here with Scotty."

Hilly made for the door, dragging both feet.

"Make sure Ella knows it's you," I said. "And you might stop and get Cararra on the way. She may need company about now."

"Go to hell," Hilly said, and slammed the door behind her.

"You'll have to forgive her, Scotty. She doesn't take orders well, not even from me."

"She was just telling me how she gave you orders during the war."

"Was she?" Lacey stopped by the wagon-wheel table, opened a box of cigarettes, and took one out. There was a lighter next to the box, but she didn't reach for it. She stood and waited.

I walked to the table and collected the lighter. It turned out to be a trap. When I lit Lacey up, she blew smoke in my face.

Ella and I may have been the only two at the ranch who hadn't preened for the evening. Lacey had repaired her hair and makeup since I'd delivered Jewel to her that afternoon. Or was it more correct to say that, like her daughter, she had changed costumes? Her hair was perfect now, one of those subtle pilings that looks like the wind did it in its spare time. Her makeup was also subtle or—what was even better—seemed to be subtle. The overall effect was wasted on the longhorn living room. And, as it happened, on me.

"Have one yourself," she said. "You look as though you could use a cigarette."

It gave me an excuse to break free of her gaze, so I took a cigarette and lit it. A very smooth Dunhill.

Lacey was pacing again before I'd taken my first drag. "How about a drink? I've a bottle of Taittinger iced. No? Well, perhaps we'd better stay alert. That fire you mentioned, was it set by Mr. Remlinger?"

"He's one suspect. The other's a mare with a nervous disposition. She may have started the fire as a way of getting attention."

"Good luck to her," Lacey said without breaking stride. "I must say, one thing I'll never get used to is the American tendency to joke at inappropriate moments. I used to think it reflected nerve. Now I see it as a symptom of congenital immaturity."

"Relax," I said. "Tell me about your days in Coastal Command."

"What would you like to hear?"

"What kind of planes did they fly?"

"All types. Anything they could get their hands on in the early days. American junk like the Lockheed Hudson and other obsolete machines. Types that were no good for frontline service."

"Any C-47s?"

"We called them Dakotas. Not as evocative as your nickname for them: Gooney Birds. Yes. Everyone used Dakotas for supply and liaison. They were as common as sparrows."

"Ever install a gust lock on one?"

"Many times, Scotty." She was smiling at me, the gracious hostess. "Tied them down, filled their petrol tanks, greased their filthy undercarriages. Guns were our proper business, but Hilly liked her girls to help out. Kept us out of trouble.

"That was her intention at least. It didn't work with me. I had too much of the kind of energy you couldn't use up loading guns. I ended up pregnant—preggers, we used to say—by a doomed pilot of a Fairey Swordfish. Hilly saw to everything, the hasty wedding, the compassionate discharge for medical reasons. She even broke the news to me when Barry was killed trying to sink some German battleships in the channel.

"After the war, Hilly looked me up. I'd made a real start in British pictures by then. I could afford to take her on. She was at sixes and sevens with the fighting over. Some people were that way. The war saved them from being odd types who don't fit in. Then the war ended, leaving them odder than ever. She was good with Jewel though. Maybe Hilly's the one responsible for Jewel's artistic temperament. What do you think, Scotty?"

"Could be," I said. Lacey was wearing me out with her nervous striding back and forth. Her always pale skin had taken on the luster of china. Slightly damp china. I knew I wasn't the cause of her jitters. Her furtive glances toward the curtained front window told me so.

Lacey ground her cigarette into the pine flooring. "What else would you like to know?"

"How you got Pioline to drive back here the night he died."

"He came back to find bouncing Bebe Brooks. Isn't that true?"

"No. They were just two ships that didn't pass in the night. Pioline came back here to see you. I'm thinking you arranged to meet him out at the airport. Then you deliberately failed to show up."

"Why would I arrange to go out there when we could have talked right here?"

"Your business was too private to discuss around Jewel and Hilly. That's probably what you told Pioline. But it was just a bluff. I mean a stall. You never had the slightest intention of meeting him at the airport. You wanted to delay him until dark. And you wanted him back here, so you could beat him to the field and clamp that vise on the tail of his plane."

"I was here, Scotty. I was here when Marc drove off. I was here when the plane crashed. Ella saw me."

"She didn't find you right away. Not in all the confusion."

"I was looking for Jewel."

"That's what Ella thought, too. It turns out Jewel was looking for you. It scared her to death that she couldn't find you."

"You're splitting hairs, Scotty. I couldn't have made it to the airfield and back in time."

"Not on foot. Not even in a car. But you could have done it on horseback. Cross country. On the mare that gets night sweats. You borrowed her, right from under the noses of the only two ranch hands who weren't off drinking in Sherwood. You took your own bridle and did without a saddle. You snuck her out through the gate in the wire the ranch hands use."

"You were a long time getting that idea," Lacey said.

"Serves me right for never making a Western. I should have remembered how well you handled yourself on Friday afternoon, when the horses got spooked during the shooting. A little bareback riding would have been nothing for you. Jewel gave me the pointer I needed just now, when she told me how you'd tried to teach her to ride.

"You rehearsed the whole thing the night before the crash.

That told you the timing would be tight. So you worked out the little business with Hilly, the stall she used on Pioline on the front porch."

Lacey had stopped listening. "What else did Jewel tell you?"

"That Pioline raped her five years ago. That's what you threw at him on Friday night. First just a hint of it so he'd wait for you out at the airport. He called here when you didn't show, but it wasn't to send Hilly after Brooks. That was Hilly lying for you. Did she even take Pioline's call? Did anyone bother to answer it? You certainly didn't need to. You knew Pioline would come back to have it out with you. What did you threaten him with? When he bumped into Brooks he made a joke about being hung. Hanging would have been easier than what he got."

"What he got was easier than what he deserved. Are we agreed on that much, Scotty?"

She stopped and stared at me again until I said, "Yes."

Then she went back to her pacing, her attention divided. "Jewel actually told you Marc had raped her?"

"Yes."

"I wonder if that's a good sign, that she can tell a relative stranger finally. It took her years to tell me, and then it didn't seem to help her. I didn't help her. I was years more deciding what to do. When Marc brought me your wife's script, I saw my chance. The story of a vengeful queen. Why not the queen of slick, empty films? It was my chance to get close to Marc again and my model for what I had to do."

"Are you confessing?"

"No, just telling you. It doesn't matter. I won't admit to any of this ever again. I'll stick to my story that I arranged to meet Marc to complain about Bebe's behavior. You'll never prove the gust lock wasn't left in place by accident. No jury would take the word of a pilot over that of a movie star."

"A pilot you were willing to kill. You couldn't have known Ford wouldn't be on the plane."

"I knew Ford wouldn't be at the controls. That was all I cared about. Not about his life. Ford lied for Marc during our divorce fight. He knew about every trip Marc made to his Palm Springs hideaway and the name of every whore he took along. Ford knew all that and swore he didn't. Male honor. Now male honor can work for me for once. You won't drag Jewel's tragedy into the light of day. Not you, Scotty. And without that, you don't have a case."

"You're forgetting Nicole Cararra. She saw something Friday night. She's been blackmailing her way into a career ever since."

In the distance, a shot sounded. It was followed by another, equally faint, from the same direction, from the corral.

"What did Cararra see? You riding off to the airport? She couldn't have reached the corral in time, not if she hung around to wave good-bye to Brooks. You were on your way by then. She must have seen you coming back, after dark, with the bridle in your hand."

"She'll never tell you," Lacey said. "Not her. Not with her ambition."

"It's what she told Remlinger that has your head in the noose."

Lacey stopped by the front window, reached for the curtain, and drew her hand away. "What did she tell him?"

"What Pioline had done to Jewel. Not in so many words, but enough for him to figure out that Pioline was the target, not Brooks. Remlinger snatched Jewel today to check Cararra's story."

"That bitch. Endangering Jewel to save her own neck."

"Isn't that what you've done to Jewel? You've endangered Ella and Cararra and everyone on the ranch. You're the only one who's known what was going on here. Why didn't you shut the production down and take Jewel away somewhere safe?"

"Where would that have been?" Lacey asked. She was still telling me the truth. More than telling, she was showing me, with the fine sweat that glistened on her. She came to where I stood, near the center of the room, and stayed put.

"You didn't keep the production going because you needed the money," I said. "That was another bluff. You hung on here—hung on for dear life—because you were scared. You couldn't go back to Los Angeles with Remlinger on the loose. You went out to the crash site Friday night all set to do a big hysterical scene. When you got there, you found out you had plenty to be hysterical about. Beverly Brooks had begged a seat on the plane you'd sabotaged. You'd given a homicidal maniac a reason to track you down."

"The slut," Lacey said, almost to herself. "The insatiable slut. Why couldn't she have stayed with her sorry husband for one night?"

Shots rang out again, half a dozen of them, much closer. I drew my gun, and we both waited.

"Is that it?" Lacey asked. "Did they get him?"

"Your mourning act wasn't for the newspapers, was it? It was so you'd have an excuse to hide in here, with Lange's little army circled around you. Those tears you wept weren't for Pioline. They were for you. You were mourning your own death."

"Remlinger's dead now," Lacey whispered. "He's finally dead. There's nothing you can do to me now. Please God, tell me I'm finally safe."

The answer she got was the front door bursting in. Remlinger followed it, his gun drawn and aimed at me. He had me cold, but I raised my automatic instinctively. As I did, Remlinger's barrel swung from me to Lacey. We fired at the same second. In the corner of my vision, Lacey pirouetted wildly. Remlinger took a quick step back, slamming the open door against the wall. I fired again, and he pitched forward as Dillon had done, staring hard at nothing.

Lacey had somehow stayed on her feet. She gaped at me with eyes only a little more alive than Remlinger's. I laid her on the sofa.

If Ella had written the scene, Lacey would have had a last line, something to win back a little audience sympathy. "It's better this way," maybe. Or she might have said Jewel's name.

She said, "Marc," and died.

41

Tyler and two of his deputies showed up next. If the sheriff was happy to see me breathing, he held it in.

"It's what I told you would happen," he said, looking down at Lacey. "This is on your head."

"Her head, Sheriff," I managed to say. Her bloody red head. "She killed Brooks and Pioline. Was anyone else hurt?"

Tyler was blinking at me and Lacey alternately. He pulled himself together. "One of my men was grazed. One of yours was killed. I'll show you."

He left one deputy to watch the house. I asked him to send the other down to the cottage grove to tell Ella the worst was over.

Tyler led me down the opposite slope, toward the barnyard, where men were still trying to put out the fire Remlinger had started in a shed. By the fire's light, I saw Bud standing over two figures on the ground. One was the man I'd expected to see, Lange, only he was alive. He was sitting in the dirt, cradling the head of a second man, or what was left of the man's head.

"Knific," Lange said when he noticed me. Tears were streaming down his face. Tears from a stone, anyone who knew him would have said. But no one knew him now.

"He saved my life. I froze. Remlinger would have had me if the kid hadn't come up, blasting away. Did you get the bastard?"

"Yes," I said.

"All this time, I thought he was going to finish me. Instead he killed the kid."

Remlinger had killed Knific and finished Lange, I thought. Tyler was thinking the same thing. He patted Lange on the shoulder, caught my eye, and jerked his head toward the main house.

"Ready to tell me why Lacey did it?" he asked as we trudged up the hill.

I was ready to lie about it. I'd already worked up a story that might satisfy the law. I hadn't served all those years under Paddy Maguire for nothing. Lacey had plotted to kill Pioline and Ford because of her bitterness over her divorce. She'd gotten Brooks by accident. Period. No mention of Jewel's rape. That was between Jewel and her psychiatrist. Or Jewel and her painting.

I didn't get a chance to try my story out. The deputy I'd sent down to talk to Ella was back, trailing behind my wife and Jewel and Hilly. Before I could stop her, Jewel was telling Tyler everything.

"Of course she has to tell it," Ella said, leading me away. "She's been alone with it too long."

Sirens were wailing in the distance. Feeling nostalgic suddenly, I scanned the smoky sky for planes. Ella drew me back across the years with a hand on mine.

"This is the end of your movie," I said. "Sorry."

"The time wasn't right for telling Boudica's story. Some other day maybe. Poor Lillie. I wonder if she read the script through to the end."

The next morning I drove Ella and Jewel to the county hospital to see Daniel Irwin. I'd promised Jewel I would, but I hadn't expected her to call in that marker, not after all that had happened.

"There must be more to Irwin than meets the male eye," I said to my wife when we'd delivered Jewel safely to Irwin's room in spite of the determined efforts of the press corps.

"It's not what you think, Scotty. Jewel explained it to me last night. She knew she was involved in Bebe's death. She wasn't sure how, but she still felt responsible. She needs to apologize to Irwin for being the cause of his loss."

Over Ella's head, I could see Jewel standing next to the novelist's bed. She'd taken his hand. I couldn't see her eyes, but what I saw in Irwin's told me that Ella was wrong for once.

She was generous enough to admit it, once I'd turned her around to face the tableau. "You're on a roll," she said.

To give the new couple some privacy, we strolled the hospital's hallways. Ella smiled at the people we passed, but her thoughts were back in Irwin's room. "Two people broken up like that," she said, shaking her head. "It'll be a miracle if their jagged edges happen to fit together."

"Ours did," I said, taking her hand and intertwining our fingers.

"We're the million-to-one kids. Or does every couple feel that way?"

"I hope so."

Though it wasn't the spot for it, we kissed. Afterward, Ella gave me an especially knowing look. "I suppose now you'd like to see a movie."

"I know a nice drive-in in Indiana," I said. "*West Side Story* may still be playing. The kids can have the front seat."

Before Ella could answer with more than a smile, we became aware of a voice calling my name. It belonged to the lady of the yellow message slips, the one who'd caught me on my last visit to the hospital. She didn't have a slip today, as my caller was holding on her line.

It was Paddy Maguire. I'd phoned in my report around midnight, giving it to Peggy because her husband had been out "catting around." I'd been expecting Paddy's follow-up call. This wasn't it.

"Scotty, I need you down here right away. It's about the Marilyn Monroe business."

"What business?"

"You mean you haven't heard? She was found dead. Overdose of sleeping pills. Have you been hibernating?"

"We've been a little preoccupied," I said.

"So I'm told. Listen, Scotty, they're calling Monroe's overdose an accident, but the whole thing smells to high heaven. How soon can you be here?"

I looked at Ella, stroked her sun-blond hair, and thought how close Beverly Brooks had come to inheriting the franchise. Now she'd be eclipsed in death as she had been in life.

"It's all yours," I said. "We're on Route 66 heading east."

Then I hung up.